She stepped off the bottom step and almost tripped over an uneven patch of floor.

She aimed the beam of light at where the window should be. What on earth? A bookcase blocked out her expected light source. Miles was the only one who could have done that, but why would he?

The cold penetrated deeper, spurring Hope toward the furnace. Her foot caught on something soft but unyielding. She stumbled and ended up sitting on the *something*. Her hand recognized the contours of a mattress. A mattress that should have been stuffed in a corner, not lying out in the open.

Once again, she sent the light spiraling over the basement, but nothing else seemed out of place. She brought the beam back to shine on the mattress and *a body*.

Her heart beat triple time before she recognized the body resting on its side, a scant two feet from her hand. Miles! Why was he sleeping in the basement and not upstairs? Her hand reached out toward his arm. Should she wake him or let him sleep? Common sense won—he had to be freezing. He didn't even have a sheet. This time her palm brushed his sleeve before she gently shook his shoulder.

A hand caught her wrist in a cruel grip.

She bit back a cry of pain.

A second later she was flat on her back—Miles' face above hers. But not the face she loved. His eyes were so dark they were almost black. His beautiful lips were drawn back in a snarl. A snarl that revealed one-inch incisors. The hand that held her down sported claws.

Praise for Faith V. Smith

"A cast of characters who are colorful, entertaining, and memorable. She gives us three beautiful (and drool-worthy) vampires—Zache, Hawk, and Miles—a detective sidekick, Gideon, who is amusing and personable, and a spunky heroine who is devoted to both her career as a surgeon and to the mysterious detective she hardly ever sees during the daytime."

*~BD Whitney, **BookWenches***

"Ms. Smith gives us a hypnotic, uber sexy, not-quite-human hero and a heroine who's a combination of innocence and bravado. In this unique read we find unexpected creatures of the night who are compassionate, heroic and enjoy brother-like friendships, and villains that are worse than our worst nightmares. A very enjoyable read with great plot and super characters, a story any lover of paranormal romance would enjoy. Just keep the tissues handy for the dramatic ending. I can't wait to read the next adventure in the series."

*~Larkspur, **Long And Short Reviews**, Rated 4* books.

"Faith Smith weaves a story that is full of action, romance, and vengeance. The hero is strong and mysterious, and the heroine is beautiful and intelligent. This book has an interesting story-line, not the usual run-of-the-mill vampire story."

*~Scarlett, **Review Your Book**, rated 4 stars*

"This is a hot and sweet paranormal romance that I thoroughly enjoyed. Miranda and Zacke are wonderful characters, strongly written and well thought out. The memorable supporting cast is magnificent. Who couldn't fall in love with such charming men? *KENSINGTON'S SOUL* has all you could want in a book—a tortured hero, a trio of gorgeous sidekicks, and a guileless yet spunky heroine. The pace was good but at times I felt it was taking just a little too long to hunt down the bad guy. The plot is well developed and the story flows seamlessly. I'm looking forward to Zacke's friends' stories. I'll recommend this to everyone I know who enjoys a thrilling paranormal romantic mystery."

~*Theresa Joseph,* ***The Romance Studio***

"I really enjoyed the twist Ms. Smith added to make this traditional vampire story unusual. The hero is sexy and heroic with loyal friends, fighting the truly hateful antagonist alongside his charming sidekicks. The love story between the hero and the bright feisty heroine is touching, endearing and inspirational. Filled with intrigue, the story has all the components necessary for a tantalizing adventure."

~*Maureen Sevilla*

"Smith covers plenty of ground in her latest novel—the first in a series—infusing charming Southern flavor into an action-packed vampire tale. It's not the same old bloodsucking story, and Zacke and his merry band of vamp (and mortal) brothers are a fabulous addition."

~*Lauren Spielberg,* ***Romantic Times Book Reviews***

"In *KENSINGTON'S SOUL*, author Faith V. Smith writes a wonderful romance between the conflicted vampire hero, Zacke, and the spunky mortal heroine, Miranda. The well drawn characters reveal loveable personalities, inner demons, and secret desires. Smith expertly paces the conflict and passion, blending supportive minor characters and a formidable antagonist into a satisfying climax. The Savannah setting provides a wonderful backdrop to the story's eeriness, history, and sensuousness. Readers will fall in love with Zacke and Miranda. Thank goodness you won't have to say goodbye to them after you close the book, the first in Smith's Bound by Blood series. Highly recommended."

~*Jennifer Akers,* ***www.MyShelf.com***

Dunbar's Curse

Bound By Blood:
The Legends, Book II

by

Faith V. Smith

This is a work of fiction. Names, characters, places, and incidents either are the product of the author's imagination or are used fictitiously, and any resemblance to actual persons living or dead, business establishments, events, or locales, is entirely coincidental.

Dunbar's Curse: Bound By Blood:
The Legends, Book II

Contact Information: info@thewildrosepress.com

Cover Art by *Rae Monet*

The Wild Rose Press
PO Box 708
Adams Basin, NY 14410-0706
Visit us at www.thewildrosepress.com

Publishing History
First Black Rose Edition, 2010
Print ISBN 1-60154-755-2

Published in the United States of America

Dedication

As always, to my darling Rick,
who if he still walked an earthly realm
would say “I’m proud of you, baby!”

To my awesome daughter Amanda, thank you for
doing all the menial tasks of housework
so Mama could get this finished.
You can never know how much you mean to me!

Acknowledgements

To my fabulous editor Callie Lynn Wolfe—
you positively rock, woman!
Thanks for loving my characters as much as I do!

Special thanks and hugs to Maureen Sevilla, Sandy Morris, and Nancy Pirri,
who were my sounding boards for making sure all the questions were answered.

To Nancy Swanson, the best production assistant,
I couldn't have done this without you!
To Rae Monet, you never cease to give me the best cover in the world.
Thank you both.

To Gini Rifkin, thank you for reading and critiquing,
and to Sarah Hansen—woman, I owe you big time!

To all I may have missed, thank you and to God be the glory!

He came to her in the mist of dreams, possessing her innermost thoughts. He warmed her heart and scorched her body with his touch.

Chapter One

Hope's arms felt weighted down with slumber, the heavy comforter threatened to smother her within its folds. She clawed the material away from her face and head, until a cool wash of air bathed her hot flesh while she tried to slow her racing heart.

He had visited her again—the man who filled her nights with shadows of reality.

The dreams began months ago. They taunted and tantalized her with such intensity, she feared she might be losing her mind.

Her body still quaked from the latest assault on her senses. Her nerve endings screamed with arousal and unfulfilled desire. A desire she experienced only in her dreams. Tonight, in the hazy world of sleep, she had fought against the hands touching her flesh. Pulled away from the lips that craved entry into her soul. Struggled and won against the fever of desire burning her insides. Now, she felt bereaved—empty—without him.

Hope shoved the covers to the foot of the bed and climbed out of the old-fashioned four-poster. She padded barefoot to the window and knelt on the cushioned window seat. Sheer lace curtains allowed her to view the street in front of her two-story house.

Her heart caught and then sped rapidly into a twisted dance of terror and excitement.

He was there.

He stood in his usual spot. His tall frame

overshadowed the gate of the white picket fence surrounding her property. Low-hanging branches of moss-covered oak trees cloaked him in mystery. Yet, she could still make out the arrogant tilt of his head. His chestnut hair flowed loose over his shoulders and down his back. The white shirt he wore hid the deep bronze of his chest—a chest she had caressed in daydreams and during the night hours. She couldn't see his eyes, but she knew they would be glowing a deep jade—just as they always did right before he took her in her dreams.

The haunting and handsome specter, for that was all he could be, looked up at her window. The smile he normally bestowed on her noticeably absent. He raised his arm and extended his hand palm up. She ignored his gesture. Hope turned away from his entreaty and returned to the wreckage of her bed. She hoped the rest of the night would be free of the dark stranger. Why did his spirit stalk her? What did he want?

****

Miles watched until Hope returned to the solitude of her bed, a bed he hungered to share and not just in her dreams. Until tonight, he had always satisfied her desires. Why had she pushed him away this time?

His nails lengthened into talons. Hope was safer without his carnal appetite, even in her dreams. Making love to her by thought transference wasn't what he wanted anyway, but at least she would be safe.

He'd loved her for so long, he didn't dare allow himself the pleasure of making love to her for real. Lately, it was all he could do to keep the beast within him chained.

He flipped back the ruffled cuff on his sleeve. Once again, the dawn would bear witness to his lonely bed. It didn't have to be that way. There were women who would warm the chill of his body with wanton limbs—even without pay. Miles yearned for more. He wanted what he couldn't have. Why didn't he just take what he desired? He knew why. But his bludgeoning arousal didn't like his answer.

He needed to seek his bed, but first he would ensure Hope's safety with a protection spell.

Once he spoke the words, a flick of his wrist sent a breeze waffling through the night air. At first gentle, it grew stronger, sending the folds of his cape cascading away from his body into a gyrating dance.

Miles closed his eyes, aligned his body with the moving air, and willed the wind to take him before the morning light began to break. When he reopened his eyes, dirt covered his body. His sigh disturbed the red Georgia clay. Fatigue swamped his limbs before slumber stole the life from his eyes.

****

Hope Morgan stepped across the threshold and into the three-story home of her boss and mentor, Dr. Miranda Kensington. She managed a small smile at the charming and handsome man who answered the door. The brief kiss Miranda's husband bestowed on the top of her hand smacked of old-world manners—impressive and not often seen in this day and age.

She retrieved her hand and then smoothed the skirt of her medieval costume. She hated parties, and Halloween parties were especially abhorrent to her. Once as a child, she'd been scared senseless while treat-or-treating. Somehow she'd become separated from her mother, but other than the fear, she couldn't remember what happened after that. Ever since, she'd lost her appetite for candy and the holiday. The date also held more recent bad memories. It reminded her of her parents' deaths. They had perished in a plane crash the previous year just a few days before October thirty-first.

“So glad you could make it tonight, Dr. Morgan.”

The soft tone of the man waiting patiently for her to follow him penetrated her thoughts.

“My apologies, Detective Kensington. I uh…”

“No need to apologize and please make it Zacke. And with your permission, I’ll drop your title. You’re not the first guest here to feel slightly overwhelmed. My wife’s parties can be a bit of an overload.”

Hope welcomed the warmth in Zacke’s voice—she would let him go on thinking the numerous guests made her nervous. No need to spill her hang-ups in public. It wasn’t his fault she’d rather be at home, or that Miranda had insisted she come to the party.

Hope moved forward slightly and gazed around the living room of the Kensington home. Silver cobwebs dotted each corner, and antique furniture gave the room a gothic air. A massive mahogany sideboard, flanked by a fireplace held a black cauldron and boasted finger sandwiches as well as an assortment of munchies.

Black curtains adorned the tall dormer windows, with plastic spiders nestled strategically in their folds.

She smiled once more at Zacke, who bowed slightly at the waist before leaving her to her own resources. The buffet table seemed a good place to start. Her caseload caused her to miss both breakfast and lunch. She crossed the room and caught the faint whiff of chili. Aha, that must be what the cauldron held.

Cups and a large bowl of red liquid sat on a table next to the sideboard. Miranda should be congratulated on the authenticity of her party. If Hope didn’t know better she would swear the cut glass bowl, acting as a centerpiece, held blood.

She looked around the room but didn’t spot her boss. Miranda was probably with the twins, a boy and girl who were almost two years old. Between the hospital grapevine and what Miranda had shared with her, Hope knew the children had arrived nine months to the day after she and Detective Kensington were married. A bit of mystery surrounded their wedding, but Hope didn't put much stock in the vampire rumors, which still floated around the hospital.

Hope had grown up in Savannah. The stories of the city's dark side were nothing new to her. Halloween always brought them back in force.

Her tongue crept out to circle her lips. Maybe she would sample the fruit punch.

She picked up the ladle and carefully filled the crystal cup. Hmmm—the sweet liquid helped to dissipate the parched feeling in her throat. She turned back to see additional guests had arrived. She also spied Miranda and Zacke standing just outside the living room threshold. They made a lovely couple. The detective, with his dark hair and tanned good looks, towered over his auburn haired, blue-eyed wife.

Hope picked up a strand of her own hair. She examined it much like she would a specimen under a microscope. It held none of the rich tones of her boss's copper locks. Its dark color with bits of silver intertwined looked like an advertisement for Lily Munster.

She dropped the offensive reminder emphasizing her lack of interest to the opposite sex. She'd never been able to maintain a relationship for more than a couple of dates—at the most an occasional, catastrophic third.

Disgust at her own shortcomings, when it came to men, made her wish she'd never agreed to show up tonight. Well, now she'd fulfilled her obligatory duty.

The growing crowd and caterers slowed her

haste toward freedom. She rehearsed the words she would say to Miranda and her husband until she finally reached their side.

"Miranda, I really appreciate you inviting me, but I need to leave."

"Hope, you just got here." Miranda caught Hope's arm in a gentle but firm grasp. "Besides, there's someone I want you to meet."

Hope stifled a groan. Miranda was trying to play matchmaker, and she really preferred not to be her guinea pig. "Miranda, could it wait? I'm really not feeling well."

Her boss's smile faded, her disappointment evident. Detective Kensington patted Miranda's arm before he spoke into the awkward silence. "Maybe *another time* would be better."

Hope felt lower than a crack on a sidewalk. She really hated hurting other people's feelings, and she really hated hurting Miranda. Her boss had gone out on a limb to help Hope get on staff at the hospital. Why she'd chosen the least qualified of applicants, Hope didn't have a clue, but she was grateful. The last six months had been wonderful. It had given her an outlet for grief and helped to stave off loneliness. She knew she would probably regret it but… She plastered a smile on her face. "Hey, it's okay. I'm sure I'll feel better in a few minutes. So fire away with the introductions."

Miranda's crushed look took on the appearance of the self-assured surgeon Hope knew and respected. "Great, now if you'll just follow me."

Follow, she did; right to the doom she knew awaited. One look at her and the unsuspecting guest would flee. It had happened before, more times than she cared to remember and it would happen again as long as well-intentioned people continued to try to fix her up.

Hope climbed the stairs behind Miranda and

Zacke. The second floor was as lovely as the first. It also carried on the old world theme. Oak floors, covered by several oriental rugs, ran the entire length of the long hallway. Wall sconces held lit candles. Their flames glowed brightly and with a mysterious zeal.

Miranda stopped at the last doorway on the left side of the hall and opened the door. "This is my office away from the hospital. It also serves as our private sitting room. I think we'll be more comfortable in here."

Hope crossed the threshold into the room. Icy fingers caressed her spine—must be the atmosphere. The desk lamp and tall floor lamp were dim beacons—not quite reaching the corners of the room.

The room looked empty. Had her blind date already flown the coop? She wouldn't be surprised, but they usually waited until they met her first.

"Listen, ya'll, I appreciate you wanting to set me up." Hope smiled at their combined looks of *oops, she's on to us*, before she continued. "But evidently your victim has better things to do."

"Oh, I'm sure he's just running late." Miranda punched Zacke in the arm. "Isn't that right, Zacke?"

The detective didn't bat an eyelash when his wife followed her blow with a pinch to the same abused spot. "I'm positive you are right, my love. But just in case we are both wrong, I will definitely be talking to—"

"Evening, Zacke, Miranda. Sorry I'm late. I had trouble finding something for dinner." The words were softly spoken in a sexy baritone.

Hope's nerve-endings went haywire. She had heard that voice before. But when and where?

"Miles, there is someone we want you to meet."

A shadow moved away from the window—a window that remained closed. How had the man gotten inside without her seeing him? His face remained a silhouette of darkness as he made his way to their hosts. She watched him lift Miranda's hand to his mouth, kiss it, and then gently replace it at her side. He then turned to Zacke who raised a sooty brow before he clasped the man in a bear hug.

Well, the man seemed congenial enough. Maybe the evening wouldn't be a total disaster.

"Hope?"

Hope turned her attention back to Miranda and away from her thoughts. She didn't wait to be introduced. She might as well get it over with. She stepped forward and offered her hand. "Hi, I'm Hope Morgan."

The man turned, his back now to their hosts. The blood pumping to fill her heart's arteries and ventricles stuttered to a halt. He took her proffered hand. Her pulse leapt to life once more, the beat so frantic, she feared she would faint.

The man in her dreams stood before her.

Had she lost her hopeless grip on sanity? The dreams were nothing more than sexual frustration and fantasies. The man who stood outside her home night after night, a figment of her wild imagination, could not be standing in front of her.

However, the kiss he placed on her palm seared her soul with its reality. She snatched her hand from his gentle but possessive grip. Her legs trembled as she backed away from this specter of her mind. Her hand found its way to her throat. The pulse she found didn't reassure her. It only made her realize this wasn't a dream. The man who made her body scream for and then delivered delicious fulfillment did indeed stand before her—a flesh and blood reality.

She had to leave. She had to escape before he pulled her into the web of insanity awaiting. For to acknowledge his existence would be to acknowledge the hold he had on her heart and soul.

"I'm sorry. I can't stay." Hope jerked her gaze from the object of her terror. She spared one brief look at an open-mouthed Miranda and a frowning Zacke. She then turned and tore out of the room like all the bats of hell were on her heels.

****

Miles stood in shock as Hope ran from the room. His gaze riveted on her fleeing form, his heart, a frozen and desolate lump in his chest. God above, he had terrified Hope. He had to go after her. Hope didn't need to be out alone—tonight of all nights. He forced his useless legs to move and started for the door.

"Hold it right there, mister. What did you say to her?"

Miranda's commanding and irate tone stopped him in his tracks, but he shook off the apology he owed his hosts and friends. However, he couldn't shake Zacke's vise-like grip.

"Miles, what just happened?" Zacke's tone remained soft, but the eyes blazing blue fire demanded an answer.

"Nothing happened. You were here. The woman introduced herself and then ran like a thief in the night." He turned to Miranda and softened his irritation. "Miranda, I promise you. I didn't even put a thought in her head." When she opened her mouth to speak, he answered her unspoken question. "Nor did I show her my fangs. I have no idea why Hope ran."

Miranda walked around Miles, studying him like a bug she wanted to squash. Did she know he lied? Too late to call back his words, not when he needed to persuade Miranda he had done nothing wrong. He had to leave. He had to convince Hope she wasn't losing her mind.

"Do you swear you're telling me the truth, Miles?"

"Yes. Now may I go?"

"Go where?"

"After Hope. And next time you decide to play cupid, make sure your prey have not already met."

****

Miles chose to walk to Hope's house instead of utilizing his usual method of travel. The air had grown colder since his tardy arrival at the Kensington residence, but he welcomed the brisk flavor of fall. Maybe it would cut through his jumbled thoughts.

What could he possibly say to Hope to persuade her he hadn't just walked out of her dreams? How could he look into her green eyes and not fear the condemnation he would see in their depths if he told her the truth?

Miles kicked a small pebble on the sidewalk. Just a bit farther to go and he would arrive at the gate to the two-storied Victorian, her parents had renovated not long before they had been killed. He remembered well the night Sam and Deirdre Morgan's company jet had gone down shortly after take-off. Hope had been devastated. The family had been close-knit. The love they shared, a constant reminder of how loveless his life had been. He wanted to comfort Hope, but his first priority was to protect her. To do that, he had kept his distance.

The gate loomed ahead. Miles jumped it, stiffened his shoulders, and walked slowly up the walkway. The brick pattern dissolved into a swirl of red as he racked his brain for a plausible excuse for being in Hope's dreams. Maybe he should wipe the memory from her mind.

Miles' talons bit into his palm. He hated to lose his only connection to her but what else could he do? He couldn't tell her he was a vampire. His physical presence alone had terrified her. Unless he could convince her he wasn't dangerous to her physically or mentally, he would lose all hope of staying close to her. No, now would definitely not be the time to apprise her of his creature traits.

He rang the old-fashioned doorbell and waited. His ears picked up steps coming down the stairs. The steps hesitated right before they reached the door. Seconds passed before he heard the chain being withdrawn and the click of the lock. He waited a century for her to open the heavy wood door.

"What are you doing here?"

The abrasive tone came from lips that had been wiped clean of their previous red color. The makeup that had highlighted her beautiful eyes also gone. The woman standing before him now wore baggy sweats, her dark, silver-tipped hair pulled back in a ponytail.

Hope's more than casual appearance didn't prevent the prick of lust jolting his loins. The woman could be clothed in sackcloth and ashes, and Miles would still want her more than life or death itself. "I came to introduce myself properly and to apologize for frightening you."

"So, get on with it." Hope's rude manner couldn't disguise the tears shimmering in her eyes or the tremble of her soft lips.

"Miles Dunbar at your service, Dr. Morgan."

Miles watched as Hope fidgeted with the trim on the door. Her short nails worried the wood in such a way her soft skin was in danger of being pierced by a splinter.

"Do you think I might come in for a moment? I hate to stand out here and discuss my many faults."

A slight smile crept over the perimeter of her lips. Miles applauded his choice of words. Maybe all wasn't lost.

"I guess so. I'll see if I can scare up something to drink." Hope's mother had raised her well. Even frightened and angry she exhibited manners. Her shapely backside swayed as she moved toward the back of the house. The prick of desire turned into a shard of lust.

He focused his gaze over the top of her head and willed his shaft to behave. “Nice house.”

“Thank you. My parents renovated it shortly before their deaths.”

“Yes, I know.”

Hope spun around and stopped a few feet away. “You know?”

“What I meant to say was, I know it couldn’t have been easy.”

The arched eyebrow she raised made him want to gnash his fangs, rip them out, and bang his head against the nearest doorframe. This woman was no fool; another slip of the tongue, and she would have him by the jugular. He hated lying. Something he only did when necessary. And only as a last resort.

Hope shrugged her shoulders. The jade sweatshirt pulled taut across her breasts. She turned once again and he groaned. The woman was going to kill him.

The kitchen also revealed Victorian qualities. He wondered if she had any of the gadgets Miranda and Zacke kept in their kitchen and if so, where they were hidden.

Hope grabbed two glasses from the wine rack, before she removed a bottle from the refrigerator, uncorked it quickly and poured the amber liquid. The cork was replaced in the bottle before she handed him a glass. She raised a matching goblet and took a hefty swig before setting the glass back on the counter.

“So are you going to tell me why you’re in my dreams and why you’re stalking me? Or should I just call the police and have you locked up?”

Miles choked on his wine. Had he heard her correctly? Hope thought she could lock him up. Of course, she couldn't know that a jail cell couldn't keep him prisoner. He'd laugh if his situation weren't so desperate.

He now had no choice.

He sat his glass down on the butcher-block counter and accepted the linen napkin she handed him. He proceeded to wipe the droplets of wine from his face. He hid his smile of satisfaction as she reached for the soiled cloth, and he captured her hand in his.

"What are you doing? I assure you I can defend myself. And I will, if you don't let me go."

Miles laughter erupted from his throat with such force it left him shocked. He seldom laughed.

Hope's face froze with disbelief and the beginning tendrils of fear.

"You tempt me to prove you wrong, Hope. A temptation I will forego. I would much rather do this." Miles pulled the struggling armful closer and held her immobile against his chest. He allowed himself one second of pleasure as her heart beat in time with his, before he lowered his head to the pulsating lure of her throat.

Chapter Two

Hope's world rocked when Miles' tongue slid across the exposed flesh of her neck. It exploded when his hands reached under her shirt and captured her aching breasts. He held her stationary with an assault of passion that left her breathless. His lips singed a path below her neckline and then moved back to the pulse throbbing out of control near her jugular.

He aroused her just as he had in her dreams. Who was he? Why did she just stand like a lump of clay, her insides a quagmire, when she should stop him? This man had questions he needed to answer. Answers that hopefully would prove she wasn't crazy.

"Stop it, Miles."

He ignored her whispered command and continued to suckle a spot below her right ear. "Miles, please, we need to talk."

He took advantage of her open mouth to slide his sinful tongue between her lips. When his heated kiss threatened to zap the molecules from her bloodstream, she tried again to slow things down. She pushed against his broad chest and found muscles hidden by his white silk shirt. For a moment, she gave in to desire and caressed him.

Bad mistake. She didn't need to touch him. He released her lips. Which was just what she wanted, so why did she feel bereft?

"Hope."

She jerked her head up to look into his strangely compelling gaze. It seemed to beckon her with a seductive promise. She waited to see what he would do next. Her insides melted into a mass of quivering organs, and her blood still raced through her body at the speed of light.

Miles released his grip on her waist and captured her head between his massive hands—his gaze still locked with hers. Gentle caresses to her temple, a swift but unsatisfying kiss to her trembling lips, and then Hope fell into a void of darkness.

****

Miles cursed himself as he carried Hope up the stairs to her room. He had come so close to taking her. His blood lust had mingled with the aching desire shooting through his loins so much so he felt he would burst into flames.

He looked down at the woman he cradled close to his rapidly beating heart. Remnants of desire still radiated throughout his body, but the lust to sip from her hot blood had dissipated. He felt gratitude to the powers that be. Thankful they kept the beast within him bound with chains.

He had accomplished what he set out to do. Hope would slumber peacefully tonight without his usual tampering of her dreams. In the morning, she would remember only meeting him at Miranda's and Zacke's. He would have to decide whether or not to tell them why Hope had fled.

Miles placed his cherished burden on her bed but couldn't resist the urge to kiss her lips again. For a moment, he wished he were anything but what he had become. He flicked off the depressing thought and secured the house with a wave of his hand.

He turned away from the woman who seared his heart with love and dissolved into mist. He breached the outside walls of Hope's home. His flight across the dark sky couldn't compare to the darkness in his aching soul.

****

Hope stumbled out of bed to the incessant and extremely annoying ring of her alarm clock. She couldn't remember the last time she had slept so soundly. Not even a smithering of a dream had teased her slumber. Not like previous nights when she had awakened with her heart pounding and her body hot and wanting. But for the life of her, she couldn't recall what any of the dreams had been about. For whatever reason she had enjoyed a good night's rest. However, it couldn't be from not having a guilty conscience. She had behaved horrendously at Miranda's. How could she have just run out like that? It wasn't as if she'd never had her hand kissed before. Her hosts and the poor guinea pig presented to her deserved an apology. Something she would take care of later today.

She plugged the tub and ran a bath. While water sloshed a comforting sound against the tub's porcelain bottom, she applied toothpaste to her toothbrush. By the time the tub was half filled, she had washed her face and brushed her hair into some semblance of order. She then clipped it on top of her head before stepping into the welcoming warmth of the honeysuckle-scented bubbles.

She loved the quiet of early morning, although she'd never really been a morning person. She loved to sit up late and read, even when it played havoc with her early schedule at the hospital. Summer suited her personality best, the long, humid days with an abundance of daylight hours. She hated winter. Its early darkness depressed her inner soul. Fall, announcing the specter of winter had never been a favorite of hers either. October stank of bad memories.

Hope soaped her body and then splashed water

to rinse the last remnants of bubbles away. Maybe it was for the best—her inability to recall that Halloween night so long ago.

She pulled the stopper out of the claw foot tub, stood, and grabbed a towel. A quick rub, and she stepped out. She glanced at the old-fashioned clock sitting on the antique dressing table. Good, she had time for a cup of cocoa.

****

Several hours later, she managed to catch Miranda in her office. "Hi, do you have a minute?"

Miranda's gaze held both welcome and wariness. Maybe she could smooth over last night's debacle. "I'm sorry about last night, Miranda. I don't know what to say in my defense except I was tired. I can't imagine why I acted like I did. You and your husband were so kind to invite me into your home and I—"

"It's okay, Hope. I shouldn't have sprung Miles on you like that. Please forgive me for playing matchmaker. It's just that you look so lonely at times, and I—"

"You wanted me to have what you have. That's understandable, but not very probable for me. I've always been a loner. I'm used to it. So don't give it another thought."

Miranda's eyes gleamed with possible pity. Something Hope couldn't tolerate. She loved her life. Yes, there were times she hated being alone, but she got over them. She didn't want Miranda to feel sorry for her.

"I wish you would come back and let me reintroduce you to Miles. He really is a nice guy."

"I'm sure he is, but not the guy for me. I'm not looking for a man, Miranda. In fact, I doubt seriously a man would want me for anything but a first date."

Dr. Kensington's eyes shone with tears.

Lord, why hadn't she kept her opinions to

herself? "Truly, I'm happy alone. So, don't worry. I'm fine. Please tell Detective Kensington how sorry I am about last night and pass my apology on to Miles."

Hope didn't wait to hear more. She smiled briefly and exited the office. She just needed to find a few moments to convince her heart that what she said was true.

A stabbing victim prevented her heart-to-heart.

It wasn't until that evening she had a chance to mull over her words to Miranda. A sleeve of her gown rested under her cheek to catch the tears she couldn't prevent from falling. She fell asleep still trying to talk some sense into her heart.

****

Miles' fist smashed into the tree trunk with enough force he split the knuckles on his right hand. Blood dripped silently onto the lace of his sleeve. He wanted to rip the shirt from his body as well as the other trappings he wore.

Hope had cried herself to sleep. Something she hadn't done in years. Her emotions usually stayed locked deep inside. She hadn't even cried when she buried her parents.

It was his fault.

If he'd only been quicker that night so long ago, then maybe she wouldn't be so frightened of life. Maybe she wouldn't feel so undeserving of another's love.

A light mist began to fall. Its soft touch seeped into his clothing. He had left his cape at the hospital after his last visit to the Halloween haunted house for the children in the cancer ward. A number of the children were terminal. He had tried to heal the more severe cases, but his powers weren't strong enough. The brightness that encompassed their young souls had shown him their reward for illness would be an eternal one. Some of the other children had gone into remission after he had spoken healing spells. Their eyes had glowed with laughter at his mock attempts to frighten them. Their small hands had clapped with glee at his magic tricks. His heart had quickened with joy, an emotion he had almost forgotten.

He had veiled his presence to all attending the annual haunted house except for the children. No one, not even Zacke and Hawk, his closest friends—knew about his past nightly exploits.

Miles didn't want to hear their good-natured kidding or their probable praise. He certainly didn't deserve the last. Most of his life had been shallow. He had basked in the glory of being one of England's most notorious warriors and the rewards it brought. He, along with Hawk, had followed Zacke into battle time after time. After each campaign, they celebrated with drink and wenches until the early hours of dawn. Although they had not shared Zacke's last conquest in mortal life, they were still caught in the aftermath. Gabriella Sanspree had turned ugly when Zacke laughed at her entreaties for a more serious relationship. She'd transformed Zacke and then both him and Hawk into vampires in the wake of her violent wrath.

Zacke had hated being immortal, but Miles had reveled in the women that seem to flock to him and Hawk. Seldom had there been a night he'd awakened without a woman in his bed. The fruits of his new talents had been enjoyed with as much enthusiasm as his new lifestyle.

But since he had met Hope, his entire life had changed. He'd gotten his priorities straight.

Two decades ago, he had prevented an assault on an abducted child. The men who had lured her away with promises of help when she became lost had not cared about her youth. A ten-year-old was a child—a babe in arms. Even now, Hope remained a youngster to his four-hundred odd years.

He had plucked her out of harm's way and killed her attackers. His one regret was Hope had seen the monster inside him unleashed. The horror in her eyes that night still haunted him. He wiped the memory from her mind and restored Hope to her hysterical parents. Since then, he'd made periodic trips to check on her well being.

Miles watched Hope grow from a pre-teen to a curious teenager. Her experimentation with her first kiss at the age of sixteen had almost given him a heart attack. He'd suffered fits of rage when one of the college students she dated tried to forcibly bed her. He was one step away from killing the student when Hope had taken matters into her own hands; a kick to the family jewels and the young puppy had dropped to his knees. Not the type of punishment Miles would have meted out but effective.

Miles clenched his fist together. The fissures from his fight with the tree trunk had closed and no sign of his temper remained. If only he could rid himself of guilt as easily.

He watched the light dancing behind the curtains in Hope's room. After all these years, she still slept with a light on. He had tried to soothe the fear from her by mind thoughts but had only partially succeeded.

Hope had matured into the beautiful woman she was today. Although she thought she ran a poor second to other women, Miles thought otherwise.

Her midnight hair hung to her waist when she let it down, and her eyes were the color of a dew-drenched meadow. He had watched Hope grow up, fallen in love with the mature woman, and now, he was no closer to finding a way to make her his.

Did he have the right to try?

If she knew what he was, she would never come to him willingly. Only in her dreams had he been able to get close to her. The blind date Miranda had set up had just made matters worse. Before he could woo Hope, he would need to convince her she could trust him as a man. Then and only then would he reveal what he was and pray he would be able to prove he wasn't a monster.

His entire sanity depended upon whether or not he succeeded. If he failed, he would decide how and when to end his lonely existence.

Heat caressed his back. Miles looked to the Eastern sky. The sun had started its journey toward the Heavens. How had he missed its first rays? Another reason to rethink his life. Lately he had grown careless. Something that could send him into the jaws of Hell quicker than he planned.

He shrugged his shoulders before dissolving into the dew that still fell. Tonight he would put the first step of his plan to win Hope into operation.

****

Hope left the hospital just after dusk. Rain splattered the pavement, her shoes, and umbrella as she started the short walk home. The day had been long. She wanted nothing more than a hot bowl of soup, a long soak in the tub, and a glass of wine.

Miranda had stopped her first thing that morning to see if she was okay and if she might consider another meeting with Miles. Luckily, duty called before she could say yes or no. She knew Miranda meant well, but the man frightened her.

Scratch that. He terrified her.

Yes, they had only met for a moment, but Miles looked like an ancient warrior come to life. All he needed was a broadsword anchored at his trim waist. A tunic to fit those excellent shoulders and a pair of leggings to further accentuate his hips, legs, and anything in between.

She wasn't saying she didn't find him highly attractive—she did, but the man had macho written all over him. It had taken Hope years of self-built courage to go out with someone after an incident in college. The wannabe pro football player had been full of himself also. His size and anger when she had refused to sleep with him had made her leery of dating anyone she couldn't protect herself from.

Now, she had to decide if she could trust Miranda's word that Miles was not only a gentleman but completely harmless. Lord, she felt a hundred years old. Why couldn't life just be simple? And although, she told Miranda she was content, why did she have to be alone?

Hope reached the fenced gate and stopped for a moment. Her hand gripped the slatted wood, and her breath stirred the wisteria vine that twined around the fence.

Who was she kidding? Even if she changed her mind, Miles would probably run a mile before he consented to another date.

"Evening, Hope."

The umbrella flew out of her hands. She turned and brought her hands up in a defensive position. She watched in shock as Miles caught her well-aimed blow and deflected it with a kiss to her palm. Heat singed her skin. Her legs proved useless as she fought the urge to slide down the fence. She refused to crumple in a puddle just because he had startled, embarrassed, and totally took out her defenses. So much for taking a self-defense class.

"May I have my hand back?"

He complied but she didn't care for his amusement filled gaze. Heat fanned her face as his lips parted in a smile. The next thing she could expect would be his laughter. Rightfully deserved, but it would still smart.

"Hope, I didn't mean to startle you. I'm sorry." He took her hand again. His fingers danced across her knuckles and erased the stiffness of her clenched fist.

"And, I'm sorry I tried to punch you. I don't like people popping up behind me without warning."

"I'll remember that in the future."

This time his smile caused her insides to heat. Did he realize what he could do with all that voltage?

She eased her hand free and looked around for her errant umbrella. Before she could pick it up, Miles placed it in her hand. "Thanks. Uh, I assume you have a reason for being here."

Hope could have bitten her tongue off. How much more rude could she be?

"Yes, actually, I did. Miranda and Zacke invited me to dinner. I wanted to know if you would come with me. I really don't want to go alone."

Hope didn't know what to say. Had Miranda convinced Miles to ask her out again? Or was it possible he did it because he wanted to. If the latter, then why? Did he need a crutch to stall future matchmaking? Hope shook her head.

"You can't say no."

"And what if I do?" Hope's cheeks heated again. Why couldn't she learn to keep her mouth shut around this man?

"Then I'll have to convince you otherwise."

****

Miles clenched his fists. He fought the urge to snatch Hope closer to his side. Maybe walking to Miranda's and Zacke's had not been such a good idea. But being trapped in Hope's small but seldom used car would have been worse. She had changed into a soft green sweater and a pair of jeans. Neither fit her body snugly but rather hinted at what lay beneath.

Hope lifted her head and smiled just a bit. He returned the gesture. God's glories. He'd felt like a whirlwind had snatched him out of the sky and plummeted him to earth ever since she had agreed to dinner. He had left Hope standing at her door, with the terse statement; he needed to run an errand and would be back in half an hour.

Once out of sight he'd found a secluded spot and taken to the sky. He had almost crashed into Zacke and Miranda's house in his hasty and desperate arrival.

He had thrown himself on their mercy. His frantic explanation of why he wanted them to fix a second dinner after they had already eaten had at first been met with astonishment. Laughter followed when Miles told them what he had done. But, Miranda had shooed him back out the door and admonished him to hurry, lest Hope change her mind.

Now, he wasn't sure what to do next.

"Miles, look, I think this might be a mistake. I'm gonna go back to the house."

Hope's words shocked him out of his thoughts. She couldn't go back. He needed her. He needed her more than he needed the blood that kept him alive. He had waited for this, their first date, for years.

"No!"

"No?"

"I mean, you have to go. Miranda and Zacke are expecting us."

"Are you sure? Miranda didn't say a word about this dinner when I saw her at the hospital."

"Uh, spur of the moment madness. Some type of special occasion."

Hope shot him a look that bit with disbelief. He resisted the urge to extract his fangs. He knew the lie would haunt him. They always did.

Their destination came into view. He caught Hope's hand in his. "Please, come with me?"

Hope gave a slight nod. She didn't smile, but for the moment, it was enough.

They climbed the steps to the porch and were greeted by Zacke and a smug looking Miranda.

"Come on in here, you two. You're just in time for dinner." Miranda caught Hope's hand and pulled her away from Miles. Before he could announce his displeasure, both women disappeared into the kitchen.

"So how did you manage to talk Hope into dinner?"

Miles didn't care for the amusement mingling with Zacke's curiosity. One of his best friends for centuries should have a bit of confidence in his powers of persuasion.

"I asked. You have a problem with that?" He allowed his incisors to show.

"No, and lose the attitude and teeth, Miles. You forget, I may no longer be a vampire, but I'm still able to make you toe the line in a mortal fight."

"And you just might get the chance to *fail*, if I didn't have other things on my mind."

Miles turned slightly away from the grinning detective and honed in on the conversation taking place amidst a clanging of pans and the clatter of dishes.

"So, Miranda, what was the special occasion that sparked this dinner?"

"Occasion? I don't..."

"Just as I thought. Miles made it up."

Miles allowed his vision to pick up and then follow the blur of color as Hope spun around to march back into the den.

Miranda caught her arm.

His sigh of relief sent papers flying off the desk.

"What's going on?"

"Sssh!" Miles followed his command by stabbing the air with his index finger.

"Ah, one of the enjoyments of being a vampire. But do you think its fair to Hope?"

"At the moment, I don't care." Miles blanked out Zacke's soft laughter.

Miranda led Hope to a chair and pushed her gently onto its surface. "Yes, he did. But Hope, he did it for the right reasons. Miles knew you probably wouldn't go out with him unless there were other people around. He asked for our help and we were glad to give it."

"You're right. After I ran out the last time I was here, I'm surprised he even wanted to try." Hope's fingers trembled as she tucked a strand of hair behind her ears. "Miranda, I don't know what to say or do. Miles is what most women would call hot. I mean he is *hot*, but there's more there. It's like when I look in his eyes, I see the past and possibly the future. It scares me to death."

Miles' heartbeat stuttered to a stop.

Hope couldn't know about the past.

He had wiped it clean.

Even the memories of the night of her abduction should only be vague uneasiness. Not something she could feel that strongly.

"I'm not trying to tell you what to do, but I can vouch for Miles. I've known him for the last several years, and he and Zacke have been friends forever. You should listen to your heart."

Miranda's words dragged his attention back to the women. He watched as Hope continued to fidget with her hair. He waited, his breath caught in his throat for her response.

"I know you're right, Miranda, but it's like I've always known Miles. I can't put my finger on it but he's like an addicting drug. You hate yourself for desiring it but you can't stop the want."

Miranda took a pair of potholders and removed a pan from the oven. She placed it on the counter. "So, what do you plan on doing about Miles?"

Hope straightened her shoulders before she took

a sip of wine Miranda had poured earlier. For a moment longer, she sat as in deep thought. "I think my only alternative is to sleep with him until I get him out of my system."

Chapter Three

Miles snatched the can from Zacke's hand and swallowed its contents. The beer burned an acid path down his throat. His breath locked in its journey to his lungs.

"Man, are you all right?" Zacke's concerned voice came to Miles from a distance. He fought the bile that rushed upward from his empty stomach. He shook his head to dispel the dizziness that attacked with sharp and tenacious tendrils.

He won the battle to breathe but lost it promptly when Zacke pounded his back. His knees buckled, and he caught the arm of the sofa to stay on his feet. "Enough." Miles' wheezing and desperate cry got results.

He sought a seat on the sofa and waved away Zacke's apology. A moment later, the women returned to the room.

"My heavens, Miles, what happened to you?" Miranda's inquiry made its appearance in Hope's gaze, but she remained silent.

"Why? Don't I look my usual charming self?" His attempt at humor fell flat.

"You look like something that's been hanging upside down in the rain."

Miranda's words caused an avalanche of laughter from Zacke. Miles would make sure his oldest friend paid for his amusement.

"Sorry, Miranda, some of Zacke's beer went down the wrong way."

"Don't you mean all of my beer?"

Miles' snarl went unnoticed by all but Zacke; who got the message—whatever that was worth.

"Miles, you don't drink beer."

"I know, Miranda. Just call it a lapse of common sense or something…"

Miranda moved a bit closer, picked up his hand, and checked his pulse. She leaned forward and placed a hand on his forehead. "Or something you overheard, perhaps?" Her whispered words caused heat to burn his face. "You feel a bit feverish. Could be that bug going around. I would lay off alcoholic beverages and solid food for a bit." This time her words held amusement as well as a serious overtone.

"I think you're right. Maybe I should go home and rest?"

"Oh no you don't. I cooked and you're going to sit while the rest of us have dinner."

Zacke's groan of dismay almost made Miles laugh. It served him right for pounding the life out of his back.

"Now, if everyone will follow me, dinner is ready."

Miles draped an arm across Hope's shoulders. He smiled into her upturned and startled face. He gently caressed her upper arm through the material of her sweater and wished he could touch her bare skin. He wanted to touch every inch of Hope's body. He wanted to—

"Miles?" Hope's whisper pulled him from his fantasy.

"Yes?"

"You can let go now. I think they want us to sit down."

Miles looked from Hope to Zacke and Miranda. He didn't remember moving from the den to the kitchen. Miranda bit her lower lip, probably to keep from spilling the laughter dancing in her eyes. Zacke on the other hand was less subtle. His guffaw escaped from his manufactured cough.

"All right you two. Behave like the gentlemen I know are hidden somewhere inside."

Miranda's words stopped Zacke's laughter. He hastily drew out Miranda's chair. Miles did likewise for Hope.

****

Hope allowed the rain-scented air to cool the heat of her face. The last hour had been, while not exactly torture, certainly not what she had expected. Her conversation with Miranda had been an eye-opener. She had been flabbergasted to find out the extent Miles had gone to for a date. However, nothing could compare to her mortification when she realized she had spoken aloud about the desire to sleep with Miles. Thank the Lord, no one else but her boss had heard her remark. She glanced up at the man walking silently at her side. Did she have the courage to do it? Could she make a move on Miles?

The man in question slanted a smile toward her that looked a bit weak. Not his usual electrifying beam. He had said nothing to her since they had uttered their goodbyes to Zacke and Miranda. Maybe she should say something first?

"Uh, thanks for inviting me, Miles. I know that it wasn't exactly planned, but I did enjoy myself."

"You're welcome. I had a good time also."

She had to strain to catch his whispered words. What on earth was wrong with the man? His usual elegant tones sounded stilted. He surely couldn't be shy?

Hope moved a bit closer. He evaded her outstretched hand. She tried again. This time Miles sidestepped off the pavement. Something definitely wasn't right.

She purposely moved away so he could step

back. "Sorry, I didn't mean to run you off the walkway." She waited for a response but got nothing more than a grunt.

The gate to her fence loomed ahead. "Look, Miles. I don't know what's going on, so why don't you tell me."

One minute she stood at his side. The next, her back met wood slats. "Hey, what—"

"Not a word, Hope." He placed a hand across her lips. "Not another word. Do you understand?"

Hope nodded her head, and Miles freed her mouth. She should have been frightened but instead her skin missed his touch. The scowl that marred his handsome features puzzled her. His entire attitude threw up red flags. How could he go from apprehension, if she had read him right, to anger so quickly? Maybe she needed to rethink her plans. She didn't need to get involved with someone who was a potential powder keg.

As she watched, his brows and face relaxed but what looked like sheer panic settled deep within his jade eyes.

"I apologize, Hope."

"Are you apologizing for being a donkey's ass on our way here or for manhandling me?"

A tinge of red coated Miles cheeks. "Both."

"Okay. Care to tell me why you behaved that way?"

The blush receded from his face, leaving behind a waxy pallor. As Hope watched, his eyes dilated—this time the emotion she glimpsed reeked of fright. Good heavens. You'd think she'd asked him to rob a bank.

"Uh, I really think I should just go." He raked a trembling hand through his hair. Maybe Miles really was sick.

"If you're not feeling well, maybe—"

His mouth cut off Hope's words. His tongue

teased her lips. She opened to the scorching and decadent heat of its strokes. His hand caressed the curve of her jaw before retreating. His next seductive attack sent waves of hot flame into her veins as he cupped her breasts with his hands. He gently plucked their aching crests, and her blood churned to a boiling point.

At that moment, she would have flung away a lifetime of caution for just one night in his bed. She arched her body closer to his. She felt the hard ridge of flesh pressing against her abdomen. She arched to her toes. She wanted to feel his heat against her center's ache. She slid her arms around Miles' waist and pulled him forward. Finally, she felt the throb of masculinity pulsing against the vee of her jeans. The conflagration of their bodies made her head reel. She rested her head against his chest.

She heard a faint rumble against her ear and then a growl. She stiffened within Miles' embrace. A gentle caress up and down her spine helped to dispel a sudden chill.

She pulled back and looked up. Miles' eyes were closed. Nothing seemed out of place. Maybe she had imagined the animal sound.

The arms surrounding Hope dropped away. Miles stepped back. His eyes glowed and as she watched, their color intensified, turning his gaze into emerald fire. She wanted so badly to reach out to him, but something about his touch-me-not stare frightened her.

She kept her eyes on Miles but reached behind to grasp the hook on the gate of the fence. It inched slowly upward. Miles, however, didn't move. His bearing rivaled one of the markers in the Bonaventure Cemetery.

The hook moved a bit more, its ascent making a slight squealing sound. The noise seemed to unfreeze Miles. He made a move toward her. His lips hovered a scant space from hers before he jerked back. His whispered words could have been, "Forgive me" or "I'm sorry." Hope couldn't tell and after a moment, it didn't seem to matter. Miles turned and left her standing there. His figure gained speed as he traversed their earlier path. At the corner, his form shimmered through her tears and then disappeared. Hope could have sworn she saw a trail of smoke rise up to meet the night sky.

****

Miles fled as if the demons of hell were after him. For the first time in his natural and unnatural life, he didn't know what to do. He wanted Hope so much it hurt—like someone had taken a knife to his gut. The woman he desired above all else, finally wanted him. Yet, he couldn't have her. Not for one night and certainly not for eternity. Not if he told her the truth.

Even if he garnered the courage to divulge his secret, how would he convince Hope he wasn't a lunatic? *Oh, by the way, Hope, I am a creature without scruples. A monster with fangs and claws. Your worst nightmare come to life.* Oh, yeah, she'd accept that—for all of five seconds before she ran away again, this time screaming.

Miles suppressed the chill of fear attacking his limbs and concentrated on the clouds below. Good, Zacke and Miranda's lights were still on. He needed to talk to them ASAP. He wanted someone to keep an eye on Hope while he checked on his English home.

Or run away and hide.

Miles shushed the voice screaming out loud his cowardice. He landed silently at the Kensington's back door. Zacke and Miranda were sitting at the now cleared table. He raised his hand to knock but stopped as he caught the tail end of Zacke's sentence, "Hope actually said that?"

"Yes, and you know what? I think it's great. Miles needs someone to tame him. Hope can do it—I know she can. If only Miles would—"

"If only what, my love?"

Miles didn't wait for Miranda to answer. He dissolved into vapor and materialized on the other side of the door.

"Yes, Miranda, if only I what?"

Miranda's shriek earned him a glare from Zacke. "Would it be too much to ask for you to knock first?"

"Sorry. I had planned to do just that but your conversation fascinated me. Maybe your time would be better spent talking about something besides my love life."

Miranda pulled free of Zacke's arms and advanced toward Miles. He had to give her points for not showing an ounce of fear upon facing a vampire. Of course, her fearlessness came from one undisputable fact: she had married into the family of creatures. Zacke and Miranda's courtship and subsequent early months of marriage had been fraught with threats from Zacke's ex-vampire girlfriend. Miranda had stood her ground, almost losing her life, and then stood by Zacke when Gabriella had mortally wounded him.

He would listen to Miranda because he loved her and because he knew she had his and Hope's best interests at heart.

"Miles Dunbar, I can't believe you said that to me. You and Hawk involved yourselves in my love life. Of course," Miranda paused to throw a grin toward her equally smiling husband, "I'm glad you did. So, I think turn-about is fair play. Don't you?"

Miles resisted the urge to laugh. Miranda had always been tenacious and when she had an agenda she became even more so. He caught her hand before she could poke him in the chest with her finger.

"Maybe so, Miranda, but don't you think Hope and I should decide for ourselves what we want?"

"Not if you're too stubborn to do it."

Miles kissed her hand before gently releasing her fragile weapon. Zacke reached out, caught Miranda by the waist and pulled her back to rest against his chest. He appreciated the commiserating grin Zacke sent his way.

He moved to one of the chairs, pulled it out, and straddled it. He rested his hands on the top of the chair. "It's not that I'm stubborn. There is more to my relationship with Hope than you are aware of."

Zacke arched a brow. Miranda pursed her lips but remained silent.

"I told you at your party you should be sure that your matchmaking victims had not met, Miranda. I have known Hope since she was ten years old, long before Zacke settled here in Savannah." Miles shot a look at Zacke. "Yes, I told you I went underground when you called for my and Hawk's help with Gabriella. I did, but before that, I had been popping in and out of this century to check on Hope."

He propped his head on his hands and settled his gaze on the hard wood floor. He didn't want to see their appalled faces when he told them what he had done.

"It was a long ago Halloween when we met. I was out cruising for dinner."

Miranda's sharp indrawn breath drew his gaze to her face. "No, I didn't take her blood, Miranda. What do you take me for? She was just a child at the time. Actually, I was intent on the two men who abducted her."

He ignored her gasp. "I followed the men from a bar over in the red-light district. I heard something like a kitten mewing. I turned into a deserted alley and found Hope pinned against the wall of one of the buildings. One man was fondling her chest and the other had started to remove her Halloween costume. I not only saw the terror in her eyes, but also felt it in the core of my heart.

"Hope apparently got tired of waiting on her mother to finish talking to one of the neighborhood mothers and decided to strike out on her own for more houses to trick-or-treat. She probably took a wrong turn and the men found her. Maybe she asked them for directions or they gave her candy, I don't know. I do know the men planned to kill her after they finished."

Miles' talons ached and then pushed forward. "When she spotted me, hope leaped into her eyes. I jerked both men away and prepared to beat them senseless. One of them pulled a knife. Instead of attacking me, he pulled Hope in front of him and placed the knife at her throat. I lost it then."

Miles tried to block the image of the blood-filled alley from his mind. He tried to shut out the look of renewed terror in Hope's gaze. He tried but couldn't.

"I killed both men in front of her. I tore them limb from limb. After it was over, Hope stood there, a small frozen doll, her sooty hair drenched in their lifeblood. Her pale features dotted with droplets of crimson. Her pink lips opened to emit a scream but none came forth. Her clothes were in tatters. She shivered from the night chill and shock."

Miles shrugged his shoulders. "It took me a moment or two to release the fury gripping me. I then moved toward Hope. I know what she thought. I read her mind. It flashed with the images of a monster with dripping red fangs. I reached her. I just wanted to offer her comfort and take her to safety."

A hand dropped onto his shoulder. Zacke now stood on one side of Miles and Miranda on the other. "You have told us enough. You don't have to finish."

"Yes. I do. Hope fought my hands when I

reached out to her. My actions must have caused a trigger to open inside her. She screamed and screamed until her voice was nothing more than a parody of sound. She finally fainted, giving me the chance I needed to hold her. Her body felt as light as the wind as I gathered her to me. I healed the scratches on her body. I cleaned the stench of their blood from her hair and skin. I repaired her rent clothing and wiped the memories of the night from her mind. I then carried her to her home. Her mother had not yet returned. She did so a bit later, frantic with worry over Hope.

"She found her daughter asleep on top of her bed. I kept watch outside Hope's window all that night. She awoke before dawn; her eyes a bit dazed but without the horror of the night before. I left then and returned the next night. For weeks I kept watch to make sure she suffered no ill effects from her experience."

Miles allowed Miranda to slip her hand inside his. He retracted his talons and tried to give her a reassuring squeeze. "I finally convinced myself she would be all right, and I left Savannah. I returned periodically over the years until she started college and later medical school. It was then I fell in love with Hope."

Miranda leaned down and kissed his cheek. "And what is so bad about that Miles?"

"Nothing, if I was an ordinary man. You accepted Zacke as a creature before he got his soul back. You were never frightened of him. Hope is different. She is terrified of a monster. How can I tell her that *I am* that monster?"

"I don't know. Zacke kept his secret hidden for months before I found out. You saw what happened next. It took me a bit, but I realized I loved him more than I feared him. Maybe it's too early to assume the worse. Why not give Hope a chance to know you better and go from there?"

"I'm sure you're right." Miles words were aimed at Miranda, but he sought Zacke's gaze. Silent communication flowed between them. They both knew that few mortal women could or would accept a vampire as a life mate.

He stood to his feet. "Thank you both. I trust this conversation will stay between us. Not even Hawk knows about what happened. I also need you to keep an eye on Hope while I visit my home."

Miles heard Zacke and Miranda's promises, but his mind already focused on his destination. A brief moment later, he once again took to the skies.

****

Hope's arm snaked out from under the covers and snagged her cell phone. "Hello?" Silence greeted her query. She sneaked a peek at the clock on the table. Four in the morning. "Hello!" Still nothing. The hospital switchboard would have already identified themselves. Probably a prank call. She stifled a yawn with her free hand and then glared at the phone. "Okay, I'm hanging up now. Next time, please pick on someone who doesn't have to be up at the crack of dawn."

This time she got a reaction. Music filtered through the line. Its melody hauntingly familiar. Her mother use to hum that song when Hope was a little girl. "Hope, it's time to come in." Hope's heart beat a frantic staccato against her ribcage. How could it be? "Mom?"

"Hope, it's bedtime."

Hope dropped the phone. She scrambled back into the center of the bed and jerked the covers over her head. Her arms and legs anchored the coverlet to and around her, blanketing the sound of the now beeping phone. Her body shook with terror. Her eyes burned with tears that wouldn't fall. Her mother had been dead for over a year. Someone was playing a cruel joke.

Time passed. Hope had no idea how much. Her limbs stopped trembling, and her heartbeat settled down to a slow crawl. Her eyelids began to grow heavy, and she tightened the fetal position she lay in. Maybe if she fell asleep really fast and prayed, she wouldn't dream.

Chapter Four

Miles shook off mist droplets and regained his immortal form. It'd been awhile since he'd done any serious time traveling. Going back several centuries and crossing an ocean was harder than he remembered.

He regained his equilibrium and looked around. Home sweet home or in his case, a castle. He scanned the great hall. Dust rested thick on top of the lord's table that set on an equally dirty dais.

He shrugged shoulders tight with fatigue. Maybe he should hire one of the locals to come in and keep house. Miles laughed out loud. The sound bounced off stonewalls and flung itself back in his face. Who was he kidding? No one with an ounce of sanity would come near Dunbar's Lair. Just one of the names, the locals had given his home. Maybe it had been a deserving title at one time. God and the devil only knew how many women his father had raped inside the castle or the men he had killed without provocation.

Miles' moved away from the front door and headed toward the kitchens. Hopefully, he could unearth a bottle of wine. He had a lot of thinking to do but first he needed to drown the ghosts that still lingered inside his head.

****

Miles drained the final drop of wine from the last of a dozen bottles—yes, he knew he shouldn't drink. The effects could render him dangerously ill, but he didn't care.

He squinted eyes that felt like the inside of a rock. He didn't know if it was night or day. The recessed windows near the rafters of the hall made any discernment of light almost impossible. He had no idea how long he had been in his childhood home. He had slept, awakened to drink more, and then slept again—when the gnawing ache of hunger had allowed him. He had purposely ignored his desire for blood. At the moment, he didn't care to indulge his creature side.

It didn't matter anyway. He had nowhere to go. Hope was just a dream he could never have. Miles knew his excessive drinking had much to do with his despondency but his disillusion came from his fractured soul. He'd never been one to give up but the unmistakable reality of what he was and what he could lose crushed his usual optimism.

Even as a lad, when his father would beat him for the fleetest of nothings, he had survived by believing someday he would escape. That life would get better. That day had come when he met Zacke and Hawk.

One night, previous to their meeting, Miles garnered the courage to leave his home. Disgust and determination rode his back. Earlier that day his father had raped and almost beaten a young girl to death. Miles had tried to stop the assault but failed. Shame had caused him to retreat to his chamber. His father had accosted him there and proceeded to teach Miles his place.

He had left before dawn, his back a bloody mass of welts. He had traveled almost to the next town, when his injuries forced him to seek a resting place. His soon-to-be friends had found him under a copse of trees. They bandaged his wounds and then took him back to Zacke's home. There he had received care and nurturing from both Lord and Lady

Kensington.

After healing, he had worked to get physically fit and joined Zacke and Miles in the ranks of warriors for England's king.

They had fought, wenched, and laughed together for several years before Gabriella had stolen their souls. The witch had attacked Zacke first and then stalked Miles and Hawk. Several years passed before they learned their vampire fate had also been Zacke's. Over the centuries, they had lost touch with Zacke. But when Gabriella threatened Miranda, he and Hawk had answered Zacke's call for help. All three of them fought side-by-side to stop Gabriella. The vampiress had died by Zacke's hands, but she had almost managed to take Zacke with her to Hell. His wounding and near death had resulted in him becoming mortal again. Something Zacke had always prayed for, but Miles didn't know if becoming mortal was an option for him or even if he wanted it to be.

He stretched back out on his side and hugged the bottle to him. Its dirty exterior made a poor substitute for what he needed—Hope.

****

Hope's walk to the hospital remained a blur, as did everything else after her alarm jarred her awake. Sleep had become an elusive stranger. The morbid prankster continued to harass her with early morning calls.

She had grabbed a cup of coffee from a sidewalk café and headed for her office. The now empty Styrofoam container, a potent wish that she had grabbed two, sat on her desk. Thank God she had a light surgery schedule.

She allowed her head to drop a bit lower on her elbow-supported palm. Her eyes closed despite her fight to keep them open. Sleep beckoned seductively only to be disrupted by the whoosh of her office door.

"Hope?" Miranda's soft tone reached around the half-opened door.

"Hi Miranda. Come on in." Hope sat back in her chair, rubbed her eyes, and willed her face into an alert expression.

"I'm not disturbing you am I?" Her boss's glance took in the opened files on Hope's desk. A chore she had been intent on finishing before giving into lethargy.

"No, you're fine. Have a seat."

Miranda did as Hope asked before speaking again. "I need a favor. One of the local colleges has a program where they bring in physicians from this area to talk to prospective med students. They have a rotation system and this month, Savannah Trauma Hospital is up. The seminar is today."

"That's great, Miranda." She met Miranda's slightly embarrassed and hopeful gaze.

"It's on trauma medicine. I had planned on doing it myself, but one of the twins has strep throat. Zacke's with Brierana now, but he has a meeting this afternoon with his boss, something to do with a string of purse snatchings. Do you think you could do it instead?"

Hope's heart sped up. She hated public speaking. She had made the debate team in college but that had been a fiasco. Her rebuttal on peer pressure had been met with catcalls and boos. Of course, the seminar wouldn't be the same thing but just being in the public's eye made her nervous.

Miranda mistook her silence for a no. "Look, don't worry about it. I'm sure I can get someone else to do it."

Hope swallowed her nerves. Miranda was a good boss and friend. She couldn't let her own insecurities keep her from doing her part. "Don't be silly. I'll be happy to help out."

Hope jotted down the time and address for the

seminar amidst Miranda's profuse thanks. She took the proffered notes and put them in her briefcase.

Miranda fidgeted in her seat. "I was wondering if you'd heard from Miles."

Hope met Miranda's gaze. "I haven't laid eyes on him since—" Heat stung her cheeks as it did every time she thought of that night. Sure, his kiss had been unexpected. Sure, it had singed her lips, but that still didn't excuse her behavior. Maybe that was why Miles had dropped from the face of the earth after he walked her home over a week ago. "Have you?"

Miranda turned her gaze just a bit. Not a good sign. Maybe she had spoken to Miles and he didn't want her to tell Hope. He'd probably had his fill of a woman who couldn't make up her mind. One minute, she wanted nothing to do with him, the next she was crawling over his body like ants in an anthill.

"It's okay, Miranda. I didn't really expect a second date."

Hope pulled one of the files forward and flipped back the cover. Her gaze settled on the words, but she couldn't comprehend a thing they said.

A slight rustling and the barely there scrub of Miranda's chair on the linoleum signified her boss was leaving. Hope kept her eyes glued to the print. A second later, the office door open and closed.

****

Hope left the medical arts building on the Savannah Branches campus at four o'clock. The seminar had started late. Instead of two o'clock, the starting time, Hope had been introduced closer to three. Butterflies had nestled in her stomach, stirring up a pot of queasiness. However, the notes Miranda had given her were priceless in their aid, and once she had gotten into the fascinating world of trauma medicine, she had forgotten about being nervous.

She'd managed to answer all the questions and even talked with a few med students. Not a bad way to end her workday. She had called Miranda shortly after the session ended and been told to take the rest of the day off. Since her shift normally ended at seven, she planned to enjoy the beautiful day. A bite of winter crisped the air, but the sun shone down like a generous gift.

She had parked across the campus from the Medical Arts building. Parking spaces had been few and far between with the fall quarter in full swing. Now, she was glad of the long walk. Fountains sang a welcoming tune as jets of water flowed up and down. A few birds soared overhead, and the sky was a stunning blue.

Hope moved toward the entrance to the park that divided the campus into sections. Earlier she had spied a few couples studying under leafy bowers. Now, the park was deserted. As she walked, the sun chose to dip behind a cloud, changing the previous friendly facade into a shadowy substitute. She moved a bit faster. A crackle of fallen leaves spurred her to an even swifter walk. The rustling grew louder, and Hope's heart hurtled to a stop. She peered behind her and it sped up again. Two men followed her at a rapid pace. Their gazes targeted her. She didn't like their expressions. The taller of the two scowled; his black brows the same color as his unkempt beard. The other just stared, giving her the creeps.

She turned back around and saw the parking area up ahead. Not much farther to go. She should have her head examined for being nervous. The men were probably campus visitors on their way to their car.

The blow caught Hope unaware. She staggered, her back a mass of spreading pain. Her breath hitched. A rough hand caught her arm and jerked her around. One man grabbed her briefcase and the other, the one with the fearsome stare, shoved her backward. Her back hit the hard earth. Dazed, she lay there. One of her legs bent in an unnatural position. Her head ached. She knew she should try to get up—she needed to run—if she could. She knew she should scream also, but her breath had escaped when she hit the ground. It returned now in an agonizing groan.

The men circled her. Their forms blurred in and out. She tried focusing her gaze on her nearest attacker. He moved in closer. His hands shoved the edges of her jacket aside and squeezed her breasts.

A different type of pain assailed her. A distant something of long ago fought to center itself inside her head. She repelled it and tried to dislodge her attacker's punishing grip.

A path of fire dug tendrils into her upper left arm. She tried to stall another attack with her other arm but failed when a fist slammed into her face. Her jaw ached. Another blow, this time to the side of her head, and Hope fell into a morass of darkness.

****

Miles catapulted to wakefulness from a slumber rife with nightmares. Water dripped into his eyes causing them to open. The room spun and then righted itself. Dampness trickled its way down his chin and burrowed into the material of his shirt. He cast a cautious look around—his head ached even more than it had the last time he had awakened. His gaze found two forms standing over him, one held an empty pitcher in his outstretched hand.

"Bout time you woke up, Sleeping Beauty."

Hawk Sherwood's tone reeked of sarcasm. What was he doing here and why hadn't Miles detected his presence? Of course, his drunken stupor could account for his vamp radar not going off.

He turned his gaze just a bit and stared into

Zacke's frowning face. "How did you get here and what do you two want?"

"First off, you can cut the defense crap. You should have your ass kicked. What if I'd been a vampire hunter? I could have cut your heart out before you ever woke up.

"So? What if I don't give a rat's ass, Zacke?"

"Well, at the moment, I'm not sure I do, but you need to sober your sorry butt up. Hawk and I didn't come all this way for pleasure."

"He's right, Miles. You need to get over your pity party and listen to what we have to say."

Miles didn't like either of their tones, but something about the concern and anxiety showing in their gazes made him put off the idea of kicking their butts back to the twenty-first century.

He pulled himself to a sitting position and propped his back against the cold stonewall. "All right, I'm listening."

Hawk and Zacke moved to sit on the floor beside him. The pitcher used as a wake-up call disappeared with a wave of Hawk's hand.

"Something's happened. Hope was attacked."

Miles' blood slowed to a crawl within his veins. He felt the gradual decrease of his heartbeat and heard a dull roar in his ears. His fangs erupted with a force that sliced his bottom lip. His vision blurred into a jade storm.

"Miles!"

He heard Hawk's exclamation. He knew Zacke's face would mirror the same concern—that he would lash out. Hawk could protect himself, but Zacke's transformation back into a mortal put him at deadly risk. A risk Miles wasn't willing to take.

He shook off the rage, and his heart began to beat once more—desolation a prime factor.

Hope was hurt.

Miles' talons released and retracted. "What

happened?"

"Hope was attacked on campus at Savannah Branches U, this afternoon. Apparently she was walking back to her car when the men accosted her. There's been a string of purse snatchings in the last few weeks—none of them on campus and none of them violent. Just a quick grab and run. No reason for them to have attacked Hope."

"How bad is it?"

"A cut to her upper arm, concussion, contusions to her face and back and her left knee is twisted."

"They didn't *touch* her, did they?"

"Not in the way you mean. Some kids on the way to class came up on the scene and the men ran." Zacke raised his hands. "I'm sorry, Miles."

"It wasn't your fault. Hope just happened to be at the wrong place at the wrong time." Hawk's words were matter of fact, but his tone spoke of an agitation that Miles recognized well. Hawk had always been a defender of right. He hated anything that hurt innocents. Something all three of them had in common.

"Will Hope be okay? Is Miranda with her?" Miles wasn't a fond believer in physicians. He had never needed one, but he had watched Miranda work tirelessly to save Zacke after his final and deadly battle with Gabriella.

"Yes. Miranda was at the hospital when Hope was brought in. She's been with her ever since. Hope regained consciousness and refused to stay at the hospital after her treatment. Miranda promised to take her to our house."

"That's good. Miranda will care for her and she'll get better."

"Miles, we really should get going."

"So go."

"Don't tell me you're not coming."

"Why? She doesn't need me."

Hawk stood to his feet. "Zacke told me what happened to Hope years ago."

Miles glared at Zacke.

"Do you really think you're doing yourself or her any good by being a coward?"

Miles shot to his unsteady feet. He grasped the wall and waited for the room to stop spinning. "You dare to call me a coward. I have guarded your back and Zacke's in battle for centuries." He spun slightly and faced a now standing Zacke. "Do you feel the same way?"

He resisted the rage and hurt that taunted him to slash out at Zacke. He pulled in his talons and allowed Zacke to place a hand on his shoulder.

"Neither one of us think you a coward. Hawk is just trying to get you to see reason. Fear can make us think all sorts of things, Miles. I almost lost Miranda because of fear. You fear you can't have Hope and if you refuse to see her, then you don't have to face that fear. It isn't cowardice but self-survival causing you to feel this way."

Miles allowed his shoulders to slump. The men standing with him were not his enemies. The only enemy he had was himself. A self that should leave Hope alone, but he knew in his heart that he couldn't do that. Hope beat in his blood like a fine wine breathed. He needed her to continue his existence. Life or death held no meaning without her.

"You're right, both of you. I am a coward. It's time I stopped being afraid."

Hawk stepped forward and draped an arm over Miles' other shoulder. "Good, but before we go, I think you need to wash off the stench of the last week. What say you, Zacke?"

"I say you're right. Of course, he could do it the vampire way, but I'm not sure his powers are up to it. I think he needs an old-fashioned bath.

Something that will help disperse the lingering alcohol fumes in his blood."

Miles turned to run but the wall greeted him. A wave of dizziness attacked. The wine he'd consumed was making itself known. No point in fighting the obvious. His weak limbs were no match for Hawk's vampiric strength or Zacke's fighting stance.

A short while later, Miles' head broke the surface of the lake's frigid water for a third time. Lucky he wasn't the Wicked Witch of the West or he'd be dead by now.

Chapter Five

Miles straddled a chair in the Kensingtons' kitchen. A concerned and anxious Miranda, who didn't seem to be finished with her interrogation quite yet, had already hauled him over the coals.

"I can't understand how you could just cut and run like that, Miles. Let alone drink yourself into an alcoholic stupor. You know what liquor does to your blood. We've had this conversation before."

He knew but it didn't help. If he were still mortal the affects of his binge would have been a hangover. But instead, the wine he'd consumed had crystallized in his blood. He'd survived the poisoning but only with the aid of Hawk and Zacke.

After his bath in the lake, he'd been freezing cold. Not the cold that his creature make-up warranted but frigid on the inside. The fever and delirium had started shortly after or so he'd been told. Miles couldn't remember much after his friends had hauled his wet and naked arse back to the castle.

There he'd spent almost a day fighting off the toxin in his body. The nasty concoction Hawk continually forced down his throat had finally done the trick.

With daylight almost on them, he, Hawk, and Zacke had slept the day away. He and Hawk had then fed before leaving medieval times, a time they both favored. Their tardy arrival had resulted in Miranda being more than a bit aggravated.

Miles tuned back into the conversation in time to hear Miranda words. "Well, if you knew then why did you do it?"

Miranda took another turn around the kitchen before she marched over to an amused Zacke and poked him in the chest with her finger. Her husband managed not to flinch. She did the same to Hawk and then moved around the table to Miles. He plastered his chest against the chair front. He'd been on the receiving end of that finger many times over the years.

Miranda pinched his ear instead.

Miles ignored the pained grins of the other males and braved another reprimand. He caught Miranda's hand in his. "Miranda, I'm sorry. Lately all I've done is apologize. I didn't mean to worry you. I've learned my lesson. Vampires and vino don't mix. Okay? Truce?"

"Truce, but don't let—"

"Excuse me, Miranda." Miles moved with immortal speed. Hope was awake.

****

Hope teetered on the top step of the staircase. Her knee buckled, and she pitched forward. She shut her eyes to block out a vision of her broken neck.

She landed against a hard chest and felt possessive hands clutch her close.

"God in Heaven woman, are you trying to kill yourself?"

Hope's eyes snapped open to gaze into Miles' appalled stare. She tried to move out of his embrace. The man had left without saying a word—left after kissing her breathless. He'd aroused feelings she'd never experienced before and then disappeared off the face of her world.

"Answer me. Are you trying to kill yourself?"

"What if I am? Why should you care?" She tried to twist away but her knee betrayed her again.

"Ouch!"

"Stop. You're hurting yourself."

"Again, why do you care?"

Hope wasn't sure if she wanted Miles to answer her question or not. Maybe he didn't care. Maybe the kiss had been a mistake on his part. Maybe he felt sorry for her. Oh Lord, what if Miranda really had put him up to asking her to dinner.

"No one put me up to anything. Asking you out was my idea."

Hope didn't know if she could believe him or not. Like, how did he know what she was thinking? A bit unnerving coming from a man she barely knew.

"Trust me, Hope. I'd never hurt you." Miles dropped a light kiss on her open mouth. "Now, let's get you downstairs. Unless you'd rather I take you back to bed."

Her cheeks heated with fire. Bed and Miles—two words in the same sentence she shouldn't contemplate. They painted a seductive scene in her mind. Her nipples tightened, and the spot between her legs ached despite her physical hurts.

Miles pulled her even closer. Hope bit back a gasp as his arousal caressed her center. She didn't need this. She wanted it but not now. There were too many unanswered questions.

"Miles? Hope?"

Hope welcomed the interruption. She placed her palm against Miles chest and pressed. His arms dropped away.

"Miranda, Miles was just going to help me down the stairs."

"Uh, okay, we're in the kitchen." Miranda's voice sounded doubtful. Who could blame her for thinking something else? Hope dared a look at the man who held her.

The hunger blazing from his eyes made her legs feel like over-cooked spaghetti. "I think we should go down now, don't you?"

"No. But I guess there's no help for it. If we don't make an entrance in just a few minutes, Zacke, and probably Hawk, will both be in our faces."

"Who's Hawk?"

Miles lips pulled back in a smile, softening his features. He no longer looked like he wanted to jump her bones.

"A good friend, but he can be a bit overpowering when it comes to women."

"Well, if you mean he's a flirt—it won't be an issue. I don't exactly look my best."

To hell with everyone else—they could wait. He wasn't moving an inch until he set Hope straight. "Damn it woman, why do you say things like that? You are the most beautiful woman I've ever seen."

"Then you must be blind. I know what my face looks like. I found the mirror Miranda hid in the bathroom."

Miles ached to touch the purple and black shadow beneath Hope's eye. He wanted to kiss the matching bruise on her cheek. He restrained the anger her injuries invoked. His first glimpse of Hope on the stairs had tormented him but her near fall had sent his heart into almost death throes.

As he held her safely in his arms, he only wanted to reassure himself she was all right. Not just in body but in spirit. Her verbal attack left him with little doubt. His Hope would recover. Now, he needed to convince her he couldn't be run off by her snide remarks. He knew it was her way of protecting herself.

"Your bruises are proof of your courage. You fought back. But for me they signify more. You're alive and the alternative is something I don't ever want to think about."

Before she could say anything else, Miles scooped her into his arms and descended the stairs.

He didn't give in to the groan trapped in his throat demanding release. He wasn't some pup who couldn't contain his lust. He would die for this woman. And when she was completely well, he would show her just what she meant to him, heart and soul.

****

"I forbid it!"

"Excuse me, but you don't have that right."

"Be reasonable, Hope. You're not well enough to move back to your house."

Miles could have yanked his bumbling tongue from his mouth. His command had done nothing but incense Hope. Since they had joined the others in the kitchen, they'd all tried in vain to convince Hope she'd be safer at Zacke's and Miranda's.

"Your concern over my health is admirable, but you're only using that as an excuse. I told you, I didn't know those men and it was a random act of violence. I just happened to be the victim."

"Hope, there's been more than one attack. You aren't the first, and if we don't catch them, you may not be the last."

Zacke's serious tone caused Hope to blink rapidly. Miles hoped it would make her see sense. For a woman who dealt with the harsh realities of life on a daily basis, she seemed to have blinders on in reference to her own plight.

"What do you mean? I thought it was just a one time purse-snatching."

"Well, the other victims weren't beaten. I don't know why but it seems as if they targeted you on purpose."

Zacke held out his hand, stopping Miles' almost released fanged growl.

"The police department *will* find whoever attacked Hope."

Miles gnashed his teeth at Zacke's unspoken

warning. Centuries of following the man into battle kept him from snarling out a reply. Even as a mortal, Zacke was a force to be reckoned with. He no longer had the strength or the fangs of a vampire, but he kept a stubborn will and unbreakable zeal of right and wrong. He would fight to find Hope's attackers and see them prosecuted by mortal law.

"Of course. But in the meantime, Hope needs to be safe."

"I agree." Miranda's soft tone broke through the tension-laden air. "I also think there is only one solution to the problem."

All eyes turned to Miranda.

"Hope will go home, and Miles will stay with her."

Silence reigned for the space of a second.

"That's *not* necessary." Hope squeaked her protest.

"I don't think that's a good idea."

Miles ignored the almost stifled guffaws coming from Zacke and Hawk at his pained words. Amusing didn't describe what would happen if he moved in with Hope.

"Miranda, Hope wouldn't be comfortable with me moving in. She needs her rest and you *know* I'm a *night* person."

"Yes, and that's why it would be perfect. You would be awake and on guard."

Zacke cleared his throat. The stern blue gaze assured Miles he'd get no help there.

"Hope, as much as I hate to rain on your parade, you were a victim. The perps are still loose, and they took your briefcase, with your wallet, giving them access to your address. Until we catch them, you are in danger. They could just rob your house, but if you're alone, they could finish the job they started at the university."

****

Fingers of light etched their way across the single window in Hope's basement. Miles had given in to what he knew was the inevitable, although no one had given any thought to where he would sleep during the day. He'd told Hope some cock-and-bull story about having to see a sick friend during the day. Not very original but it had worked. He just thanked God he'd come across the basement during his midnight prowling.

A grin pulled at his lips. It had taken awhile the night before but his angel had finally given an unenthusiastic yes to having a bodyguard. A reminder that she had seen their faces and would probably be targeted for that alone helped to garner her agreement. After Zacke called a sketch artist to the house and Hope had given them her remembered descriptions, Miranda had almost tossed them out the door. The woman should show some finesse. Surely, Hope had seen the glee not quite hidden by Miranda's concerned expression.

It had taken only a cup of hot tea to have Hope nodding off. Miles had helped her up to bed but left her to her own devices. He didn't trust himself to tuck her in.

He moved around the basement and found a mattress wedged into a corner and tugged it into the middle of the floor. He then placed an empty bookcase in front of the window. He could sleep in peace now but for one small detail. He waved his hand and the bolt on the basement door locked. It wouldn't do for Hope to find him—one look at his cadaver-like body, and she'd never recover.

The mattress sank beneath his weight. He rested on his side—his favorite position for sleeping above ground. His eyes closed, and he welcomed the darkness of slumber.

****

Hope hobbled to the stove and turned the flame

on under the teakettle. She'd awakened just a bit ago. A fragment of the sun still shone but night would soon make its appearance. Which was more than she could say for Miles.

The guest room upstairs had been empty. No evidence to show he'd even slept in the bed. The den also lacked her reluctant bodyguard.

A shrill whistle broke the silence. She turned off the burner on the stove and opened a tin of raspberry tea. She dumped two teaspoons into a cup and drowned the mix with boiling water. The kitchen filled with the enticing fragrance. A quick stir and Hope turned and braced her back against the counter. She raised the cup to her lips.

Tea spewed across the tiled floor. "Where did you come from?"

"I just got back."

"Well, you weren't there a minute ago, and the door was locked. How did you get in?"

"I borrowed your house key."

Miles' explanation made sense, but why hadn't she heard the door? She would swear he hadn't been there when she turned around. Maybe the pain pills were affecting her vision.

"Uh, okay." Hope moved to the table and set her cup down. She needed to mop up the mess she'd made. Before she could follow through on her thought, Miles left his prop against the back door and crossed to the broom closet.

"Sit. I'll take care of this. You don't need to be on that leg. You shouldn't even be downstairs."

He moved to the sink and filled the bucket before squirting some soap into the water.

Hope watched the muscles bulge in his arm as he lifted the bucket to the floor and proceeded to plunge the mop in its depths. His T-shirt pulled taut across his broad shoulders as he wrung out the mop head.

Hope stared in fascination at denim-molded buttocks when Miles stroked the mop back and forth over the spilt tea.

Of course, a paper towel would have done the trick but she wouldn't have enjoyed that as much as this floorshow. Heat burned her cheeks as Miles made one more circuit before replacing the mop in the closet. His strides to the backdoor to throw out the dirty water drew attention to his thighs and the bulge pressing against the zippered front.

Lord help her. This man would be spending the next several days and nights under her roof and all she wanted to do was have him between her sheets.

The door closed with a quiet click. Hope jerked her gaze up. The look on Miles face made her limbs dissolve. He knew what she was thinking.

Miles caught her in his arms and pulled her up and out of her chair. The bulge against her belly grew. She pressed closer. Liquid pooled deep inside her. A teasing caress against her throat brought her up on her toes. Her knee began a slow burn. A gentle caress to the injured limb made the ache subside. Miles cupped the underside of her knee and lifted her leg. His wide stance allowed it to rest on his thigh—bringing Hope's aching center flush against his arousal.

Miles' lips left her throat and staked claim to her lips. She opened to his kiss. His tongue laved the inside of her mouth. She welcomed the silken touch and returned its heated entreaty.

Hope fell into a tunnel of scorching desire. Her hands crept around Miles' neck and ended in a strangle hold as she held on for dear life.

"Uh oh."

Miles instantly felt the loss of warmth as Hope jerked her arms and then her body away. His chest mourned the absence of her breasts against him, his fingertips felt empty without her loveliness to touch, his arousal burned with unquenched fire.

Hawk would pay for his interruption.

He assisted a dazed Hope to a chair before he turned to face his vampire brother. "I trust you have a good reason for being here."

"Miranda wanted me to check on Hope. The other good doctor got called to the hospital."

"Hope is doing fine. So why don't you take off."

"I would, but Zacke was a tad concerned about your dinner arrangements."

The raised eyebrow finally dinged a bell in Miles' mind. He had to feed, but he didn't want to leave Hope.

He'd awakened a bit earlier than usual tonight and had planned on finding his own dinner before Hope awoke but the idea lacked appeal. In the past, women had been an easy conquest for a bite to eat, but since he'd entered Hope's dreams he'd found it harder to take what he needed from another woman. Although he continued to satisfy his hunger, guilt had ridden his back like a second skin.

Just like it would tonight.

"Thanks, Hawk. I'll go out for a bite after I fix Hope's dinner."

"Nonsense. I'm perfectly capable of cooking dinner for all of us."

"You need to stay off that leg." He shot a smile her way and turned once again to Hawk. "You want to stay for dinner?"

"Well, it depends on what you plan on burning."

Miles chuckled. Over the centuries, he and Hawk had traveled the world. A lot of that time they spent camping out under the stars. It helped to remind them of better days—when they fought for the King of England and wined, dined, and bedded women without a care in the world. However, his skills as a chef left a lot to be desired.

Miles crossed to the refrigerator and perused its

contents. "I've improved my culinary skills. How does a steak medium rare sound?"

An hour later, Hope wiped her lips with her napkin and sat back. Dinner had been delicious. Not only had Miles grilled steaks, the salad and French bread that accompanied the meat had been perfect.

"Dinner was great, Miles. Thank you."

"No problem."

"Well, I have to admit, you have gotten better."

Hope watched Miles and Hawk exchange grins.

"Hawk, if you don't mind, could you stay with Hope, while I run an errand?"

"Certainly. It'll be my pleasure."

The shrill ring of the phone broke into the men's conversation.

"I'll get it. You stay seated, Hope."

Hope's gaze followed Miles' backside as he strode from the room.

"Bossy isn't he?"

"Just a bit."

"But you know, Hope, he's one of the kindest guys I've ever met. I've seen him give his last penny to help someone."

For the first time, Hope really looked beyond the handsome good looks of her guest. His amber gaze radiated honesty and concern.

"That's not the first adjective that comes to mind when I think of Miles." Her cheeks burned at all the words that could describe his sensual hot looks and body, not to mention an attitude dating back to archaic times.

"If kind doesn't work then how about—"

"Arrogant?"

"Guilty as charged."

Hope's face stung even more. The man should wear a bell around his neck. He walked way too quietly for her peace of mind. He did a lot of things that disturbed her orderly life.

"Who was on the phone?"

"Some man named Guy. He said he's your manager at Morgan Rarities."

"Yeah, he is. I'll see what he wants."

Hawk stood up when Hope did, and Miles helped her walk into the den. There he eased her to the couch near the phone. She should probably get a portable but no one but Guy called her at her home number. The hospital used her cell phone.

Hope picked up the receiver. "Hello."

"Hope, I just found out about what happened. Are you okay?"

"Guy, I'm fine—just a bit sore. Is everything all right at Morgan's?"

Guy cleared his throat. Not a good sign. He always did that when he had something he didn't want to say. "Hope, who was the guy that answered the phone? I didn't know you had anyone visiting."

"The guy is Miles Dunbar. He's been assigned by the Savannah PD to be my bodyguard. There really wasn't a reason for you to know. Now, if we could get on with our business."

"Well, our last few shipments have been missing some items. I'm sure it's just an oversight from the shippers, but I wanted to talk to you about installing more security at the shop and warehouse."

"It probably wouldn't hurt. Dad planned to do just that before he and Mom—before the accident. Can you tell me more about the missing items?"

The throat clearing was more audible this time.

"I know you have company but I'd really prefer to talk to you in person. Could I drop by in a bit?"

Hope rolled her eyes. She wasn't up to dealing with Guy's insecurities tonight. He'd stepped into his dad's footsteps as manager of her parent's business after his dad passed away. He'd only been the manager for six months when her parents had been killed. Guy had brought up then that he wanted to have weekly meetings with Hope, but she just didn't have the heart or time to give to the business. Truth of the matter, she couldn't stand to step inside the ornate front doors. The halls echoed with her mom's laughter and her father's teasing tones. She'd finally compromised with a monthly meet and talking by phone in-between if needed.

"I'm really tired, Guy. How about I meet you at the shop tomorrow afternoon?

"All right. See you then."

A resounding click irritated her ear. Guy wasn't happy, but he'd just have to get over it. Hope replaced the receiver and looked up at Miles. Apparently, he'd been there during the entire conversation.

"You okay?" Miles voice flowed over her like hot mulled wine. The man looked good, felt good, and made her feel like one hundred percent woman.

"Hope?"

His tone now resembled aged whiskey. A bit rough but vibrant. She needed to get a grip. Just because he made her bones feel like melted snow on a sidewalk didn't mean a thing.

"I'm fine. Like I told Guy, I'm just tired. I think I'll go up to bed."

Miles cleared his throat and tried not to think of the lust consuming his body. He prayed the massive arousal Hope's thoughts had invoked would go unnoticed. "I have to go out for a bit, but Hawk will be here if you need anything."

"Okay. I'll see you tomorrow."

"Count on it."

****

A few hours later, Miles let himself into Hope's house. This time he actually used the key. He might as well get used to entering the mortal way. If he'd been one second off earlier that night, Hope would have seen him materialize out of thin air. Not the type of thing he wanted her to know, at least not yet—probably not ever.

"Hey, how was dinner?"

"It was okay. It stopped the hunger."

Miles and Hawk walked back into the den. Miles confiscated the couch, and Hawk sat in the recliner.

"Everything go okay here?"

"Yep. It's been quiet, I actually dozed off for a few after I made sure Hope was asleep."

"Good. She was exhausted. I think that manager, Guy, upset Hope." Miles allowed a bit of fang to show. "I personally didn't care for his attitude."

"Why?"

"He's a bit condescending. *"I'd like to speak to Ms. Morgan."* Not even an *if you please.* I don't know, he just rubbed me the wrong way."

Hawk laughed. "My friend, I think any man who wants to talk to Hope rubs you the wrong way. You've got it bad, and I don't see it going away."

"So?"

"So, when are you going to tell her what you are and that you love her?"

"If I tell her I'm a vampire, then I'll never get to tell her I love her. And if I tell her I love her first, then I'll just lose her when I tell her the other. Either way it's a no-win situation."

The afghan previously residing over the back of the recliner smacked Miles in the face. "Hawk!"

"Stop growling. I can't believe you would have so little faith in Hope or yourself. You know, I've done some thought reading myself. The woman cares for you more than she'll admit at the moment—even to herself. You fascinate her and it's not all sexual."

"Since when did you add a PhD in psychology after your name?"

"Ah ha, touched a nerve, didn't I?"

"Yes, you did."

Hawk scrubbed a hand across his face. "Think about telling her, Miles. Now, I'm gonna head out and see if I can't find me a bit of company for the rest of the night."

Miles knew company meant a late night snack and bed. He wished Hawk luck with his night's adventure before locking the house up with a safety spell. He turned off the lights and headed up the stairs. He'd just peek in on Hope before he did a bit of investigation on Guy Evans.

A light shone under Hope's door. Of course that didn't mean she was awake. He could scan the room but that might not be a good idea. He could get more than he bargained for. Hope in the innocence of sleep was more seductive than a nightclub full of strippers. And although he ached to see her, her bedroom wasn't the safest place. The kitchen would be better.

"Hope?" Silence met his ears. "Hope, are you awake? Can I get you anything?" A faint sound met his hearing this time. It wasn't bedclothes rustling. It sounded more like a whimper.

"Hope." The whimper grew louder followed by the distinct sound of weeping.

Chapter Six

Miles materialized by Hope's bed and cursed silently. In his anxiety, he'd given no thought to what his Houdini act could do to Hope. However, his fear she would shriek was foundless. Her entire body was encased under the coverlet. Maybe she'd had a nightmare. Lord knew she had a right to them.

He caught one corner of the cloth and lifted. The sight that met his eyes tore at his heart. Hope lay in a fetal position, her eyes tightly clenched.

His hand shook slightly when he reached out to touch her face. Her eyes snapped open, their pupils dilated and glistening with tears. As he watched, a silver droplet escaped and crept down her ashen cheek.

"Miles?"

"What's wrong, Hope? Are you hurting? Can I get you a pain pill?"

She caught his hand and squeezed it hard. If he'd been a mortal it would have hurt.

"Move over." Miles knew it was probably a mistake, but he slid his body onto the rumpled sheets and his arm around her shoulders. The silk of her nightshirt caressed his fingers, a blatant temptation to explore the satin smoothness beneath its surface.

But first he needed to find out what was wrong. His innocent bundle of seduction hadn't even protested him climbing into bed. Something definitely was going on.

"Tell me. Did you have a bad dream?"

Hope hiccupped before using the edge of the sheet to wipe her eyes. "I only wished it had been a nightmare."

The panic in her voice caused Miles' hackles to rise. Someone or something had terrified Hope. He willed his fangs and claws to stay hidden. "Why not tell me about it? It might help."

"For the last week or so, I've been getting phone calls during the night." Hope's voice shook. "The first time, I thought it was just a prank caller but then I heard someone humming the song my mother use to sing to me as a child."

Hope moved closer to Miles. He willed his body to behave.

"I don't know how they knew about the song but before I could ask, I heard my mother's voice telling me it was bedtime."

Miles brain went into overdrive. Deirdre Morgan's lullaby had always been done in the privacy of Hope's bedroom. The slightly off key rendition of "Rock-A-Bye-Baby" had been the only thing to get Hope to sleep after her near abduction. Mrs. Morgan had only sung it to Hope for a few months before she declared she could go to sleep on her own. Not even Hope's dad had been privy to those tender moments. Only Miles in his quest to make sure Hope was safe had been a witness.

"Are you sure that's what you heard? Maybe you were dreaming?"

"No! The calls always come in on my cell phone. I tried to call the number back but it always comes up as unknown."

"I'll talk to Zacke about this tomorrow. In the meantime, you need to get some sleep."

"Yeah, I have that meeting with Guy tomorrow."

Miles' fangs connected with the force of his animosity. He didn't like Guy. Something about the man didn't ring quite right. He couldn't pinpoint it. It could be the fact that he was sure the manager wanted to sniff up Hope's skirts, but regardless, he still planned on finding out all he could about the man.

"Why don't you call Guy and ask him to come by here tomorrow night for that meeting? I really don't want you to go out on your own. I have some previous obligations tomorrow during the day but I'm all yours tomorrow night."

"I don't really need a babysitter, Miles."

"I think you do." Before Hope could protest, Miles kissed her open mouth. "Now get some sleep, woman."

****

Miles awoke not long before sunrise was scheduled to make its appearance. He couldn't remember the last time he'd slept during the night hours.

His arm burned with pins and needles. He turned toward Hope. Her hair, which had been tied back earlier, had escaped its confines. Midnight tresses flowed over his captured arm and inched their way across his chest.

Hope murmured in her sleep and pressed closer, her hand dangerously near to his awakening arousal. Before becoming a vampire, Miles had always enjoyed making love in the morning. A distant memory, but one his body certainly recognized.

He moved her hand back to her thigh. He needed to get out of bed.

Hope's sleep-warmed body and her innocent but seductive moves were powerful tools for trouble. God above knew he wanted to make her his in every possible way. He wanted to sheath himself deep within her virginal depths, but he wanted Hope to know what he was and to be awake when he made love to her. To take her now when she wasn't fully aware would be a mistake. One Miles was sure would haunt him long after he exulted in his release.

His unsteady hand dislodged Hope's hair, and he eased his other arm from beneath her body. Good. Now all he had to do was slide off the mattress.

Miles silenced his groan as Hope turned fully on her side and slung an arm over his chest. Now what? He eyed the taunting limb as if it were a snake. Before he could come up with a plan that would allow him to keep his sanity, Hope moved in for the kill by pressing closer. Her breasts with their sleep-ripened tips set off alarms inside his body. His fangs grew, his blood pumped rapidly, and his arousal screamed for release.

He was sunk. It seemed that no matter which way he turned, the fates were against him. To hell with them and his outdated chivalry.

Miles pulled Hope closer. His lips found the mesmerizing pulse at her throat. He caressed it with a heat that threatened to engulf him. He could feel the flow of blood in her veins. It called to him like a siren's song. His teeth nipped and then licked the reddened skin. Too dangerous. If he wasn't careful, he'd do the unforgivable and sip the rich, warm nectar until he was satisfied. The result would be a weakened, almost to the state of death, Hope.

He willed his mind away from the bounty of her blood and allowed his hand to cup the underside of her breast. The soft flesh filled his hand and caused his engorged shaft to jerk. He was fast losing control of the situation, but he didn't care. He caressed the tip of her breast between his thumb and forefinger. The nipple elongated and so did his teeth.

Hope moved restlessly when he covered her body with his. He unbuttoned the nightshirt and bared the flesh he longed to taste. His fingers once again teased a pebbled tip before his lips captured his treasure.

Hope's eyes flickered open. Her gaze a mixture of confusion and desire. His teeth raked and then laved her flesh with a heady combination of lust and love.

Her body writhed beneath his, bringing the core he sought in direct contact with his erection. He pushed gently against her center. When she didn't protest, he pushed her long nightshirt up past her waist. Her nether hair was drenched with droplets of heated want. His hand sought and reveled in silken warmth before he withdrew. He found Hope's gaze. Her pupils were dilated even more. Her lovely lips parted in a temptation he couldn't refuse.

He explored and tasted the sweet confines of her mouth as one hand continued to palm her breast. His other hand once again sought haven between her legs, pressing against the small nubbin of flesh swollen with desire.

Miles retreated from the succulent lure of her mouth. His goal now—to taste Hope's core.

Miles stripped off his T-shirt and tossed it to the floor. Hope's hands caught and caressed his bare shoulders. Tendrils of heat scored a path down his back and launched an answering fire in his buttocks. His erection strained against the confines of his jeans. His hand sought the button at his waist but before he could release it, warmth of a different kind engulfed him.

Sunlight poured in from the sheer curtains in Hope's bedroom. Dammit! He'd been so lost in desire he'd forgotten about the sunrise.

Hope pulled him closer, her body a magnet for his still pulsing arousal. He couldn't leave her like this. It wouldn't be fair.

His fingers caressed her with an intensity that had Hope's backside leaving the mattress. He eased his middle finger into the center of her desire. He stroked in and out of her silken depths as he continued his frontal assault.

He captured her renewed whimpers with his mouth. He ignored the shards of flame attacking his body. He owed these few moments to Hope and to himself. For too long, he'd denied his love and desire for her. He'd walked away from making her his time after time. At least when she reached her release this time, he'd be there. Not a mystical dreamlike creature but in the flesh.

But Miles' time to leave without causing permanent damage to his flesh had almost run out.

Hope's body rose and fell with her exertions to attain release. Her body stilled for one second of time before her inner muscles tightened around Miles finger. The strength of her climax threatened to cut off the blood supply to his digit. Her release flooded his fingers with liquid heat. He eased his hand from between her legs and forced his mouth from her lips.

Her breathing slowed and eyes that had closed with the anticipation of fulfilled desire reopened. "Miles?"

"It's okay my love. This time was for you. There will be others. Now sleep."

****

Hope stretched with contentment. She'd actually slept long and hard. Her bedside clock showed past noon. Her stomach rumbled with the beginning yearnings of hunger. She might as well get up. She had that meeting with Guy today.

No. Miles had asked her to change the time and place of the meeting. Hope racked her brain for details of that conversation. Her hand crept to her throat. He'd been in her bedroom. He'd witnessed the aftermath of the phone call, and he'd—Her cheeks heated. Surely she'd dreamed she and Miles had made love.

A quick look at her unbuttoned nightshirt and the twisted material confirmed it hadn't been a dream. Hope's head hit the pillow with a soft thud. Miles had satisfied her but had left before she could do the same for him.

Insecurity arose despite her attempt to tamp it down. The desire glowing in his jade eyes had been real. He'd wanted her, yet something had stopped him from taking her completely.

That something would be one of the first things she ask him when she saw him. He'd stated prior commitments for today, which meant she'd have plenty of time for a long luxuriant bath before she launched her plan of attack.

****

Several hours later, Hope lit twin tapers of light on the dining room table. She dimmed the overhead fixture and returned to the kitchen. Meat sauce bubbled in a saucepan and noodles rested in an ironstone dish. She'd chilled a bottle of wine after her bath. It now sat in an ice bucket on the counter. She planned to move it to the dining room in a few minutes. First, she wanted to check on dessert.

Rich chocolate-coated strawberries had been the best idea she could conjure up without going to the store. Even if Miles didn't have a conniption fit about her leaving the house alone, her knee just wasn't up to walking any distance or driving.

The bath had soothed the residual ache and eased the stiffness. She hoped the care she'd given it would allow her to wear the high heels she'd unearthed from her closet.

She hated the torture devices, but the dress she'd chosen would be totally ineffective without the right shoes. She closed the fridge door and glanced at her watch. Almost seven. Surely, Miles would get home soon. If not, her plans for dinner would be spoiled. She planned to have dinner out of the way and her little talk with Miles, before Guy arrived for his nine o'clock meeting. She'd preferred to cancel the meeting altogether but Guy had not been happy with that idea or the change in their meeting time. He'd try to browbeat Hope into coming into the shop after she refused to have dinner with him.

No way.

The last time she'd combined business, dinner, and Guy, she'd been treated to his brand of flirting. Not to mention his irritating habit of interrupting her. Of course those faults were much better than his "Don't worry about it Hope, I'll handle all the business."

Part of it was her own fault. She'd given Guy free reign after her parents had been killed. Morgan Rarities was just a reminder of what she'd lost. But maybe it was time she started to take an interest in the business. Her folks would have liked that, although, they'd always made it known that Hope's medical career had to come first.

Tonight would be the first of a lot of things for Hope. After she seduced Mr. Make-My-Bones-Melt, she'd set Guy straight as to who owned Morgan's.

She eased her feet into the heels and grabbed the chilled wine. Gingerly she made her way into the dining room. The click of the kitchen door caused her heart to stall. Miles was home.

"Hope?"

"I'm in the dining room." Hope waited with trembling hands. Her courage deserted her like a rat jumping a sinking ship. She didn't have a prayer of a chance of getting Miles flat on his back and in bed. Who was she kidding?

"Hi."

The soft baritone hit Hope midway between her abdomen and her heart. Her breath hitched and her heart thudded. Miles moved farther into the room, his face carved into a mask of sensual sin.

"Hi yourself. I was beginning to wonder if you were going to make it home for dinner." Hope was proud her words didn't lodge in her throat. No use in letting the man see how nervous he made her. "I hope you're hungry."

Miles was starving—but not for food.

His lovely innocent had baited her sexual hook with a lure he couldn't resist. Not that he could resist Hope in any form of dress, but tonight if she'd set out to knock his fangs out, she'd been successful.

Jade green silk clung to the curves Miles wanted to touch. The sleek design had him wanting to encircle her waist and share the grip the material had on Hope's hips. The neckline plunged, not far but just enough to give him a glimpse of the handful he'd suckled last night.

Legs that looked great in jeans looked like weapons in sheer nude hose. The three-inch heels caressing her feet would bring her lips almost to his.

"Starving would be more like it."

Hope's cheeks turned a lovely shade of rose. A perfect match for her lipstick. Her lashes flickered, but Miles didn't think she was flirting. He could read her mind to find out what she was thinking, but he liked the game just the way it was—both of them guessing.

"Well, I hope you like spaghetti."

"That's fine. Is there anything I can do to help? You really should be resting that leg."

"Oh, my leg is doing much better, thank you. And I don't need any help. Why don't you sit down, and I'll be right back."

Miles inhaled and exhaled, trying to calm his breath and raging erection. Dinner first and then dessert. No need to rush. They had all night, and he planned to make the most of the night hours. He opened the wine and poured the red liquid into fluted goblets. It reminded him of the night he wiped

Hope's memory of his dreams. Never would he have thought he'd be able to make love to her like he had last night.

Now, if he could only get up the courage to tell her what he was, then he'd have it all or he hoped he would. Maybe she wouldn't—

"Thanks for pouring the wine. I trust the year's okay. It's all I had on hand." She sat a plate of pasta in front of Miles and fixed one for herself.

"The wine will be great, Hope. Why don't you sit down?"

Miles stood and moved to her side before sliding the chair back and seating Hope. He allowed his hand a quick caress of her cheek before returning to his chair. The next move belonged to Hope. She'd started the game, and he would be patient.

Miles nibbled on a sauce-drenched noodle. He prayed his stomach wouldn't reject the food. But, whether it did or not, he wasn't about to disappoint his dinner partner.

He met her expectant gaze. "The pasta is good. You did an excellent job."

"I'm glad." Now it was his turn to watch her take a bite. Tomato sauce dotted her lips and the front of his pants tented as she used her tongue to capture it.

"Miles, I was wondering. I went into the guest room to see if you needed anything washed, but I couldn't find any clothes."

His lust did a slow dive. He didn't know why Hope was talking about laundry but he'd better come up with some type of excuse. "I uh, didn't want to make extra work for you so I had my clothes dry-cleaned."

"All of them?"

"Yeah, why?"

"I guess I just never knew someone who had their underwear sent out before."

Miles could feel the heat stinging his face. How could he tell this delightful and inquisitive woman he didn't wear underwear.

"Did I say dry-cleaned? I meant I took them to the laundromat."

Hope twirled a length of noodle around her fork. Her brow furrowed in concentration. He wondered if she actually bought his story. How many more lies would he have to tell before he found his backbone?

A clattering fork brought his attention back to Hope.

"Miles, why don't we cut to the chase? You made love to me last night, and I want to know why you left before we finished."

He observed the wine glass he set down, amazed it didn't topple over. Hope's agenda had been plain—she wanted a seduction, but he had no idea she would ask him why he'd left. His mouth felt as if his tongue was ten times its normal size. He needed another drink but feared his trembling hands couldn't hold the glass.

"Miles?"

"I heard you, Hope. I just don't know what to say."

"Well, that's a first. I've never heard you at a loss for words before. What makes what happened last night different?"

Suddenly, it jelled in Miles' head.

"Last night *was* different. You are *different*, Hope." Before he knew it, he was out of his chair and around the table. "Never in my entire existence have I met a woman like you. You pour light into the darkness of my soul. You open a window where there wasn't one. You make me feel emotions I thought long gone."

Miles pushed Hope's almost full plate aside and slid her chair back. He sat on the table's edge and pulled her up. He closed her parted lips with his finger. Too much of a temptation. He needed to say the words. The words he'd held inside for so long.

"Hope, there's something you need to know. I'm not what you think I am. I'm a—"

Chapter Seven

The doorbell pealed. Hope jumped. Miles cursed. Whoever was at the door was going to pay for this interruption.

"Oh Lord, that's Guy. I totally forgot he was coming by tonight."

"Guy?"

"Yes." Hope touched the hands he had clamped to her shoulders. "Remember, you asked me to change the meeting to tonight? I did."

The doorbell rang again. "I have to let him in, if I don't he'll just keep ringing until I do."

Miles eased his hold but dropped a kiss on Hope's lips. "Go answer the door. We'll finish this conversation later."

Hope walked on trembling legs to the front door. Her mind dipped and swirled with questions. Had Miles truly said those words to her? All her life she'd wanted a fairytale romance. A knight in shining armor. Someone who would protect her, to love her, and to make her feel special. She'd never said the words out loud but they were always there beating a refrain in her heart. Now, was it possible she'd found that someone?

The doorbell became more insistent. Hope just wanted it to stop, for Guy to go away, and let her finish out the fantasy of her lifetime.

She unbolted the lock and pulled the door open to reveal her manager's indignant face.

"It's about time, Hope. I was beginning to think

you weren't home. What took you so long?" Guy barged over the threshold and into the room.

"Evening to you too, Guy. You're early."

"Well, I didn't figure you'd mind. I mean you have to be bored to death, here all alone."

"Actually, I don't think Hope's been bored at all. Have you darling?"

Miles' arm slid around Hope's waist, and his fingers caressed her hip. Lord, the man had incredible timing.

"Uh, I guess I should have called first." Guy's face turned the color of a summer tomato. He shook his head and held out his hand to Miles.

Miles didn't look pleased, but he returned the greeting.

"I'm sorry if I interrupted anything. Maybe I should come back another time."

Hope pried Miles' hand off her hip. "Nonsense, you're here now. Why don't we go into the den and talk business? Miles, I'm sure you can find something to do for a few minutes."

Hope really didn't want Miles to leave but the glowering look he was wearing only made him look that much more seductive. His eyes glowed a bottomless jade, and his previous kissable lips were chiseled into an almost pout.

"Yeah, guess I could clear the table."

Hope shook her head. His tone sounded like a disgruntled child. A child with a body of a cover model. Okay, enough. She needed to get this meeting over with so she could find out what Miles wanted to tell her before they were interrupted.

"That would be great, Miles, thank you. Have a seat, Guy." Hope eased down onto the recliner's surface. Guy moved to the couch and sat. His expression not much happier than the one Miles had worn. At least she didn't have to worry about him sitting too close. With all the male testosterone floating around, there was bound to be an explosion if she let things get out of hand.

"That man is your bodyguard? He doesn't act like one, Hope."

Guy's clenched fists radiated the anger she could see in his eyes. "Yes, he is, and his behavior has no place in this business meeting. Now, you mentioned some items missing from shipments. When did this start, and do you have a list of the items?"

"There were several pieces of jewelry along with a few medieval artifacts. I didn't think to bring a list. I can run one by tomorrow if you like. Or we can have lunch, and I'll bring the list then."

Not on her life or his. "Why don't you email me the list? I'll go over it and get back to you on what we should do."

Guy cleared his throat. "I'll get the list, but I don't want to bother you with too much detail. You're still recovering. I just wanted to run the security idea by you."

"Guy, I'm fine. I'm in no danger of expiring from what happened. I'm also more than capable of dealing with the list and the security system. Get me a list of security companies you're considering, and I'll query them and compare their stats and costs."

"I really think that I—"

"Sorry to interrupt you two, but I thought you might want a glass of wine."

Hope didn't know if she should slap the smirk off of Miles' face or thank him. "That's very thoughtful, Miles."

Miles handed Hope a goblet and then offered one to a reluctant Guy. "Thanks, now if we could get back to business, Hope."

Her sexy and definitely not subtle Miles set the empty tray down on the end table and moved to Hope's side. Too bad she couldn't shoo him out of the room like a pesky fly. The man knew he was a distraction, and his *take-that* look to Guy as he sat on the arm of the recliner just made it worse.

"I agree, let's wrap this up. I want the information on the missing items and the security systems by noon tomorrow."

She waved away his protest. "I know. I've been totally absent from the business in the last year, but I plan on being more up to speed on what's going on at Morgan Rarities."

"But you—"

"Yes, I've never been there full time, not since I worked summers during college, but Mom and Dad kept me abreast of what they wanted for the company, and they taught me how to do things their way, Guy."

Hope stood and watched as Guy stumbled to his feet. "I hope we can work together to keep Morgan's the wonderful company my parents built. I won't be looking over your shoulder, but I do expect to have final say on most of the decisions. I think that's what my folks would have wanted, don't you?"

Guy's features did a one-eighty. He lost his belligerent scowl and managed a slight smile. Good, she really didn't feel like fighting or extending the meeting any longer.

"Of course, Hope. It's your company. Just let me know what you want me to do."

"I want you to continue to manage Morgan's, but I want to be involved." Hope moved toward the doorway and prayed Guy would follow. She also prayed Miles would keep his mouth shut.

A few moments later, Guy was gone, and Miles leaned against the den threshold.

"Go ahead, say what you're thinking."

"About what, Hope?"

"Guy. You certainly weren't very warm and fuzzy toward him."

"I didn't know I was suppose to be." Miles looped

his arm around Hope's waist. "Now, if he'd been a bit less rude and hadn't interrupted our dinner, I might have been more polite."

He pulled her closer. "But at least I didn't kill him."

Hope's grin threatened to split the sides of her mouth. "Yeah, well, I'd make you clean up the blood."

Miles' guffaw came from out of nowhere. Hope stood amazed. The man seldom laughed. But she liked the humor on him. His face softened into bronze etched lines, and his eyes went from dark jade to a green that made her want to wallow in their depths.

Hope's feet left the floor, and her legs found anchor around Miles waist. "What are you doing?"

"Finishing a few conversations."

"I like the way you think."

Miles' lips locked on hers. A kiss that lasted the time it took them to reach the couch. Hope welcomed the cool leather against her heated skin. Her nerve endings screamed for him to touch more than her lips. Her mind yelled *don't stop this time.* Miles' tongue wooed her with its caress. She gave him back each touch, and when he released her mouth, she felt lost.

Miles slid farther down on the couch taking Hope with him. A twist of his body and she lay beneath him. One of his hands caught both of hers—his hold possessive but gentle as he raised her arms above her head. Again his lips captured hers. This time the rhythm of dance changed. The slow tempo was gone, replaced by a blast of sensual chords. He stoked her mouth with firm strokes, sending a heat wave down to the ache between her thighs. Hope's body dampened with desire. She needed to touch Miles. She wanted him to touch her—to fill her with himself. She pulled back from his kiss.

"Miles, please."

"Please? Tell me what you want Hope."

"I want you. I want you inside me."

Bells went off above their heads. It took her a moment to realize it was her cell phone. Not now. Maybe whoever it was would hang up. The phone continued its discordant noise.

"Miles, the phone."

"Ignore it." Miles lips burned her throat before tickling the tender spot below her ear.

"It could be the hospital."

"Ignore it."

The phone rang a second more before it stopped.

Miles nipped the lobe of her ear, sending shocks of sexual awareness down to her toes and back to her core.

"Now, tell me again you want me."

"Miles, I—"

"Hell's bells." Miles released Hope's hands and grabbed *his* phone. He snapped it open and growled. "Call back later!"

"Miles?"

Miles shook the lust from his brain. "Zacke?"

"Yeah, I was calling Hope, hoping to reach you."

"Well, now's not a good time."

Zacke's laughter did a good job of deflating Miles' remaining arousal. "Hang on." The phone made a clunking sound on the table. He cupped Hope's flushed cheek with his palm and dropped a hard kiss on her mouth. "I'm sorry, love."

Miles exited the couch without lingering against the warmth of Hope's curves. He caught her hands in his and helped her to sit up. The dress's askew neckline plagued him with regret.

"Miles, you still there?" Zacke's now not so humorous tone jerked him back from his wayward thoughts. He caught up the phone and jammed it against his ear. "I'm here."

"Good. I've got some information for you on Hope's manager. Do you want me to come over there or do you want to meet me at the station?"

"I'll meet you." He closed the phone and reluctantly turned to Hope. God knew he didn't want to leave her. There was still so much to say. So much he wanted to do with and to her. But, he also needed to get the lowdown on Guy. The man was even more irritating in person than he'd been on the phone the night before. Miles wanted to strangle him, and his one-eighty when Hope said she wanted to be more involved in the business didn't ring true. Guy had been pissed. He'd covered it well but why would he get that upset over Hope's decision? She had every right to be involved. No, something certainly wasn't on the up-and-up.

"Hope, I have to go."

"Why? I thought we were going to finish all our conversations, Miles. You can't just run off. Not after the dinner tidbit you threw out."

"I know, but it's business."

"That was Zacke on the phone. What could you possibly have to do with police business?"

Miles leaned over and kissed Hope's lips. A pastime he could get use to forever. "I help Zacke out with some of his cases. The serial killer case a couple of years ago was one I worked with him and his partner."

"I'm not sure I knew that."

"No reason for you to. Our job was usually consultation and sometimes following up leads." Miles pulled back from Hope's out-stretched hand. If she touched him, he'd never leave. "This shouldn't take long. We'll finish our conversation and other interesting things when I get back. Okay?"

"Sure. In the meantime, I think I'll email Guy and remind him to send me those lists."

Miles blew Hope a kiss and then walked quickly

to the kitchen. The porch had adequate bushes for cover. He protected the house with a safety spell and a moment later, he was airborne.

****

Miles used the back alley Zacke always used for a landing when he was a vampire. He then found his way to the squad room. The place was quieter than the last time he'd been here. Of course, in those two years, he'd been all over the world in his quest to get Hope out of his mind.

Zacke had been given his own office in the interim and that was where Miles headed. He knocked once before opening the door and stepping inside the small cubicle. "Hey."

"Hi, you made good time. Any problems getting away from Hope? And did you get someone to stay with her while you're gone?"

"Quit worrying, Zacke. I placed a safe guard on the house. Do you think I'd leave Hope defenseless?"

"No, but I'm wondering if we shouldn't put a safeguard on Hope against you."

"Uncalled for, my friend. You wooed Miranda your way, and I plan on doing my own version of Romeo with Hope."

"Don't hurt her, Miles. I've grown fond of the little doctor, and Miranda would stake you herself if you upset Hope in any way."

"I know. I hope and pray that won't happen."

Zacke gave him a commiserating look. "I believe you. Now, sit. I found some interesting data on Mr. Guy Evans."

Miles sat. "Like what?"

"Like the man is a saint. Not even a parking ticket. He pays his bills on time and even leaves a tip every time he goes to a restaurant."

"And this is the big news?"

"Yes. Think about it, Miles. No one is that clean." Zacke grinned. "I did some more digging and found out that Mr. Clean Hands is living way above his means."

"Okay, so where is he getting the money?"

"Good question. One I wished I had an answer for. I ran cross sections of data against his social security number but nothing popped. That doesn't mean he doesn't have additional bank accounts. I just haven't been able to find them yet."

"You'll let me know when you do, of course."

"You got it. Now, tell me what's going on with you and Hope."

"I told you. I'm making her love me."

"Well, you know what they say about well laid plans of—"

The door banged opened to admit Hawk. "Miranda said I might find you two here. What's up?"

Zacke motioned Hawk to the computer.

"I take it you don't have a clue as to how he's getting the money?"

"No, that's what Miles and I were discussing when you came in. Among other things."

"Other things? As in when he's going to tell Hope he's in love with her?"

Miles had a feeling the roasting that was coming would leave his skin singed. "Whoa. Wait just a minute. I really don't think my love life is up for comment."

"Sure, that's what Zacke said a few years ago. Now look at him. He's happy with a beautiful wife and sweet kids."

"Well, Zacke's situation was different. He was actively seeking a way not to be a vampire. I have no plans to change, so convincing Hope to accept me as I am isn't going to be that easy."

Hawk moved back around the desk. "It might be better if you just told her the truth. You know, get it out in the open. All of it. Tell her you are crazy about her."

It wasn't often Miles got one up on either of his friends. "Just so you know. I did tell Hope I loved her." He relished the open-mouth stares coming his way. "I also was this close," he held up his thumb and forefinger, "to telling her what I was when that idiot in a manager's clothing interrupted us."

"Miles, I'm stunned. That's awesome news." Hawk pounded Miles on the back. Both men noted his flinch of pain.

"What's wrong with your back?"

Miles resisted the urge to squirm. It wouldn't do him any good. Hawk could read his mind and Zacke could read his face. "I uh, got a little burned earlier today."

"How did you do that? The only kind of burn that would leave it still painful this long would be from the sun."

Miles face heated.

"How on earth did you allow the sun to get you?" Zacke's incredulous tone made Miles want to cringe.

"And what had you so preoccupied that you didn't realize the sun was up?" Hawk's question made Miles want to run. No way were they going to let him out of there without an answer.

"I uh—"

"Never mind, I think we both can guess. Miles, how could you let your lust overrule your common sense?"

"It wasn't like that, Zacke. Hope got a phone call that upset her. I stayed with her until she fell asleep and must have dozed off myself." He shook off the hand on his shoulder. "The next thing I knew, I was making love to Hope. Before I realized it, the sun was streaming in through her bedroom window."

"Well, I hope you learned your lesson."

"Yes, Hawk. I did. The next time I try to make love to the woman I love, I'll pull the damn curtains closed. I'll also make sure I don't tell you guys anything."

The laughter when it came didn't irritate Miles as much as he thought it would. His friends had every right to question his sanity. He'd spent part of the day doing the same thing. If he was out of commission from burning his body to a crisp then who would protect Hope? "All right, enough already." Miles allowed his incisors to show bringing Hawk and Zacke's amusement to a slow end. "So now what? Do we just wait until Guy makes a wrong move?"

"Yeah, that's about it, but I think having someone trail Guy when he goes out at night would be a good thing. Don't you Hawk?"

"I agree, I suppose you want me to play the bulldog?"

Zacke exchanged grins with both Miles and Hawk. "Yep. Miles has his own agenda, and he needs to stay with Hope. I'd do it but Miranda and I have frequented Morgan Rarities a few times in the past year. The man knows me and that I'm a detective."

Miles stood. "Thanks, both of you. I appreciate this more than you know."

"Well, you can pay us back by telling Hope the truth and making sure you stay out of the sun."

"I think those are two things I can safely promise." Miles shook hands with both men. "Stay safe out there on the streets. I'm headed home."

He followed his words with action. He decided to skip feeding tonight. Miles hated that he'd left Hope the night before. Although, he knew Hawk would die protecting her if the need arose he still felt guilty. He despised his need for blood, but his fear that his lust would drive him to feast on Hope's beauty had been real.

As of tonight, he'd put that fear to bed.

No longer would he use mortals as a dinner

entree. Zacke had managed for centuries to avoid the taste of human blood. It was time for a change. He would talk to Zacke about getting his own blood bank started.

Miles made sure no one was around before he took to the sky. Gone was his desire to navigate the darkness looking for something—anything—to fill the hole in his heart. He had a place to go now. And he planned to talk to Hope and get everything out in the open before the next sunrise.

****

Guy finished dressing and then placed a hundred dollar bill on the hotel's bedside table. The hooker had been worth the price—if only for the hour she'd taken his mind off of Hope. How dare she dress like a slut and parade around in front of that imbecile Miles? He'd had such plans for his and Hope's relationship to grow; especially when she'd agreed to monthly meetings. Now, she'd shown her true colors. Not only was she trying to take back control of a company she had no business running but she'd also flaunted her relationship with another man in his face. Both were facts he'd not forget or forgive.

Chapter Eight

Hope huddled inside her terry cloth robe. Sometime during the night her dinosaur of a furnace had gone out. It was probably just the pilot light but even the few minutes it would take her to light it would seem like an eternity. The temp had dipped during the night, sending Savannah into the below-freezing range. Not unheard of but certainly not welcomed.

She tapped on Miles door, but didn't get an answer. She'd given up on waiting for him to come back the night before and now this...

Maybe he'd gone out again, but that made no sense. It was too early, barely sunrise, and besides, Zacke would have had Miles' head for leaving her alone. Not that she was really worried. The men who robbed and attacked her had probably left Savannah by now. They were most likely in Atlanta and laughing their butts off about not being caught.

Still, it was strange Miles hadn't left a note. He always told her the night before if he was going to be gone during the day. Maybe he was still with Zacke.

Well, no sense wondering about her absentee bodyguard. The furnace needed to be fixed, so Hope made her way down to the kitchen and grabbed a butane lighter and flashlight from a kitchen drawer. She didn't want to take a chance on tripping on the stairs. The stairwell light had burned out a few weeks ago, and she hadn't gotten around to replacing it. The basement's one window should provide her with adequate light for the grungy job once she got down the stairs. Thank Heaven, her knee was feeling much better. So much so, she planned on going back to work in a few days.

Hope turned the knob to open the basement door and found it locked. She didn't' remember locking it, but... She shivered again as she fished out a key from her junk drawer. First thing she planned to do after she lit that pilot light was to relax with a cup of hot tea. She unlocked the door, clenched her hand around the banister and started a slow descent. She wasn't really mad about Miles not being there, more like angry with herself. She'd stayed on the couch waiting for him to get home, but the next thing she knew she'd awakened on top of the bed, the coverlet pulled over her. Hope didn't remember going to bed so that meant one thing. Miles must have carried her up the stairs. She wished she'd been awake to enjoy his arms around her, and she wished they had gotten around to finishing their conversation. She really wanted Miles to make love to her.

She stepped off the bottom step and almost tripped over an uneven patch of floor. She aimed the beam of light at where the window should be. What on earth? A bookcase blocked out her expected light source. Miles was the only one who could have done that, but why would he?

The cold penetrated deeper, spurring Hope toward the furnace. Her foot caught on something soft but unyielding. She stumbled and ended up sitting on the *something*. Her hand recognized the contours of a mattress. A mattress that should have been stuffed in a corner, not lying out in the open.

Once again, she sent the light spiraling over the basement, nothing else seemed out of place. She brought the beam back to shine on the mattress and *a body*.

Her heart beat triple time before she recognized

the body resting on its side, a scant two feet from her hand. Miles! Why was he sleeping in the basement and not upstairs? Her hand reached out toward his arm. Should she wake him or let him sleep? Common sense won—he had to be freezing. He didn't even have a sheet. This time her palm brushed his sleeve before she gently shook his shoulder.

A hand caught her wrist in a cruel grip.

She bit back a cry of pain.

A second later she was flat on her back—Miles' face above hers. But not the face she loved. His eyes were so dark they were almost black. His beautiful lips were drawn back in a snarl. A snarl that revealed one-inch incisors. The hand that held her down sported claws.

Miles wasn't Miles. He was a monster. One of the beings she vaguely recalled from childhood nightmares. Only this time the nightmare was real.

He lowered his head bringing his sharp teeth too close for comfort. "Miles? Miles!"

Shades of color began to recede from his vision. Miles shook his head and tried to focus. The roaring in his ears quieted when he heard a whimper. He shook his head again. His vision sharpened, and he became aware of other things. His hand pressed against cloth-covered breasts. He looked down—into the tear-filled, petrified gaze of Hope. Oh, God above. What had he almost done? What had he done?

"Hope, angel, I'm sorry. I won't hurt you—I promise."

Hope's expression didn't change. One tear rolled off her bottom lashes and crept down an ashen cheek.

"I swear, love. Please. If you don't believe anything else, please believe me. I wouldn't harm a hair on your head."

The woman beneath him, the woman he'd tear his heart out for, closed her eyes. He watched as she took a deep breath and then another. Finally she opened her eyes. "Then if you don't mind would you take your hand off my chest and let me up?"

"Oh Lord." Miles moved so quickly he almost fell. He reached out a hand to help Hope sit up and prayed she'd take it.

She didn't.

Maybe if he moved back a bit more. The space of the room separated them before he found additional courage to speak. "Hope, I know this seems strange but I can explain."

Hope slid her legs off the mattress and then stood slowly to her feet. She took a step forward and stumbled. The look in her eyes stopped him from going to her. The tears receded, replaced with a gleam of anger. Good. Anger he could handle. Anger meant she would get over her fright. Whether or not she forgave him was another matter.

Once her feet were steady, Hope straightened up. Her shoulders went back.

"Hope?"

"Unless you're going to tell me this is some kind of sick joke, I have nothing to say to you."

"Let me explain."

"Explain what? That you thought it would be a hoot to dress up as a vampire. Even as a joke that makes no sense. I mean who sleeps in fangs and claws. And that brings me to another matter."

Hope advanced toward Miles. "Why were you sleeping in the basement in the first place?"

"I uh, like it."

"You prefer sleeping in a frigid basement instead of a nice warm room?"

"Yes, I do."

"You know what, you're crazy."

Hope moved closer. "What I don't get, is why or

how you could play such a cruel joke, especially after acting like you cared about me—like I was someone special."

"You are."

"Yeah, well, you have a strange way of showing it, Miles Dunbar."

She now stood directly in front of Miles. Even quicker than his eyes could see, her hand moved. The blow across his face wasn't hard but it still hurt—all the way to his heart.

"That's for half-ass making love to me."

Before he could react, Hope turned on her heel and strode across the basement. She went into a small room at the back.

"Damn it! Where did I put that lighter?"

Miles heard metal straining as Hope continued to curse. Not like his Hope at all but then again, she had every right to be upset. He moved closer to the doorway.

"Sorry, sleazy, son-of-a—"

Blessedly the sound of metal, slamming this time, prevented him hearing the rest of Hope's words. She'd be amused to know, if he ever got the chance to tell her, his mother had actually been an English lady.

A couple of minutes later, Miles jumped back to avoid Hope running over him. It would hurt her a lot more than it would him physically.

"Hope, can't we talk?"

"There's nothing to talk about."

"Yes, there is." Miles didn't try to put his arm around her. He liked having all his limbs attached. "Let's go upstairs. You'll be warmer and I'll try to explain what you just saw."

The scowl she leveled on him didn't bode well for this or any *future* discussions. He didn't want to think about what could happen to their future *relationship*.

"Fine. If you think you can dream up a story I'll believe, then go for it."

Miles followed Hope up the stairs, his steps a lot slower than hers.

He closed the door to the basement. Hope placed a kettle of water on the stove. The slow rise of steam tempted him. It would be so easy to dissolve into its mist. But, disappearing wouldn't solve his problem. It also wouldn't solve Hope's. The men who had attacked her were still out there, and he couldn't leave her alone.

Hope went about fixing her tea and ignored Miles. Only after she took her first sip did she look his way. "I'd rather not have this conversation at all but if we have to, let's do it in the den."

Miles followed Hope and bit back a groan when she sat in the recliner. She was putting the same distance between them as she had with Guy the previous night. Not good.

"So talk."

Miles wasn't sure how to start. Should he tell her everything—even about the almost abduction when she was young? No! Just the fact he was truly a vampire would be more than enough to send her running. If he told her everything it would send her over the edge.

"You think I was playing a joke—I wasn't." Miles paced the confines of the room. "Some things are hard to believe. My story is one of those. I don't know how much to tell you. You're going to think I'm lying through my teeth or ready for an asylum."

He chanced a look her way. Hope's face resembled marble. He'd hoped for just a bit of softening if for no other reason than she felt sorry for him. Fat chance of that.

Miles' pacing took him to the door's threshold. He leaned back against the sturdy wood. Hopefully it would keep him from fleeing like the coward he was.

"Why don't you just spit it out, Miles."

"All right. My full name is Lord Miles Sinclaire Dunbar. I was born in the year 1589 in England. I was a warrior for King James and during a campaign in Scotland, I was turned into a vampire."

Hope's expression of rock hard indifference didn't change but her eyes widened just a bit.

"I'm over four hundred years old, and I'm in love with you, Hope."

"Love? You don't know the meaning of love. If you did you wouldn't be spouting all these lies."

"They're not lies. It's the truth. If you don't believe me, then ask Miranda."

"Don't drag her into this insane comedy. Why would you expect her to lie for you?"

"Not lie. Tell the truth. I expect it of her because she's been up close and personal with a few vampires herself."

Hope jumped out of the recliner. "Oh yeah, like whom?"

"Zacke for one. He was a vampire when she married him."

"And he's miraculously not one now? Oh please."

"It's true. Zacke was almost killed trying to get his soul back and become mortal again."

"And I suppose you believe the Wicked Witch of the West is real too? What about the Easter Bunny, Miles? Do you believe in him? Santa Claus? Tell me, how long have you had these delusions?" Hope stalked him like she had in the basement. "Or is this just an easy way to get out of what could have been a serious relationship? Do you do this to all the women you make love to? Feed them romance and then a bunch of lies?"

"No. I don't!" Miles caught Hope by the arm before she could slide past him into the kitchen. "Call Miranda and Zacke. Call Hawk. They'll all tell you the same."

"I don't think so, Vamp Boy, and if you value those teeth of yours, you'll let go of my arm."

"And if I don't?"

"I'll take a pair of pliers and yank them out."

Miles dropped Hope's arm like it was a hot poker. The woman was livid and just might do it. If she caught him in the middle of the day he'd be helpless. His stomach churned at the thought of waking up fangless.

"I'm going to get dressed and go to the hospital. Do me and yourself a favor—don't be here when I get back!"

****

Hope stormed down the corridor toward Miranda's office. Of all the imbecilic tricks Miles could pull, this one burnt the candles off the cake. Did he really think she was that stupid? Then again, maybe she was. For one moment, she almost believed him. Until he said Miranda knew he was a vampire. No way, no how, would her boss, and friend, keep something like that, if it were true, from Hope. Not that she thought it was. Of course not. Vampires weren't real. Just a figment of romance authors and movie moguls' minds—despite all the myths her beloved city of Savannah oozed.

She knocked once and without waiting for an answer opened the door. Miranda wasn't there.

Dang it.

She needed to talk to her.

Now.

She needed answers.

Now.

Hope couldn't go back home until she got Miles' preposterous explanation straightened out. Of course if Miranda said she didn't have a clue as to what Miles had been rambling about, then that meant the one man who could make her forget everything needed a straight jacket. Not something she wanted to think about. And if for some reason Miranda verified his story, Hope seriously wondered if she ought to be the one locked up.

Maybe Miranda was in the cafeteria? Hope exited the office as fast as she entered—only to be brought up short by a hard object.

"Hope, are you all right?"

"Yeah, just didn't see you," Hope answered Zacke's slightly out-of-breath question.

"I'm not surprised. You were in quite a hurry. Where's the fire?"

"No fire. I just need to speak to Miranda."

Zacke loosened his grip on Hope's shoulders. "Why don't we go into her office and wait. She's finishing up a surgery."

Hope must have looked puzzled.

"Mac, the surgery tech told me." He placed a light but persuasive hand at the small of her back and gently moved her back into the office. "Have a seat. I'll grab us something to drink." He moved to the mini-fridge Miranda kept stocked and pulled out a couple of cans of soda.

Hope took the proffered can and pulled the tab back. She took a quick drink before meeting Zacke's gaze. "You know don't you?"

"Know what, Hope?"

"What I want to talk to Miranda about. Miles called you, didn't he?"

"Yes, he did."

She wiped a stray drop of liquid from her bottom lip with her thumb. "So, are you going to tell me?"

Zacke seated himself on the edge of the desk. She still had to look up to see his eyes but it was better than craning her neck.

"That Miles is a vampire? I think you already know the answer to that."

"I don't know what to believe. My mind tells me

there are no such things, but I can't fathom why you, a police detective, would back up his story if it wasn't true."

"I wouldn't. Believe me, Miles told you the truth."

"But that would mean—" Hope's hand crept to her throat. "He really is a vampire, I mean really—the fangs and claws are real."

"Yes, they are."

"But that would also mean that you—" Hope didn't know how to finish her sentence. The calm man seated before her didn't look like he could ever have been a monster.

"That I was once a vampire? Guilty as charged. Hope, you have to understand that neither myself, Miles, or Hawk wished that curse on ourselves. It happened—due to the jealousy and revenge of one woman."

"Okay, say I believe you and Miles. How is this possible? I mean physically?"

"I can tell you that." Miranda's soft tone cut through the tension-laden room.

Hope had been so intent on Zacke's words she'd missed the door opening.

"Hi, hon." Miranda placed a light kiss on Zacke's mouth before she leaned back into his embrace.

"A woman changed Zacke and the others into what they are, or in his case was." She pointed toward her husband, then continued. "Gabriella was evil and didn't care whom she hurt in her quest to get Zacke back. She turned up in this century, and yes, my husband is older than he looks." Miranda smiled at Hope and patted Zacke's hand. "She kidnapped me. I know it sounds like something out of a movie but it happened. Zacke managed to kill her but he almost died himself. It was only by the grace of God he survived. We're not sure how he became mortal again but that too we believe was a miracle."

Hope felt like she was in Neverland. Miranda looked sane but the entire conversation sounded like something you'd dream about.

"I know, it's hard to believe, but I think you and I both can relate to the medical facts."

"Medical facts?" Hope wondered if the breathlessness she felt at Miranda's words showed in her voice. Facts she could understand—myths, no. Was there a plausible reason Miles was a vampire?

"Yes. Before Zacke almost died, he came down with what we thought was a flu bug but it wasn't. He'd started having some strange symptoms, totally opposite to what he should have been having as a vampire."

Hope's mind whirled. Her interest caught despite the mixed feelings of the last few hours. "What type of symptoms?"

"His stomach ached really bad. Several months before, he also began to sweat like mortals do. Zacke's vampire blood seemed to lose its ability to heal his body. The only reason the man came clean to me about being a vampire—"

"Miranda, that's not true. I was going to tell you."

"Yeah, well, Detective, it took a bullet in your shoulder before you decided to tell me the truth." Miranda turned back to Hope. "For me, his wound healed at an amazing rate. Zacke told me he should have been healing ten times faster...but I digress. After he healed, I took blood samples trying to see what was going on. His white blood cell count was off the charts. I was frantic and still didn't have any answers. Then he almost died, from the wounds he received. They were horrific and filled with poison."

Hope sat forward on the chair's seat. "What caused the poison?"

"Gabriella's claws contaminated Zacke's blood.

His red cells went haywire, separating and finally just being eaten alive by the white cells."

Miranda moved from Zacke's arms. "I felt so helpless. The blood transfusions I started doing at home when he first got sick, didn't seem to help. I thought if I kept giving him more then maybe I could stop the poison. Nothing worked! The white cells destroyed the new blood. I couldn't understand why Gabriella's blood was so poisonous and Zacke's wasn't."

"So the link is in the blood itself."

"Yes. How, I don't know. Some strange blood disorder we've never heard about. Who knows, but the transformation from mortal to vampire for Zacke, Miles, and Hawk has something to do with the chemical makeup of the blood."

"But what about the fangs and claws?"

"I don't know. I never got that far in my research. Once Zacke became mortal, I just stopped looking. Maybe it's something we both can look into."

"Maybe." Hope's tone sounded desolate even to her own ears.

Miranda placed her hand on Hope's shoulder. "I don't think having fangs and claws is something that makes them monsters. As with any man or immortal, it's what they do with them that counts. Miles has always been a crusader. I've seen him go out of his way to help others. He's not a mean person, so don't judge him for what he is but for what he stands for, Hope."

"Thank you both. I have to admit I'm still in more than a bit of shock. I mean I have a real-life vampire sleeping in my basement. That's kinda strange."

"It can be or you can just chalk it up to one of the things that you'll have to learn to put up with if you love him."

"I never said I loved him."

"Not out loud but it's there, Hope. You can't run from it. Believe me, I know. I tried to rationalize my feelings for Zacke before and after I found out what he was. But the bottom line—it didn't matter. I fell in love with the man who risked his life constantly to save mine. Miles would do that for you if the need ever arose. Give him and that part of him a chance."

"I should at least go back and talk to him." Hope stood up and then sat back down. "I don't know the first thing about vampires. What do they eat? How do they get blood? Does he need it? There are so many things I don't know."

"You can always ask Miles those questions."

"I could but I'm scared."

Zacke eased off the desk and squatted by Hope's chair. "There's nothing wrong in being afraid, Hope. But don't let your ignorance of things you don't know keep you from seeing what's real."

Hope's mind played a video of all the time she'd spent with Miles. Even in those few blood-curdling moments in the basement he had not hurt her. Frightened her almost to death but he hadn't harmed her in any way.

"At the moment, I'm not sure I'll ever know what's real again."

Chapter Nine

Miles paced from Hope's front door to the kitchen door once again. He'd retraced his steps so many times he was almost dizzy. Thirty minutes had turned into an hour and then another. He wanted to stamp the floor with his feet. To tear the paneling from the walls and to do some major damage to someone—himself.

He'd called Zacke right after Hope left that morning. Zacke had promised to catch up with her at the hospital. The hour he'd waited then had almost worn a groove in his fangs. He'd been on the verge of braving the sunlight with the aid of sunglasses, hat, and his cloak, when Zacke called to say Hope had left the hospital. His firm assurance that she was no longer angry and planned to keep an open mind about what she'd learned had soothed his worry for almost an hour.

Noon had arrived before he'd called it quits and gone to the basement. His eyes had been gritty from lack of sleep, his limbs almost useless with fatigue, his heart however, felt as if it'd been harpooned with a sword.

Miles had willed himself to wake at dusk. The moment he opened his eyes, he knew Hope had not returned. The house felt dead. And for the last couple of hours he'd watched both entries into the house in vain.

What would he do if she didn't come back? Of course she would eventually—it *was* her house. But what if something had happened to Hope?

God above! He should have gone after her this morning. If not then, right after he'd awakened. He'd wanted to give her time. Time to come home on her own. Time to realize he wasn't a monster but a man who loved her above all else.

Miles resisted the urge to destroy the closest object at hand—an antique Tiffany lamp. Hope would have his heart on a platter. The door's threshold made an unsatisfying thud instead. He shrugged his shoulders and began to extract the splinters from his knuckles.

Ten slivers of wood were discarded in the trashcan before his ears heard the sound he yearned for—Hope's footsteps. He arrived in the kitchen almost simultaneously with Hope opening the door.

"Hi."

Hope's scream ripped through the house.

"Miles! Stop sneaking up on me."

Hope's tone held just a smidgen of humor. Miles didn't care—he'd take whatever he could get. "I'm sorry, Hope."

He moved a step closer. She didn't run. "I'm sorry for a lot of things."

"That word seems to be in your vocabulary a lot lately."

"I know. Can we talk?"

Hope's chin went up, and her eyes flashed with something too brief for Miles to catch. She was playing her cards close to her chest, and it scared the hell out of him.

"I have a better idea. I talk and you listen."

Miles didn't know what to make of that idea, but he certainly wasn't going to argue.

"Fine by me."

"I don't begin to understand all I've been told. If the truth be known, I'm wondering if ya'll all didn't fall off a turnip truck, but since Miranda and Zacke seem to be fairly cognitive, I'll have to take their word that you are a vampire."

"You will?"

"I thought I told you not to talk."

Miles nodded his head.

"Okay, so there are some questions I need to ask and some arrangements to work out if you plan on staying here."

"I'll answer anything you want."

"Good, but before we start, have you had dinner?"

Miles mouth dropped open. What did Hope mean? Dinner as in food or in his case, blood. Was it a trick question?

"I ugh—no."

"I didn't think so. There's a cooler on the porch with some bags of blood. I stopped by Miranda's house before I came home. She gave me some from the supply she keeps for you and Hawk when needed. We'll have to see about setting up some type of blood supply for you. Because if you plan on staying here you are not going to be biting people."

Miles wanted to shout halleluiah. Hope actually sounded matter of fact. Could his dream of her accepting him really be happening? "I wouldn't dream of it."

"Go ahead and do whatever you need to do. I don't want you to get hungry while we're talking."

Nope, her tone conveyed she still wasn't comfortable. "Okay, I can take the cooler to the basement. It would probably be better there since I can eat when I first wake up."

Hope walked to the fridge and took out a bottle of wine. "That's another thing we need to discuss—your sleeping arrangements. I'll be going back to work and there's no sense in you sleeping in that cold basement."

"I don't mind the cold. I don't really feel it, you

know."

Hope's grimace spoke volumes. Maybe he shouldn't volunteer information.

"I didn't know, but I do need to know more about your physical habits." She poured some wine into a goblet. "I don't want to be surprised like I was this morning."

"And God above knows I don't want that to happen either."

"Good. Now, for the last time, go have your dinner."

****

Several minutes later, Miles left the basement and reentered the kitchen. He'd devoured two bags of blood. He wasn't taking a chance on his beasty side getting out of hand. Back when Zacke had needed blood he'd inject it with a syringe straight into his jugular vein. Miles didn't want anything remotely sharp against his throat so he'd used a cup he found in the basement.

Hope sat at the table, her glass of wine barely touched while her fingers traced through the beads of condensation on the crystal.

"That didn't take long."

"I hurried. Mind if I sit?"

"No, go ahead." She motioned to the chair across from her.

"I'm ready to answer any questions you have."

Hope took a sip from her glass. "Okay, first off, how often do you need to feed? I guess that's the correct word."

"It's fine. I usually eat once a day after waking, but I can go a couple of days in-between."

"So if I put a mini-fridge in your room with blood, you'll be okay?"

"That'll work. Next question?"

"Do you always sleep like you're dead?"

Miles smiled. He couldn't help it. Hope was

adorable when she worried her lip with her teeth.

"Most of the time. I try to go to bed right after sunrise. My body lets me know when it's time to wake, usually right after the sun goes down—unless I'm disturbed like this morning."

Hope caught her lip again and bit down slightly. "I was wondering, what makes your fangs and claws grow."

"If you are asking what caused them in the first place, I don't know. But when I'm hungry, angry, or sexually aroused, they seem to have a mind of their own."

Hope's cheeks turned a lovely shade of pink. "Did they—uh—the other night?"

Miles reached across and caught Hope's hand. He held his breath, hoping she wouldn't draw back. "Yes. But you'll never have to worry about me hurting you, Hope. I'd pluck them out myself before I'd harm one hair on your head."

"I hope that includes my neck." Hope's tone definitely held amusement this time. Her lips even held a slight smile.

"I can't promise I won't nibble on it, but I'll never take what's not offered—not from you."

"What do you mean?"

Miles held on to her hand. The next part could be tricky.

"I'm not the type of vampire that likes to sip from a man's neck. I prefer my dinner to be feminine."

Green eyes turned dark. "Wait a minute. You mean up until tonight, you've been getting your blood supply from women?"

"Technically, yes. But, I stopped a couple of nights ago."

"Let me get this straight. You stopped two nights ago. So where in the Hades did you get your blood the night you were in my bed?"

"Hope, it's not what you think."

"Really, then tell me what it *is*." Hope pulled her hand free and pushed her chair back. "Miles, I was having a hard enough time having you live here while I thought you were human."

Miles cringed. She'd certainly stuck a nail in his coffin.

"I am now trying to reconcile having a vampire as a houseguest/bodyguard. How can you not expect me to misunderstand how the man or vamp—whatever—who told me he cared for me more than anything or anyone, makes love to women to satisfy his blood hunger?"

Heat surged into his face. What could he say? It was the truth. How could he undo the damage?

"I never said I made love to them, Hope."

"So what—you just latched onto their necks with no foreplay."

Miles wished for that pair of pliers to twist out his bumbling tongue. "God, how do I make you understand?"

"I don't know. You tell me."

"There are vampires out there that are monsters, Hope. I've seen them take blood until their victims were bled dry. They would laugh and go on to their next prey. I may have to drink blood to survive but I have never hurt anyone doing it."

His nails, thankfully without claws, drummed on the tabletop. "Hawk and I both felt that if we fed our need while we were intimate with a woman then we could give her pleasure at the same time."

"Sure of yourselves, weren't ya'll?"

"Yeah, I guess we were and that's a good thing. At least we treated them like lovers and not appetizers."

"Please Miles, that's not funny. Look, I'm tired. I didn't sleep the day away. I'm going to bed."

"I was hoping we could get some of this settled."

"We did. You're a vampire, and I'm seriously in danger of losing my mind. Look, maybe by the time you get up tomorrow night, I'll have a handle on what I'm feeling."

Hope walked close to Miles but avoided touching him as she exited the kitchen. He followed her but kept his mouth shut. Maybe things *would* be better tomorrow. Lord, he'd never thought they'd get this far in discussing his vampire state.

Hope's steps were slow, and she favored her injured knee as she climbed the stairs. Miles hoped he hadn't irretrievably damaged the future he still prayed he had with Hope.

****

Hope pulled the drain on the tub and watched the swirling water disappear. Two hours had gone by since she'd left Miles. No amount of pillow punching had sent her off to la-la land. She'd finally given up and ran a bath. Yet, still her mind refused to shut off.

Miles and his immortal state had her stomach tied in knots. The few sips of wine she'd consumed in an effort to boost her courage had soured. She finished drying off, shrugged on her robe, and pulled the belt tight. Maybe if she read for a while. She had a good suspense novel that had been on her to-be-read list for a long time.

Once propped up on her pillows with the book open to the first page, Hope refused to wonder where Miles was or what he was doing. The house had been silent as a tomb—bad choice of words—except for the running bath water. If he'd gone out, she'd not heard him. Of course, that didn't mean anything. Miles probably had other ways of leaving without using a door.

Stop it! Forget about the man for at least tonight. Finally her mind complied. Her gaze actually saw the words on the page, and she was soon drawn into a world of kick-butt heroines, murder, and mayhem.

****

Hope fought her way out of a dream, where she wore four-inch heeled boots and had a gun trained on a bank robber, to grab her ringing cell phone.

"Hello." Music assaulted her ears. This time the haunting melody didn't throw her into a panic. She'd grown used to the almost nightly calls. "Listen, I don't know who you are but if you don't quit harassing me, I'm calling the police."

"Hope, it's bedtime."

Goose bumps peppered her arms, but Hope wouldn't give into the terror. "I mean it, don't call back." She slammed her cell shut and tossed it across the room. Hope burrowed down in the center of the bed and tried to close out the world.

"Hope?"

"Go away Miles."

"Look, I heard the phone. Was it that same caller?"

"Yes. Now, go away."

"Are you all right?"

"I'm fine. I just want to go back to sleep. Okay?"

"Sure you don't want me to come in?"

"I'm sure. Good night, Miles."

****

Miles waited until he got back to the den before he slammed his fist into the wall. Sooner or later, he'd have to stop abusing the walls. Hope was going to eventually notice the splintered wood.

Why wouldn't she let him in? The phone call had to have upset her. Why wouldn't she let him help?

His fangs burst forth in a rush of loathing. He knew why. Hope was more frightened of him than she was of the phone call. How could he make her understand that he'd die before he harmed her? What would it take to convince her he was sincere?

First thing come sunset tomorrow, he was going to get with Zacke about the calls. Jealousy had eaten away at him the night he'd gone to the station, so much, so, he'd hadn't told him everything.

Miles' body dissolved into particles of air before he materialized in Hope's backyard. The moon's crescent didn't disperse the shadows from the trees, but he welcomed the darkness. It soothed him almost as much as lying under the earth. He needed to get a handle on his feelings. Rage wouldn't help Hope. Finding the person behind the calls would.

For that he would need Zacke's help. Modern technology wasn't actually his strong suit. Hawk, on the other hand, had taken to the computer age like he had wenching way back when. He was the one to convince Miles to get a cell phone. Of course, Hawk's job called for him to be accessible to his students. After Gabriella's death, he'd had applied and been accepted as a lecturer at one of the colleges in Savannah. He was also a student himself working on his PhD in history. And why not, they both had an up close and personal view of history while it was being forged.

Maybe he was too set in his ways. Maybe it was time for a change. If he planned to make a life with Hope he needed to fit into her world.

His mind made up, Miles relocated back to the den. That was the only room with a television. If he remembered correctly from nights he'd spent at Zacke's, this time of night, infomercials would be on in full force. Maybe he'd check out laptop computers. It wouldn't be a bad idea to own one.

****

Hope sneaked a peek into the guest room but wasn't surprised when she didn't see Miles. The man had a stubborn streak a mile wide. If he thought it would unnerve her to have him that close then he was wrong.

She padded her way to the kitchen and a much-needed cup of tea or maybe she'd settle for a diet cola. Lord knew she needed the extra caffeine.

A moment later she sat at the table and took a hefty swallow of cola. After the disturbing phone call and Miles' plaintive attempts to get her to let him in, Hope had done a lot of thinking. Although Miles had been with a woman since he'd moved in, there hadn't been any love involved. He'd taken blood from the woman because he had to. She still wasn't sure if she wanted to know how far he went with his victims but maybe it didn't matter.

He used the blood she'd brought, and he'd been in the house virtually all night as much as she could tell. So he wasn't going out to feed.

He'd also sworn he cared for her.

Yes, he was a vampire but he hadn't asked for that status. Had he hurt her physically?

No. Right the opposite.

He'd made her feel safe, loved, and totally satisfied. Maybe it came from all his experience over the centuries, but he'd made her feel desirable. He'd also made her want to crawl his body and literally kiss him to death. Of course that wasn't feasible, since he was already dead, nor was it practical. If she kissed him to death, he couldn't make love to her.

Hope giggled. How ridiculous did that sound? Life had certainly turned sideways since she'd met Miles. She took another swig from her can. Should she give him a chance? That question had turned in her head for the last several hours. Could she be sure he wouldn't turn on her?

She looked deep inside herself, and remembered the care he always heaped on her and the countless times he'd apologized. No, she really didn't believe he'd willingly hurt her—physically or emotionally. But what if he couldn't help it?

So, what to do about the man who made her crazy?

Hope tossed the empty can in the recycling bin. First things first—she was going to get the man out of the basement and upstairs. Then she'd work on getting him to make love to her for real next time. Miles had told her himself that his fangs and claws came out when he was aroused. The thought frightened her, but she needed to know for certain if love could tame her beast.

****

Several hours later, Hope signed a final credit card slip.

Success. She'd bought new furnishings and a mini-fridge for Miles' new room, plunging into her money market account like she was a millionaire. Whereas the old Hope would have been appalled at such extravagance, the new Hope didn't care.

"Please have everything delivered by three this afternoon, if you can, Mr. Poppam."

"You can count on it, Miss Hope." The gray-haired storeowner came out from behind the sales counter. "I'm just so happy to see you smiling again. This last year's been hard on you, but your mama and daddy would be happy to see the light back in your eyes."

Hope hugged the little man back. He was right, it'd been way too long since she actually enjoyed life. Miles had done that for her.

"You tell that young man of yours, he'd better treat you right or he'll answer to me."

Her cheeks heated. "What makes you think I have a young man?"

Mr. Poppam tweaked her cheek. "Because you have the same look your mama had in her eyes when she and your dad starting spooning."

Hope didn't know whether to laugh or cry. It was funny to hear her and Miles referred to in context to spooning, but cryable because it was so apparent to others that she cared for Miles.

She gave the elderly man a kiss on his cheek and then walked out of the store. It had been good to see Mr. Poppam again. He'd been a family friend ever since Hope could remember. She'd stopped many an afternoon at Poppam's Furniture Emporium after grade school on her way to Morgan's Rarities. He always had a stick of candy stashed away just for her. Even in high school, when she'd been dieting like most teenage girls, he'd talked her into having a little something to tide her over until dinner. Lord, just seeing him again brought back wonderful memories.

Hope hated that over the last year she'd gone out of her way to avoid Mr. Poppam. She'd see him out and about and there were times he'd stop her to chat, but for the most part he and his friendship had been dismissed. It had hurt too much to see him and remember. Just another reason to be glad she'd met Miles.

A low rumble from her stomach caught her ears and a quick glance at her watch confirmed it was lunchtime. Maybe she'd make a day of it. Have lunch at the little Mexican restaurant she loved and then drop in at Morgan's. After everything that had happened in the last day or so, she'd forgotten Guy had not emailed her the lists as he promised.

The clock in the square had just chimed one o'clock when Hope walked out of the restaurant. Replete and just a bit tired, she thought about just walking on home. The delivery trucks would be there in a couple of hours and she could grab a nap if she hurried.

Still, if she planned to become part of the business again, she needed those lists. Hope shrugged her shoulders. Nothing else for it but to stop. Maybe she'd get lucky and Guy would be gone to lunch. The new girl he hired as his secretary could give her the lists, and she could get out without a confrontation. If Guy ran true to course, he'd fuss because she wanted the lists and tell her again that she didn't need to worry about the store. Or start in again about Miles.

Oh, please, let him be out.

Hope crossed the street and stopped in front of the building that had been her second home growing up. Morgan Rarities was housed in an older part of town. Cobblestone streets ran into the paved walk in front of a graceful two-story house made of rose-colored stone. Tall windows faced the street and set adjacent to double oak doors.

Her heart skipped and started back. It'd been a long time but she was ready to put her grief aside. Hope's right hand reached out to turn the brass doorknob but she stopped. The closed sign faced the street. That wasn't right. Maybe someone forgot to turn it around when they opened. She gripped the knob this time and opened the door.

Silence greeted her ears. Where were the chimes that signaled arrivals? Her mom had chosen the delicate porcelain bells, the same color as the exterior, and they had hung from the door's threshold for over thirty years.

Hope closed the door, flipped the sign over, and turned back around. Where was the girl that should have been greeting customers? Even if she was gone on a break, Guy should have been there.

This certainly wasn't the way to run a business. Certainly not the way her parents had operated one. Guy better have a good reason for leaving the business unattended. She moved through the front showroom and down a long carpeted hallway. Her parents' office set at the end but her goal was the manager's office halfway down the hallway.

Hope didn't bother knocking. She opened the

door and found it empty. Where on earth was Guy? Maybe if she couldn't find him, she could find the lists. Before she could look for them, a giggle reached her ears. Had someone come in the store behind her? She reentered the hallway to go back to the front of the store but a second, louder giggle—followed by low male laughter detoured her steps.

Both came from her parents' office. No one should be in there. She'd locked that office herself a few days after her parents were buried.

Again, she didn't bother to knock. The door opened and Hope gasped. A blonde straddled Guy's lap, bare to the waist. The bimbo turned and gave Hope a startled look. "I'm sorry, we're busy at the moment, can you come back later?"

"I don't think so. Get dressed and get out."

The woman looked at Guy who just shrugged his shoulders. She snatched up her bra and jacket but didn't bother to clothe herself before marching past Hope.

"Oh, and in case I didn't make myself clear. You're fired."

Guy waited all of one second before launching what Hope knew would be a ridiculous explanation. "Hope, I'm sorry you had to witness Brittany's behavior. I've warned her time and time again I would not tolerate that type of goings on in the office."

Hope bit back a snort. "Guy, what kind of pushover do you think I am? You had your hands up her skirt. She was straddling your waist and you weren't fighting her off."

"Well, she—"

"Stop, right there. I know what she and you were doing or going to do. If it wasn't for the fact I need a manager, you'd be out the door too." Hope approached the desk. I want the key you have to this office, and I want you out of this room. How dare you use my parents' office for your foreplay."

"Hope—"

Hope's nails bit into her palm. "Don't 'Hope' me. I mean it, Guy. Get out of this office. Get me the lists I need and if I ever catch you in a situation like this again you'll be fired."

Hope watched as Guy got up from the chair and came around the desk. He withdrew a key from his pocket and handed it to her. She backed up to give him access to the door, closed and locked the door after his exit, and followed him to his office. Silence reigned as he riffled through some papers on the desk and then handed her a folder.

"Is there anything else, Hope?"

"I meant what I said. Is that clear?"

"Perfectly.

****

A glass hit the wall and shattered, water dripped slowly down the wall. "How dare Hope give him orders? How dare she come into Morgan's and treat *him* like something she wanted to grind under her shoe? Just like her parents had treated his dad before he got sick and died. The man had barely enough to live on and now Hope was trying to do the same thing to him. Did he understand? Yes. Perfectly. And he would enjoy devising the perfect punishment for Hope.

Chapter Ten

Miles opened his eyes to darkness. He'd slept longer than his usual daytime coma. It'd been past dawn when he turned off the television and made his way downstairs. He'd then spent another hour wondering how to approach Hope.

Sleep had finally captured him. He'd drifted off with visions of computers, cell phones, and Hope dancing in his head.

A quick stretch and he jumped up from the mattress and headed for the stairs. Hope planned on going back to work the day after tomorrow, and he needed to make the most of the next few hours.

His nostrils flared as he found the scent he sought. Hope was home. The honeysuckle scent teasing his senses caused discomfort in his loins. He suppressed the urge that made his shaft want to harden. He needed to woo Hope emotionally before he finally claimed her body.

Arrogant as that sounded to his own ears, Miles knew that eventually Hope would be his. She had to be or what he called his miserable soul would disappear from his body.

He followed the sensuous lure of her fragrance to the guest room he'd yet to utilize. The door stood open, and he had a lust inducing view of his woman's shapely backside as she bent over a cardboard box. What could be so fascinating? He looked around and for the first time, noticed the room's décor.

Gone were the previous feminine trappings. A

king size bed, complete with a canopy stood sentinel in the middle of the room. Hunter green curtains, the same shade as the bed drapings, covered the windows. A brass floor lamp stood in one corner and a smaller replica rested on a oak bedside table. A recliner in the same color motif sat near one set of windows and a massive entertainment center stood against the wall midway between the recliner and bed.

Miles eyes almost bulged at the thirty-six-inch flat screen TV filling the center shelf. Books on various subjects adorned the other shelves. If he had chosen the furnishings himself he couldn't have done a better job.

He started to ease away from the door's threshold and his eyes caught the only bit of white in the room. A small refrigerator set on the opposite side of the bed. A crocheted something covered the top of the metal surface and a vase of flowers claimed a spot in the center of the cloth. Miles blinked back the unfamiliar moisture from his eyes.

Hope had been busy and by the looks of it, she still slaved to turn her home into a vampire's comfortable and safe haven.

Her delectable fanny still arched in the air, but her upper body now rested almost entirely inside the box.

Miles bit back his laughter but couldn't stop his feet from crossing the carpeted floor to the object of his desire.

His arms slid around Hope's slender waist. She jerked. His hands moved under her sweatshirt. Her body trembled. His fingers eased inside her bra and cupped her breasts. Hope's inhalation allowed him access to pebble hard nipples. Desire pulsed its way from his fingers to his shaft. The rigid and seeking flesh pressed against her shapely buttocks.

Miles waited for Hope's protest or cry of horror.

His breath caught when instead, she leaned back against his arousal. He withdrew one of his hands and traced the junction of her thighs. Denim prevented him from touching her intimate flesh. He wanted to get closer. He wanted to ease into her center and feel the evidence of her desire.

Hope's moan, deep and sensuous, turned his insides to mush. Never in his wildest dreams had he thought to hear her respond this way—knowing what he was. His heart stammered and then beat furiously. He didn't deserve Hope but Lord how he wanted her.

Miles pressed even closer to the tantalizing vee of her jeans. His hand cupped her sex. Her legs trembled against his. Her body arched again and straightened—giving Miles access to her throat. He laved the soft skin with his tongue before nipping it lightly with his teeth.

Hope's whimper stoked his desire. She turned and stretched upward. Her face tilted toward his. Lips the color of ripe cherries seduced him. He caught her mouth in a kiss. He branded her lips with his love and then sought the heated warmth inside.

Once again he cupped her breasts. He flicked her nipples with his fingers but it wasn't enough. Miles pulled away from her lips.

"Hope, I want to..." He caught the edge of her sweatshirt and pulled it up and over her head before dropping it to the floor. The lacy edging of her bra caught his eye, and then his hands quickly unhooked the beautiful barrier. It landed on the mini fridge.

Hope didn't know how things had gotten that far or how she was even allowing it to happen. She only knew Miles made her feel things she'd never known were possible. His touch incited her to wild imaginings. She wanted to loop her legs around his waist and press her aching cleft to his seductive rock hard arousal.

If she were in her right mind, she would be running for safety. If she were not crazed with love and lust for this man, she'd be screaming for help. If she didn't believe she could trust him, she'd be hunting for her pliers.

Miles lips left her mouth and exchanged places with one set of fingers. Hope's knees buckled as his teeth nipped her aching crests. He followed with a swipe of his tongue and her toes curled.

Her body suffered sensual shock when his other hand trailed a path of fire to her waist. A quick twist and a slight tug and Hope felt the warmth of his touch sliding downward to touch her aching center.

Miles' groan caused her to open eyes that had closed against the assault of his desire. His eyes glowed emerald as he met her gaze.

"Hope, you have no idea what you do to me. I want to touch—to taste—every part of your body."

Hope's heart soared with the pleasure his words brought. She felt loved and humbled and maybe just a bit exuberant that she could make this man want her the way she wanted him.

She touched his face. "What's stopping you?"

The growl that caressed her ears didn't frighten her. It made her feel powerful and so totally seductive. All thoughts of anything left her mind when Miles slid his hand under the edge of her panties.

She sucked in air as he touched the curls hiding her sex.

"Breathe, love. I want you conscious when I make you mine."

The teasing note in his voice didn't cool the heat his touch elevated.

"Open for me. Let me feel the heat, Hope."

Hope did as he asked and widened her stance. His hand cupped her and then his fingers touched her with fire.

A cry of longing left her lungs and escaped her lips as he brought her close and then rocketed her into an abyss of pleasure.

"Hope, I want to love you completely. Will you let me?"

She struggled to find a lung full of air to answer. No more reasoning—no more resistance—no more excuses. She loved Miles.

"Yes."

A blur of motion and Hope found herself prone on the bed. Miles' hands moved with such speed her jeans and panties were off before she knew it and cool air bathed her heated skin.

His lips caught hers again before he pulled back—much too soon.

"Are you sure, love? There'll be no going back. If I take you now, it'll be forever. I won't let you go. No other man will feel the seductive lure of your body, and no other man will sheathe himself inside you."

Miles' hand caressed her cheek. "Can you live with that? Can you live with me? I don't want just a lover. I want a wife."

Hope's mind reeled. Had Miles just proposed? Things were moving so fast. She loved him, but to be his wife? What would that mean? In most cases marriage meant *until death do us part.* Marriage to a vampire? He'd live forever and she'd die old and ugly. She looked into the face of the most handsome man she'd ever seen. His green gaze held what looked like hope and fear. His dark brows arched as a frown took shape.

"Hope?"

She opened her mouth to tell him…what? What could she say?

"Miles—"

Glass shattered somewhere downstairs. Miles moved and Hope found herself on the floor. He stripped the coverlet off the bed and tossed it over her.

"Stay here."

Then he was gone. She didn't see him leave. He just disappeared right before her eyes.

****

Miles materialized downstairs. He sniffed the air. His fangs burst forth as he caught the scent of his prey. He followed the adrenaline-laced blood scent and arrived in the kitchen. Glass from the backdoor littered the floor. He jumped through the new kitchen window and followed receding footsteps.

Night had fallen completely while he and Hope were upstairs. Good. His vision sharpened, and he saw two men jump the fence and run toward a pickup truck. He started after them.

"Dang it! Ouch!"

Miles turned his vision back to the house. Hope hopped on one leg, holding her foot in her hand. The rich aroma of her unique blend of blood tantalized his nostrils. He hurled the temptation aside.

Hope needed him—not his fangs. He glanced back at the men who had already climbed into their vehicle. The truck's motor revved to life. Squealing tires signified a hurried departure. Miles clamped down on his anger and retracted his fangs and claws. He could chase them but he'd rather return to Hope. Besides, he got their tag number. Zacke could hunt them down. Miles had better things to do.

****

Hope's head pounded with a combination of light and sound. Miles, Zacke, and Hawk were carrying on a loud conversation right outside the kitchen door. A police cruiser's lights, she assumed Zacke called for one, spun a dizzying circle of color through the window.

"There, that should make Miles happy."

Hope honed in on Miranda's words and then looked to where she gestured. Her right foot had a length of gauze wrapped around it. A bandage she didn't need. The piece of glass embedded in her foot had been miniscule. She'd already plucked it out and dabbed the small cut with alcohol by the time Miles returned to the house.

He'd been more concerned about her foot than the men who had broken the window. His lack of concern bothered Hope just a bit. Shouldn't he be more worried? If the men were the same ones who attacked her in the park, shouldn't he be a bit anxious about their escape?

It wasn't that she wanted him to go after them. He would have been out-numbered—could have been possibly hurt or maybe not. She should have asked more questions during their talk the night before.

"You okay?"

"Yes. I'm sorry, Miranda. I appreciate you placating Miles. The man took one look at my foot and almost had a conniption. I'm not sure if it was the injury or the blood."

Miranda laughed. "Bless his heart. I'm sure it was a shock. I know he was worried but horror probably topped his emotional list."

"What do mean?"

"Bear in mind, I never saw Zacke do it, he became seriously ill not long after we were married and then was transformed back into a mortal, but he did tell me how the blood/lust thing works between mates."

"Do tell. Miles mentioned the word mate. I'm not quite sure I like that term."

"It does smack a bit of male chauvinism. But remember our guys come from a different time. They didn't even know what bra burning was way back when or anything about women's lib."

"I know. I guess it's another thing I'll have to get used to."

Miranda patted Hope's hand. "You will. Just

give it time. You don't have to rush into a deep relationship right now—regardless of your strong emotions. Get to know one another first."

Hope's sigh sent an unused piece of gauze sailing across the table's surface. "I'm not sure I have a lot of time to get to know him."

"What do you mean?"

Should she tell Miranda about Mile's proposal? Why not? She needed some clarity on what to do.

"I mean that right before those goons threw a rock through my window, Miles told me he wanted me as his wife."

Miranda smiled. "That's wonderful, Hope." Her smile dimmed just a bit. "Isn't it?"

"Yeah, I guess. In the sense that I love him to distraction it is, but—"

"Uh oh, that's not a good sign."

Hope got up from her seat and limped toward the fridge. "You want something to drink?"

"You aren't going to change the subject are you?"

"No, I just suddenly have a parched throat."

Miranda giggled. "Men can do that to you."

She retraced her steps with two diet colas in hand. She gave one to Miranda. Back in her chair she popped the top on her drink and took a quick sip. "Okay, call me vain, call me selfish, call me whatever, but I have a problem with me getting old and ugly and Miles staying the hunk he is."

Miranda's eyes grew wide. "Yeah, I know about that. I wondered too, but in the beginning of our marriage, Zacke was set on getting his soul back and becoming mortal. Then we weren't even sure he'd live long enough for either of us to age. I can see your dilemma."

"You can? You don't think I'm being just plain old self-centered?"

"No, I don't. Have you talked to Miles about this? Forgive me for being nosy but did you tell him you would marry him?"

"No. I hesitated long enough for him to frown. Then we were rudely interrupted. For the life of me, I'm not sure what I would have said. I love him, but—"

Miles, Hawk, and Zacke converged on the kitchen door. Hope prayed Miles hadn't heard what she'd said. She also prayed he wasn't able to read her mind—something she'd wondered about before. Again, she could slap herself for not asking these questions earlier. Something she desperately needed to do before their relationship went any further.

"Hey, did ya'll get everything taken care of? Get a bead on the bad guys?" Miranda's questions helped Hope get a leash on her emotions. She took a deep breath and smiled up at the man whose hand now rested in a possessive gesture on her shoulder.

"You okay, Hope?"

"I'm fine. I told you it was just a small cut. Nothing to worry about."

Miles leaned a hip against the table. "I worry. You're my mate, that's what I do."

Hope's cheeks heated. Why on earth would he say that in front of everyone? Nothing was settled yet.

Miranda gave her a commiserating smile, as Miles accepted the good wishes of Zacke and Hawk.

"So when's the wedding?" Hawk's question made her cringe.

"I'm leaving that up to Hope."

At the moment, Hope wasn't sure who she wanted to strangle more—Hawk or Miles. She'd make up her mind later. Everyone was waiting for her to say something.

"Is anyone going to tell me what happened with the guys who broke my window?"

Silence followed her question. Miles withdrew his warmth. He only moved a couple of feet away but it felt like the length of a football field. Zacke and Hawk looked confused, but Miranda, bless her heart gave her a thumbs up for courage.

"Sure, Hope, sorry. We are running down the tag number Miles gave us. The truck is probably stolen but with the look Miles got at them, we do have a bit of description to put out on the streets. Although, it's probably not enough to match them to the description you gave us of your attackers in the park. Still, hopefully, we'll get more leads from that."

"Yes, and in the meantime, I'm going to be doing fly-bys on a regular basis in and around this neighborhood. If they come back on foot or in another vehicle, I'll know it."

"Thank you Hawk, you too Zacke. I appreciate what the police are doing, and I'm grateful for your help."

Still nothing from Miles. What did she expect? His feelings were probably hurt but until she could talk to him, she couldn't give him an answer or even get too happy over his proposal. Hope just wasn't sure if she could marry him—knowing what he was. They also hadn't talked about children. Could he father a child? Would the child be mortal or a vampire?

Tension pounded the back of her neck and did a slow crawl over her skull to rest right above her eyes. Hope rubbed her forehead.

"Here, take these for your headache."

Miles stood at her side. She hadn't noticed him getting her a glass of water or finding the tablets she kept for pain.

"Thank you." She took the glass, and her heart hurt when Miles purposely kept from touching her hand. Lord, she hated this. Hated hurting him and she hated being a coward.

"Well, if ya'll have it all handled, I guess we should go." Miranda followed her words by standing.

"Oh, sure. I hate that you came over for nothing."

"Nonsense. I like getting out every once in awhile. Getting to chat with you outside work is good for both of us."

Hope accepted and returned Miranda's hug. Zacke dropped a quick kiss on her cheek, and Hawk gave her a salute.

Miles, still silent, followed the group outside. Hope braced her arms on the table and rested her head on top of them. Her simple orderly world had turned totally tornadic.

No longer a woman alone, she now had a man who wanted her as a wife or mate. The word mate sounded so primitive and for the life of Hope, it made her insides heat just thinking of being Miles' mate. How could she go from one extreme to another? And what on earth was she going to do about Miles?

"Hope, why don't you go on up to bed? I'm going to clean up the rest of this mess and fix the door."

Hope jumped. Drat the man for his silent approach. "I can help, or I could if we had anything to fix the door with. There won't be any place open this time of the night to get the materials."

Miles actually smirked. "I don't need manmade materials."

"Oh? Well then, how do you propose to fix the door?"

"Like this."

Miles walked to the injured door, pressed his hand against it and then closed his eyes.

Glass filled in the empty window frame.

He then dropped a kiss on Hope's open mouth. Before she could enjoy the lustful delight, her mind grasped one thought. He'd moved again without her seeing him.

Against her body's protest and probably her

better judgment, she broke the possessive and intoxicating kiss.

"Hang on a minute, Vamp Boy. I've got some questions."

"All right. But first I want an answer to mine."

Chapter Eleven

Hope's breath left her lungs. Oh Lord, what was she going to tell him? Before her brain could come up with an answer, the devastatingly handsome man lifted her from her chair, proceeded to carry her out of the kitchen, through the house, and up the stairs. Would he take her back to his room? Did she want to continue where they left off earlier? Should she forget about all her questions?

No! She had to know where she and Miles stood on several issues. Love wasn't just about being compatible in bed—she needed to know if they could make a marriage work.

Miles bypassed the guest room and moved down the hallway. Her door opened by itself and once they were inside, closed the same way. Miles laid her gently against the pillows on the bed and then moved to sit in a chair across the room.

"Hope, I need an answer."

Hope stalled. She scooted into an upright position, glanced at Miles, and looked away—only to bring her gaze back to an extremely ruffled looking vampire. His usually well-groomed chestnut hair was disheveled. A frown between his brows made the confusion in his eyes stand out more. His stock in white shirts had suffered also. The one he wore had a rip in one sleeve and smudges of dirt down the front.

"Now, Hope."

"Miles, I can't answer your question until you

answer some of mine." Hope prayed he couldn't detect the tremor in her voice.

His sigh whooshed into the silent space her words brought.

"Okay. You do have a right to ask all the questions you want." Miles set a bit straighter in his chair. "But you may not like the answers."

"I understand. And you may not like mine."

Miles stood to his feet and crossed to the bed. "May I?"

"Sure." Hope's queen size bed seemed to shrink when Miles sat on the edge of the mattress.

"Go ahead. Ask your questions."

"First I need to know if you can read my mind."

Miles lips creased in a slight smile. "Yes, but I do try not to do it."

Heat attacked her face. "I don't like it but it's an interesting concept. Now, how are you able to just disappear?"

This time his smile was full-blown. "I just think about where I want to be and then my thoughts transfer my body to that place."

"I guess that's just a vampire thing. It could come in handy at times."

"Yes, it has and still does."

"I'm wondering, can you be hurt or killed?"

"Not usually physically hurt. If we are, we heal quickly. I think Miranda told you about Zacke's gunshot wound."

"Yes."

Miles reached out and took her hand. "We can be killed. Not by all the old myths you read about or see on television or in movies but if you take out our heart and then chop off our heads, we do die."

"Well, I guess since my medical bag isn't missing, you're not really afraid I'll do some unscheduled surgery."

Miles laughed. "My only fear is that you won't

answer my question the way I want you to."

Hope tried to digest all Miles had told her. The man was virtually indestructible, handsome as all get-out, and even with her dragging her feet, he still wanted her for his wife. Most women would jump at the chance to be married to this man, and Hope wasn't immune to the lure of what life with Miles could be. But there still remained a couple of more unasked questions.

"Can you father children and will they be a mixture of us?"

"Good question. I'm fairly certain I can be a father. There's nothing to prevent it as far as I know. Zacke was still a vampire when he got Miranda pregnant. And although he'd been experiencing mortal traits, he was still one of us. I don't know if our children will be half mortal, half vampire, or completely one or the other. I just know that I'll love them no matter what."

"Thank you for being honest. In the scheme of things if we do have children, it really won't matter as long as they are healthy."

Miles placed a kiss on Hope's forehead. "Do you have any other questions?"

Hope looked up at Miles. "What do we do when I get old and you stay the same age you are now?"

"What do you mean?"

"I mean that I'm going to get old, arthritic, and more ugly."

Laughter exploded into the room. Hope snatched her hand back. Miles ducked the blow she aimed at his head.

"Hope, darling, you will always be beautiful to me."

"Well, that's well and good but somehow when I'm eighty and look like your grandmother, it's not gonna make me feel better."

Miles strived for a somber look. Hope was

seriously upset. He didn't blame her—he blamed himself. He should have already thought of what would happen in the future. Life and death went hand in hand. If he planned on having a life with Hope, then he too had to face a life someday without her. He would never transform her in to what he was. Hope loved sunshine and light. She'd suffer and eventually hate him for taking those away.

"I'm sorry. I guess I never thought about how you would feel. Don't hit me, Hope. I only thought about how my life would be without you. Selfish, yes, but I never thought beyond my own feelings."

Hope reached out to him. He took the hand she offered and when she moved closer, he accepted the warmth with a hopeful heart.

"I should apologize. You give me your heart and I give you my petty insecurities. Not a fair exchange."

He draped an arm over her shoulder and pulled Hope even closer. "Maybe not, but from where I sit, I'd be getting way more than I ever deserved."

Soft lips caressed his. Miles didn't question her change of heart. He just took what was offered. He returned the kiss. He nibbled and then stroked the pliant flesh offered—repeatedly—before breaking the kiss.

"Hope, in answer to your question about us growing old. I have a solution."

Hope's well-kissed mouth fell open.

Miles closed it with a quick touch of his index finger. "Too much temptation, love."

"You have a way to keep me from getting older?"

Miles cleared his throat. "Not so much that but a way that I can grow old with you."

"I'm listening."

"What if for every gray hair, every wrinkle you get, I get the same?"

"How's that possible? You died at what age?

Thirty-something, right?"

"Right, but with makeup and plastic surgery, it can be done."

"But why would you want to?"

Miles caught and gripped Hope's hands. "Because, I love you more than life. I want to make you happy. If that means aging then so be it."

Hope's gaze still held confusion. "But Miles, will you be content to just start over after I die?"

He released his grip on her hands and pulled Hope up to sit on his lap. "I don't plan on starting over."

"I don't understand."

"When I lose you Hope, I'll lose my heart and my soul. When that dark day happens, my life will be over."

"No! Miles, you can't. You have to promise me that you won't kill yourself."

"Sorry, that's not a topic open for argument."

Miles silenced her protest with a quick kiss.

"I'm tired. I've been tired for a long time. I've kept myself busy with several projects. Now, my life will consist of keeping you safe, happy, and well-loved for the rest of our lives."

"What about any children we have? What will we tell them?"

"We'll cross that bridge when we get to it."

Miles gently pushed Hope off his lap and swatted her lightly on the backside before standing up himself. "Now, I suggest you do whatever women do to get ready for a wedding. I assume or fervently hope I've put your fears at rest."

"I'm not happy with all your solutions, but I'll be more than overjoyed to start planning our wedding."

"Good, I'm not getting any younger you know."

Hope's laughter caressed Miles' ears. Yes, life could be good, and he planned on making the most of the years they would have together.

****

"I'm so happy I could cry, Hope." Miranda's voice indeed sounded as if she had tears in her eyes.

"Well, be happy and be helpful. I have a feeling Miles won't stand for a long engagement."

"I agree. So have you decided where you want to get married?"

A few moments later, Hope hung up the phone and turned to a grimacing Miles.

"I guess that conversation means you don't want to just elope?"

"No, but you'll be happy to know that I talked Miranda out of a big church wedding." Hope blinked back a mist of tears.

"Okay, I give in. If you want a big fancy wedding we'll do it."

"That's so sweet but no thank you. It wouldn't be the same without my dad giving me away or mom sitting in the front pew of the church. The plane crash destroyed that dream."

"I'm sorry."

"It's okay. Bad things just happen sometimes. I still miss them like mad but it's getting better."

Miles pulled her into his arms and kissed her. The man certainly knew how to get her out of a somber mood. She'd lighten his.

"This should make you happy. I thought we could have the wedding right here at the house. Nothing big or fancy but I think a twilight wedding would be beautiful, don't you?"

"Hope, *you're* beautiful. We could get married in the basement for all I care. I just want you to be mine as quick as possible."

Hope giggled. "Not much on patience are you?"

"No. Not when it comes to you and getting you in bed."

Hope's cheeks stung with heat. "Well, I never said we had to wait."

"Call me old-fashioned but now that you've agreed to marry me, I want to wait until I have my ring on your finger. If you agree."

"I can't say I'm not disappointed, but thank you."

"For what?"

She traced the line between Miles' brows. "For caring enough to give me the choice. Not too many men would do that."

"Remember I come from a time when wives were revered for their chastity."

"And you're sure I'm chaste?"

"Yes."

"And you would know this how?"

"If I answer that I'd be in trouble." Miles' laughter rumbled forth and for the life of her, Hope couldn't help but laugh along with him.

Her adorable vampire looked like a mischievous child with a big helping of male testosterone thrown in.

"Fine. So I guess I'll just have to move the wedding from Christmas Eve to next June."

"Not if you want to keep me happy."

"Oh and what happens when you're not happy?"

"My fangs and claws come out."

Hope searched Miles' gaze carefully. The deeper green that signified a change of mood wasn't there—neither was a glimpse of a fang. However, she did spy a glint of humor. "You are so bad."

"Count on it, sweetheart." Miles looped an arm around her waist. "Come on, you need to eat. You didn't have anything last night, and I bet you didn't eat much today."

Hope wondered how Miles could possibly know she'd nibbled on cheese and crackers for lunch and skipped breakfast entirely. She'd need to do better if she planned on hitting the hospital floor running in the morning. But today she'd slept a bit later than usual due to the hoopla from the break-in and then began making notes on what she needed to do to put a small wedding together.

Miranda said she'd take care of the caterers, and Hope had placed an order for flowers with a local florist. She needed to haul down the Christmas decorations from the attic, but she would get started on that chore after the weekend. The house would really be lit up when the decorators arrived a couple of days before the wedding but there were a few things she wanted to put in place herself. Last year she'd forgone the Christmas cheer, but the antique bows and garlands would be lovely for the wedding.

Hope released a long sigh. So many things to do, and she would need to go shopping for a wedding dress. It might be a small ceremony but it would be a day she would always remember.

"Guilty as charged, but I'll order a pizza and pig out."

"Not appetizing. How you mortals can eat that stuff is beyond me."

"Well, my darling vamp, your fetish for blood products confounds me also." Hope glanced up and caught Miles' startled look. "But you know what? I love you anyway."

"Likewise, my love, but do you love me enough to get married this weekend?"

"Miles! There is no way we can do a wedding this weekend. Everyone is tied up with after-Thanksgiving plans. In fact, Miranda wants us to come over Thursday for dinner. I don't know how she did it but both she and I are off for Thanksgiving.

Hope grabbed her cell phone from the kitchen table and hit speed dial. She ordered a large pizza with everything except mushrooms and anchovies.

Miles stood waiting as she got the total and thanked the guy before hanging up.

"Pizza will be here in about half an hour."

"Good. That'll give me time to eat my own dinner, and I need to pop in to see Zacke."

"For what and what do you mean, 'pop in'?"

Miles' lips creased in a smile. "I just need to touch base with him."

"Okay, so now tell me about the other."

"Just that, I'm going to drop in at Zacke's and Miranda's."

"You going to do that mind transference thingy?"

Miles actually snickered. "No, I actually planned on flying."

"Whoa. You forgot to tell me that you could do that."

"Sorry. Guess it slipped my mind."

"Sure it did. So when do we go?"

"Not we, me. You need to eat."

Miles stole the protest forming on her lips. By the time she'd gather her wits, he'd disappeared.

Dang it. Mortal or vamp, men were still the most irritating creatures on earth.

****

Ten minutes later, Miles followed Zacke to the den. Miranda had been putting the last touches on their dinner when he'd arrived but abandoned her preparations for an inquest about the wedding.

Women no matter what era went totally on point when it came to marriage plans. He knew perfectly well she and Hope spent most of the day calling back and forth about this and that. So why did she need him to give her his version?

Fortunately, Zacke rescued him from flowers and cakes, etc. He gently rerouted Miranda back to the stove by telling her the rolls were burning.

Zacke closed the door to the den.

"Thanks, I owe you one."

Zacke laughed. "Actually, you owe me several, but I'll let it slide. You were beginning to look a bit harassed."

"That bad?"

"Yep. Why didn't you convince Hope to elope or get married at the courthouse?"

"I thought about it, but she's had so much taken from her in her lifetime, I didn't want to spoil it for her."

"It's amazing how women take to giving orders when it comes to weddings."

"Yes. I remember your sweet little wife threatened me with a broom if I didn't get it together."

"Lord love her and Hope."

"Guess that's the bottom line. We do *love* them."

Miles flopped on the couch. "Have you been able to find out anything about Hope's phone calls?"

"Not yet, have they stopped?"

"No, I wish they would. Someone's still calling and playing the music to a song her mother used to sing when Hope was small. They cap off the call by playing a tape that has her mom's voice telling her it's bedtime like I told you before. I should have followed up on this sooner, but I forgot."

"Yeah, and I bet Guy and that green-eyed monster did a whammy on your memory."

"Okay, I was and still am jealous. I don't like him."

"I don't blame you. Something's not right, but I'm still no closer to following his money trail."

"So what's next? I suppose I could kill him and then hire someone to manage the business for Hope."

"And I'd have to arrest you."

"Bad idea. I have a wedding coming up."

"You know, he could just be out for what money he can get and be totally harmless in every other way."

"The little weasel needs an attitude adjustment if you ask me."

Zacke nodded his head. "I'm of the same opinion

but in the meantime, if Hawk agrees, what do you think about having him work at Morgan's as a night guard?"

"That could work. Hope told Guy she would look into a list of security companies he wanted her to hire."

"I have a feeling those companies have been bought off or at least one of the guards has."

Miles wanted to rip Guy in two. The man had a lot to answer for but he'd allow Zacke first strike. If the police department failed to catch the man embezzling funds or stealing stock then Miles planned on paying him a visit.

"So will you talk to Hawk?"

"Talk to me about what?" Hawk's question fell into the room a second before his body materialized.

"How would you like to go undercover?" Zacke grinned.

"I have a feeling this has something to do with Guy Evans."

"You'd be correct. We want you to tell Guy Hope hired your firm for security and that you'll be working the night shift."

"I'll be glad to help. I haven't had any luck with trailing him. If he's up to anything, he's doing it during the day when I'm asleep."

The next few minutes were taken up with implementing their plan and discussing further Hope's harassing phone calls. Miles stood and crossed the room to Hawk. "I appreciate what you're doing. I know we have no concrete evidence against him, but every cell I have screams he's the one. I'm not sure how far Guy will go in his quest to cheat Hope, but I want him stopped. Since Zacke won't allow me to kill him, then you'll be our eyes and ears to get the evidence we need."

"It's in the bag, Miles. Just do me a favor."

"Name it."

"Make sure Hope doesn't play matchmaker for me at your wedding."

"Who clued you into the wedding?"

"Hope did. I stopped by there before coming here."

"Did she say something about fixing you up with a date?"

"Not verbally, but she had this appalling glow in her eyes and it makes me uneasy."

Miles and Zacke guffawed.

"It's not funny. Both of you want to be leg-shackled. I don't. I enjoy my life like it is and don't plan on changing it for any woman."

"Famous last words, my friend." Miles clapped Hawk on the back. "But, I'll make sure that you don't get shanghaied at the wedding."

"Good."

"Well, I'm out of here. Hope was waiting on a pizza when I left, and I need to make sure she eats. That woman is already causing my hair, if it could, to turn gray."

Zacke smiled but his eyes were serious when he asked. "Did you come up with anything to placate Hope about your aging problem?"

"Miranda must have told you."

"Yeah, we don't keep secrets from one another."

"No problem, I figured Hope would talk to her." Miles closed his eyes for a moment before opening them again and meeting his friends' gazes. "I did come up with a plan. I'll use artifice to age right along with Hope and when she dies, I plan to follow her."

"You're sure?"

"Yes, I am Zacke. I watched Hope grow up for decades, then I fell in love with her without a clue she would ever be mine. When I lose her, the reason for my life will be gone."

Although the other two men remained silent, he

could read their faces. Hawk looked shocked. Zacke's expression, bless his heart, held understanding.

Miles threw up his hand in goodbye and then left to go back to Hope and home.

Chapter Twelve

Thanksgiving's dawn held the promise of being a beautiful day. Hope resisted the urge to skip as she took her cup of tea to the guest room. Miles would be getting ready for his long day's nap, and she wanted to talk to him first.

She eased the door open and promptly lost her breath. Miles stood near the bed, naked as a jaybird. His expression when he turned his head and looked at her held amusement.

No doubt due to the embarrassment heating her cheeks.

"If you keeping staring, love, I may have to take you up on your thoughts."

"Dang it, Miles. You said you wouldn't read my mind."

Miles stripped the top sheet off the bed and wrapped it around his waist. "No, I said I would try not to. I couldn't help it. Your thoughts were screaming in my head."

"Stop it. It's your fault. No man should look like you do."

Miles' smile was sheer devilment. "So I've been told by a number of women."

Hope advanced to the other side of the bed. She grabbed a pillow and watched in amazement as it floated out of her hand.

"No fair."

"Yes, fair. If you hit me, we'll just get into a tussle. That will lead to me groping several of your body parts—which would lead to something else. If I even halfway make love to you now, we'll both end up in this bed. I'm eventually going to have to sleep and you'll have to stay with me."

"Why is that?"

"You'll be too exhausted to get up."

The image his words invoked turned Hope's knees to gelatin. No point in arguing with the truth. The man knew what he was talking about.

"Now, give me a kiss before you start your cooking marathon."

"That reminds me. I came up to tell you, we have to leave for Miranda and Zacke's around six. Is that okay?"

"It's fine."

Hope moved around the bed and allowed Miles to pull her into his arms. "It's nice of them to have dinner so late."

"Yeah, Miranda started doing that the year they got married. She wanted to make sure her adopted brothers-in-law as she calls me and Hawk took part in the holiday."

"Well, next year, we'll return the favor. It'll be great having family and friends here for holidays."

"Yes for both of us. Now, enough talk woman. The sun is almost up and—"

"I know. It's time for your nap."

Miles leaned down and touched his lips lightly to Hope's before coaxing her to open her mouth. Not that she needed any encouragement. Miles had been missing in action for the last several nights, only coming in as she was going to bed. But then again, she'd been exhausted after returning to work. The ER had been hit with a multitude of accidents, assaults, and even a couple of rape victims. Her days had been long and part of her evening hours had been taken up with addressing invitations. The engraver Morgan Rarities had used in the past for special occasions had been more than happy to rush her wedding job. She'd dropped the envelopes in the mail a couple of days before.

Miles deepened his kiss, and Hope forgot all about the wedding preparations. She felt the proof of his desire against her belly and welcomed the heat of his love as he caressed her breasts through the material of her robe. She shifted closer. She wanted to feel his touch on her naked skin but instead of taking what she offered, Miles released her lips, removed his hands, and stepped back.

His eyes shone a deep jade, and his lids began to droop. "Sorry, darling, we'll have to continue this another time."

Once Miles lay comatose on the bed, Hope pulled the coverlet over his body. She kissed his rapidly cooling lips before making sure no hint of sunlight showed through the drapes. One more lingering glance at his still form and she headed for the kitchen.

She popped half of a bagel in the toaster and sat down with pen and paper to make a list of what she needed to do. She'd promised Miranda she'd make potato salad and green beans for their dinner. She'd also promised Zacke, who Miranda said had developed a sweet tooth in place of his fangs, a red velvet cake.

The grocery store had been packed the night before when she did her shopping and with all the ingredients at hand, she hoped to get everything ready with time to spare.

That extra time would be spent looking through magazines for a dress style and adding the newest employee to Morgan Rarities' payroll. Miles and Zacke had explained Hawk's role as a security guard. She didn't like the implication that Guy could be the one stealing pieces of merchandise but she'd never thought he'd be making out with a secretary at work either. He certainly wasn't like his dad. Luke Evans had been a good soul who had loved her and her parents like his own family.

Her breakfast popped up and after slathering on butter and strawberry jam, she went back to her list.

A few minutes later when she'd placed the last bite in her mouth and finished her list, her thoughts returned to Guy. She hoped he wouldn't disappoint her or tarnish the memories of their families. But either way, she planned on filing charges against the lowlife culprits whoever they were.

****

A couple of hours later, Hope sat back down and gave a sigh of satisfaction. The potato salad chilled in the refrigerator, the green beans, flavored with a piece of bacon, bubbled fragrantly on the stovetop. She'd checked on the cake layers and they were almost ready to come out of the oven. The cream cheese icing ingredients lay ready on the countertop, and she now had time to skim through the first of the wedding magazines.

Most of the gowns were way too modern looking for Hope. She wanted something more in vogue with what Miles' bride would have worn back in the day. Her gaze caught and stayed on a cream-colored gown. The neckline was square cut and the sleeves were tight and met in a point at the tips. The dress flowed freely from the bodice down to the hem. Barely-there sequins dotted the material. A gold chain rested on the hips of the gown's model.

Hope almost drooled. This was it. The exact gown she'd had in mind. The veil and detachable train were just as exquisite.

Now, if she could find a contact number or the website, she'd place her order for all three.

The cake timer went off just as she finished jotting down the boutique's number. Hope grabbed a pair of potholders, opened the oven door, and lifted the pans out onto a cooling rack. The house phone rang just as she turned off the stove and shut the door. The phone continued its impatient ringing. What on earth could Guy want on a holiday?

Maybe, possibly, he just wanted to wish her a happy Thanksgiving. Naw—she wouldn't be that lucky.

"Hello."

"Hope?

"Who else would it be, Guy?"

"Sorry, I'm just a little upset."

Hope promptly sat down on the sofa's arm. "Has something happened at the store?"

"In a manner of speaking."

Why on earth couldn't he just spit it out? "Guy, what's wrong?"

"I went into the office early this morning and ran into a security guard. He said you hired his company as security."

"So, what's so upsetting about that?"

"How could you hire someone without telling me?"

Hope's breath left her lungs in an exasperated burst. "I didn't think I needed your permission to hire someone."

She positively couldn't have heard an obscenity on the other end of the line.

"You don't, but that company wasn't on the list I gave you."

"You mean the list that I made you give me after you beat around the bush?" Hope didn't wait for Guy to answer. "I did my own research and found a company I liked. Besides, what were you doing at the office today? Morgans is closed until Monday."

"I know that, but I had some paperwork I wanted to catch up on."

"That's well and good, but if you're having trouble keeping up with business matters, I'll be more than happy to hire an assistant for you or do the paperwork myself."

This time the expletive was cut off in mid-syllable. "That won't be necessary. I'll just take the work home with me and do it there or we could do it together over lunch."

"I'm sorry, Guy. I have plans today—holiday plans."

"I suppose it's with that bodyguard you have hanging around. I would have thought he'd be gone by now."

Hope resisted the urge to tell him to go to Hades. She didn't want Guy to leave Morgan's—not yet—and not under his own steam if evidence pointed to his guilt.

"Well, you thought wrong. Miles is a permanent fixture around here, Guy. If you haven't already gotten it, look for the wedding invitation in the mail."

"You can't be serious. How can you marry someone you barely know? For all you know, he could be a thief or a murderer."

Hope's nails bit into her palm. "Well, that could be said of a lot of people. Do yourself and me a favor, Guy. Go home. The security company is watching the business, and they will contact me if there's a problem."

"Hope, can't we—"

"Guy, I have to go. Happy Thanksgiving and goodbye."

Hope literally threw the receiver back on the hook. That man was fast becoming a nuisance. The gall of him trying to make her look like the bad guy. He had no business being in the office when it was closed or to complain about anything. He'd better watch his step, or she'd be sorely tempted to turn Miles loose on him.

A smile tugged at her lips. Miles would like that.

He'd made it abundantly clear he disliked Guy. It wasn't so much in what he said but the almost snarl on his lips every time Guy's name came up. Anyway, she'd get much more satisfaction by tearing her deceitful manager from limb-to-limb herself.

Hope put Guy out of her mind while she wrote a check to James Enterprises, the fake name the men had come up with for Hawk's fictional employer. In order to work, everything had to appear on the up-and-up. The check would go into a secondary account Zacke set up under Miranda's maiden name.

Thirty minutes later, the cake rested on a crystal cake stand. The enticing aroma of cream cheese tempted Hope to cut a small slice but she opted for an apple. She'd make Miles happy and gorge at dinner.

A glance at the kitchen clock caused a momentary panic. If she wanted to shower and dress before Miles woke up, she'd have to do it now.

****

"Ready to go?" Miles locked his arms around Hope's waist and nuzzled her neck. She tilted her head to the side and enjoyed the texture of his tongue against her earlobe. She leaned back against his frame and pressed against his noticeable arousal.

"Hope, if we start anything now, we're going to be late."

"What if I said I didn't care?"

"Woman, you are making more than my body hard. Do you know how much trouble I'm having not taking you to bed?"

"Well, if it's anything like what I'm feeling by not begging you to, then yes."

She felt the vibrations of Miles soft laughter right before he nipped her neck and released her.

"I think I have something that will make you feel better."

"I seriously doubt that." Hope knew she sounded

petulant but dang the man turned her on and then expected her to turn herself off.

"Trust me."

"*Fine, I trust you.*"

Hope allowed Miles to lead her to the kitchen. She canvassed the table and countertops. Nothing had been added.

"So, what is it that's suppose to help my feelings?"

"You'll see. Have you got a box or something to put the stuff in you're taking to dinner?"

"Sure, but I still don't understand. What—"

"You will, now get the box."

Hope turned on her heel and opened a kitchen cabinet and took out a large plastic container for the salad and beans. She shot a glance at Mr. Give-Me-Orders-and-Regret-It.

It was a good thing she loved Miles or she'd throw the container at his smug look. She pulled the lid off, loaded the food items, and closed them up. "Okay, is there anything else I can be ordered to do, your majesty?"

Miles moved to Hope's side. "Yes, grab the cake and place it on top of the container. Then you can put your arms around my neck."

"You're really cruising for a bruising, Miles. Why would I want to do that?"

"I thought you wanted to get to Zacke and Miranda's."

"I do, but what the heck has that got to do with me putting my arms around your neck?"

Miles' smile widened. "Well, it's a nice night and I thought we could fly."

Hope's mouth fell open. "You mean it? We're going to fly?"

"Yes, my love, but you have to hold on tight. I don't want to drop you."

"Oh, don't worry. I won't let go for a minute."

Her arms looped around his neck in a secure hold before her gaze fell on the food. "What about all this stuff. I can't hold it and hold on."

"Don't worry about the food. It'll be there before we are."

Hope's mouth fell open again as the plastic container and the cake holder disappeared right before her eyes. "Wow, I bet some of the overnight services would pay you big bucks to work for them."

"Probably, but I don't need the money, and I already have a job I like."

Before Hope could ask him why he didn't need money, Miles scooped her up in his arms, strode to the kitchen door, did his whatever he did to make it open, and stepped outside. The door closed behind them, and then the ground disappeared from under Miles' feet.

"Oh my." Hope's words were tossed away by the night wind but it didn't prevent her from enjoying the view. Church steeples looked close enough to touch, stars beckoned from directly overhead, and the just-rising full moon showered them with its glow.

She should probably be frightened to death, but Miles had her. He wouldn't drop her, and she wouldn't ever forget the gift he'd given her tonight.

She lost count of the rooftops they passed over and marveled at the air traffic from flying creatures. Next time she would have to bring her camera.

"Having fun?" Miles words teased her ear.

"Oh yes! I can't believe this is real. It's great."

"I take it I'm forgiven now?"

Hope bravely removed one arm from the security of his neck and touched her hand to his cheek. "Even without this fantastic flight I couldn't stay displeased with you for long."

"I'm glad. You know, you're a good passenger."

Hope hesitated but then asked anyway. "Have

you carried many people this way?"

"Only one other, my love. I brought Zacke back to his house from Johnson Square the night he almost died."

Hope for the life of her couldn't think of anything to say. Instead she kissed his cheek.

The rest of their flight was silent. They landed under a copse of trees near their hosts' front door. Miles' arms held her steady as Hope regained her land legs. She looked up to thank him and her breath lodged in her throat.

Strong, invincible, macho Miles' eyes glittered with blood red tears. "Miles, are you okay?"

Immediately his features changed. His lips slanted up into a slight smile. He blinked once, and she wondered if she'd imagined the previous droplets.

"I'm better than I've been in centuries. You've shown me through your eyes what I've lost sight of—that the night can be a joy and not just a prison."

His lips trapped hers in a gentle kiss.

"Okay you two—break it up. It's time for dinner."

Miranda's words caused them to pull apart, but Hope welcomed the warmth of his grip on her hand. He gave a smiling Miranda a kiss on the cheek and then greeted the man who she knew meant the world to him, with a traditional male slap on the back.

****

Thanksgiving dinner at the Kensingtons' was a joyful and hilarious affair. Miranda shooed her and Miles to a chair and admonished Hope not to move—she was a guest. Hawk arrived just moments after she and Miles. He entertained Zacke and Miranda's offspring by making faces out of an assortment of raw veggies while Zacke finished carving the turkey.

Silence fell when Zacke said grace and then

chaos broke out. The twins clamored for pieces of the succulent bird and fought over who would get the first piece of cake. The din grew louder until Zacke raised his voice.

"Braden, Brier, silence."

Calm settled as the twins sat back down and both looked at their beleaguered dad. "Yes, Daddy," they chorused.

Brierana, an adorable mixture of both her parents with Miranda's auburn hair and Zacke's darker blue eyes, sent a mischievous look at Zacke and then did the unbelievable. She raised a dainty hand, extended her forefinger, and slowly twirled it in a circle. A small glob of cake icing floated across the table into Brier's open mouth.

The child's mouth wasn't the only one open at the table. Braden's tremulous lips erupted in a wail. Miranda stood to her feet and looked at Zacke.

"You said this wouldn't happen. Do something."

Zacke dropped the carving knife he still held onto the tabletop. His eyes were wide with shock, and his gaze also held desperation. "I didn't say it wouldn't. I said it wasn't probable."

Hawk looked askance and then his shoulders shook with laughter.

Hope elbowed an equally amused Miles in the ribs. Brier who had swallowed her ill-gotten treat, now had tears in her eyes threatening to overflow at any moment.

"Zacke!"

"I'm thinking, Miranda." Zacke moved around the table and stopped first at Braden's chair. He placed a hand on the child's shoulder. "It's okay. You can have some cake too."

Braden's frantic howl shut off like a water faucet.

Zacke approached his tiny daughter and knelt by her side.

"Brier, sweetie, no one's mad at you." He shot Miranda a look that screamed help.

"Your daddy's right, honey, we're not mad. You just gave mommy and daddy a shock."

"That's right, but we're over it now, Brierkins. Now, why don't you tell us when you started making things like icing come to you?"

Brier blinked back tiny droplets of liquid. She turned her adorable face up to Zacke's. "I only could do it tonight. I've been watching Uncle Miles. He makes me laugh when my ball bounces by itself."

Miles groaned. "Little bit, that was supposed to be our secret."

"I'm sorry Uncle Miles. But, I didn't tell them about the tree."

Now the soup was in the fire. Miles squirmed in his chair against the combined incensed looks of Brier's parents. He didn't dare look at Hope. The woman had already tried to take out his ribcage, he wasn't giving her another chance to jab his body parts.

"It really wasn't that big of a deal. Your neighbor's cat got caught in one of the trees in your backyard. Brier started to cry, and I sorta let her help me get the cat down."

"The kitty's name is Snowball, Uncle Miles."

"Right, Snowball."

"And I wasn't a bit scared when Uncle helped me fly to the top of the tree."

"Miles how could you?" Miranda's indignant tone stabbed his heart. He really shouldn't have done it but he hated to see Brier cry.

"I didn't plan to do it, Miranda but you know it's partly your and Zacke's fault."

"And how did you arrive at that conclusion? And how did you help her?" Zacke's question carried a lethal note and much to Miles' relief just a scrap of amusement.

"I just used thought transference, it wasn't dangerous. And to your first question, she's the best of both you, and I just couldn't say no."

Laughter cloaked the dining room—diffusing what could have been a tenuous situation for Miles. Tiny giggles helped to melt away any residual tension.

Zacke placed a kiss on his daughter's nose. "All right, you're off the hook for now, miss, but we will have to talk about what happened."

"We most certainly will, young lady."

"Yes ma'am, Mommy."

Zacke and Miranda resumed their seats, food floated around the table in a mortal way, and when everyone had full plates, Miles chanced a look at Hope.

His beautiful bride-to-be flashed him an impish smile, raised one sooty brow, and then leaned over to whisper in his ear. "You can drop the *I'm sorry* act. I'm not certain Zacke or Miranda bought it. I know I didn't."

"You didn't?"

"Nope. The only thing you're repentant of is getting caught."

Miles bit Hope's earlobe before replying. "You're right. The next trick I teach her will be when to know how to avoid getting her Uncle Miles in trouble."

Hope giggled and the sound was like an angel's chorus to Miles. He wasn't sure how she would take Brier's magical debut. He'd wondered if the very real possibility that any future offspring they might have could in fact be another Brier, might make Hope reconsider their marriage.

"So, I guess that you're okay with the odds that one day we might have a child with immortal talent?"

"I'm more than okay with it. The thought of

having a miniature *you*...would make me the happiest woman in the world."

Miles dabbed a linen napkin against his burning eyes. He didn't deserve the woman sitting at his side, but he'd fight every day of a century of lifetimes to keep his precious gift.

****

Guy ripped the cream color vellum in half, placed the jagged pieces in the kitchen sink, and struck a match. He watched in glee as the paper writhed with flames. Hope's gall in sending him an invitation to her wedding would not go unanswered. She'd ruined his plans, and he would get even.

Miles Dunbar would be left at the altar; his bride-to-be would be missing in action and dead.

Chapter Thirteen

Hope tossed her briefcase on the kitchen table and then collapsed into a chair. She'd thought she'd become used to the brutal aspects of her chosen career, but human nature had definitely taken a turn for the worse today.

She toed her sneakers off, the only form of sensible footwear in her opinion, and propped her elbows on the table. Her head gravitated downward and found an anchor between her palms.

Why did people commit the atrocities they did in the name of love, lust, and greed? She'd never been able to figure that out and never would. Her mind blurred with images of blood and pain. The first victim had been rolled into triage right after Hope came on duty—a young girl who'd been brutally beaten and sexually assaulted by a family member. The young girl would recover physically, but Hope doubted she'd ever get over the psychological damage.

Tears seeped from her closed lids as she remembered the second casualty of the morning. A family on their way home from dropping their oldest son off at the airport to catch a flight back to school after the holiday had been T-boned by a drunk driver. Hope had fought tears when she told that same son, whom security had tracked down at the airport, that he'd lost his entire family.

The day's events continued with one tragedy after another. Thankfully, the rest of those patients had survived. Before leaving the hospital, Hope went back to ICU and visited Megan, the little girl who'd been molested. The once childlike features were bruised. Her eyes, which the parents told Hope normally held laughter, were vacant of any type of life.

That one case rode her shoulders all day. It wasn't as if she hadn't seen child assaults before, but this case stirred something in Hope she wasn't sure she wanted to explore. Sometimes, the stuff of nightmares were better left in the dark.

Lips teased her neck, and a shriek tore from her throat.

"Easy, love." Miles moved in closer and locked gazes with Hope. "I didn't mean to startle you."

Her heart still galloped wildly, but Mile's gentle concern warmed her chilled soul. "It's okay. I was thinking."

"And from the looks of it, it wasn't good. You want to talk about it?"

"I don't know—maybe."

Miles slid her chair back and lifted her to her feet. A quick turn and Hope was seated once more—this time on a pair of muscular thighs.

"Okay, now talk."

"It was just a really bad day at work. I can't understand how people can be so cruel, Miles. Why do we allow it?"

"Honey, there's been evil in this world since long before I was born, and there will be bad things happening long after we both are gone. I don't know why some mortals or immortals are good and some evil. Maybe it's what life's done to them. Other than trying to prevent it from happening, or in your case, patching up their hurts, I don't know what else can be done."

"She is just a little girl, Miles. Someone who should be looking forward to becoming a teenager and going to high school. Now…she'll be blessed if she manages to walk down the street without being frightened out of her skin."

Miles broke his promise—he delved into Hope's mind and reeled from the images. The blood-spattered child broke his heart. The similarities between Megan and Hope as a child tore at his insides. He probed and found that the day's events had sent her mind into a backspin of memories. Thank God her subconscious had not been able to pull forth the memory he'd erased years before. Hope's will was strong and just the fact that her mind remembered a feeling of being upset proved his preventive measures hadn't worked completely.

"…a seventeen-year-old that his parents were dead."

Miles caught the last of Hope's sentence. He knew what she referred to. That memory from the day's events sucked also. He needed to get her mind off what had happened.

"Hope, why don't you change clothes, and I'll take you out to dinner."

"You seldom eat dinner out in a mortal way."

"Well, tonight I'm going to. Now, hop to it. I know a great little Italian place that you will love."

****

Hope looked around in amazement. Miles had taken her to dinner, but she'd never imagined the restaurant would be in Atlanta—more than a good four-hour trip by car. But they hadn't traveled that way.

The flight from Savannah to the South's Big A was totally awesome. City lights and countryside night sounds had mesmerized Hope. She never felt the cold with the blanket he wrapped around her, the closeness to his body, as well as his arm encircling her shoulders. The entire trip had taken only an hour and while Miles conjured a reserved table from the *maître d'*, she'd repaired the damage to her clothes and hair.

Now, sitting at their secluded table she sipped at her glass of wine. Any moment the waiter would be bringing her salad. Miles had opted to wait for the rare steak he'd ordered.

"So, do you like it?"

"What's not to like? You've given me a night to remember."

"Good, I want you to enjoy yourself. You've been on a fast track since I met you, Hope. It's time to slow down."

"But I—"

"Staying home after being attacked was not taking it easy. It was common sense."

Miles caught her hand, and placed a searing kiss on her sensitive skin. "I love you more than life. As an immortal I can see now what mortals do to their bodies with stress and other things. You need to sleep more."

As she watched, Miles expression changed. A brooding jade replaced the gentle flecks of green. "I haven't asked and you haven't said, but are you getting any more calls at night?"

"No, thank goodness. Maybe whoever it was got tired of freaking me out."

"That's good, but I'd still like to know who it is. Zacke is checking it out. He said if they continue he's going to put a trace on your phone."

Miles expression stayed sober. "Hope, do you think it's possible that Guy might be behind those calls?"

"I haven't given it any thought but no. How could he? He's only a couple of years older than I am, and he was never around when my mom use to sing to me."

"All right."

"Have you heard anything about what's going on

at Morgan's?"

"Nothing. Hawk hasn't had any success in catching Guy in the act yet."

"So, you're all sure it has to be Guy?"

"Well, so far, he is the only one who has access to all the shipments once he signs for them."

Their waiter placed a cut-glass bowl of salad greens and raw vegetables in front of Hope.

Hope glanced up. "Thank you." The server ducked his head in acknowledgment and then left as silently as he'd approached.

Hope poured a generous amount of salad dressing and then sampled the mixture. "Oh wow, this is great. Sure you don't want just one bite?"

"Please, don't mention bite to a vampire. It stirs up all kinds of fantasies and none of them include eating weeds."

"I am not eating weeds. Lettuce, cucumbers, and tomatoes are good for you."

"Only if you're a rabbit."

Hope's ribs hurt with laughter as she concentrated on not choking on the sip of wine she'd just taken.

"See, I told you that stuff wasn't good for you."

"Okay, okay." Hope took the linen napkin Miles handed her and wiped her eyes. "Now, Mr. Definitely *Not* A Vegetarian, please continue with your thoughts on Guy."

"Not much more to say. I think he's a thief, and I don't like him."

"*Really?* I'd never have guessed."

Miles looked a bit miffed, and then his gaze danced with humor. "Okay, I'm jealous."

"Was that so hard to admit?"

"No, and truly, you're not the first one to make me say it."

Hope finished chewing a bite of tomato before she asked, "I take it the rest of your vamp pack has been teasing you." Whatever his answer was, she was sure it would be humorous.

"You could say that. More like torturing me with the image of a green-eyed monster with fangs and claws."

"Just so you know, if the situation was turned around, I'd be the same way."

Miles thanked the waiter after he placed their entrees in front of them.

"Will there be anything else, sir?"

"Not at the moment but—" Miles looked at Hope. "My fiancée might like dessert later."

"Not a problem, I'll come back in a bit with the dessert cart."

"Are you telling me, you'd be jealous of another woman?"

"In the first place, Vamp Boy, there better not be one, but if there were, I'd have no compunction in snatching her bald-headed."

"Then what?"

"I'd use my own fangs and claws on her."

"A bit blood-thirsty aren't you?"

"Yeah, guess you could say it's the company I've been keeping."

Laughter burst forth from Miles, causing the occupants from neighboring tables to glance their way.

After that, dinner became a comfortable hour of talking and teasing one another. The time flew, and after gorging on a delectable piece of raspberry-covered cheesecake, Hope was more than ready to accompany Miles on the walk he suggested.

Nightlife in Atlanta was faster paced than Savannah. There was an air of expectancy and impatience missing from her hometown. Miles did his best to keep her from being jostled by the parade of people crowding sidewalks and doorways.

Laughter, curses, and shouts filled the night.

Women with trades to ply sidled up to Miles, and he waved them off. Men also approached Hope. They were dispatched with a snarl from her fanged knight.

"You about ready to head home?"

"Yes, as much as I hate for our date to end…this really was our first date wasn't it?"

"I hate to admit it, but that's true. I've been so busy with everything else, I forgot the niceties of courtship."

Hope clung to his arm. "It doesn't matter. What's important is that we are together."

"True, my love. Now, you choose."

"Choose what?" Hope's confusion punctuated her words.

"How you want to go home."

"Well, it's probably too late to catch a real flight, the bus would take too long, and I think all the rental car places are closed, so I guess the way we got here?"

"Or we could take a quicker mode of transportation."

"That would be?"

"This." Miles pulled Hope into a secluded doorway. His lips locked onto hers and the next time she opened her eyes, they stood in her kitchen.

"Wow, that *was* quick."

"Yeah and more comfortable for you. It's chillier now than it was when we left earlier. I didn't want you to catch a cold."

"Thank you for making me forget, Miles."

"I'll always protect you in every possible way."

"I know." Hope's words sounded guttural as a yawn caught up with her.

"It's time you got some sleep."

"What will you do?"

"I might catch some late-night television or see if Hawk's found out anything. But I'll only be gone a few minutes."

"Okay." Another yawn threatened to crack Hope's jaw. "I'm headed up to bed. Be careful. Please?"

"I will. Goodnight, Hope."

"Nite."

****

Miles materialized inside Morgan Rarities by the front counter. Security lights dimmed the luster of the treasures on display. He closed his eyes and grinned. Hawk was on the roof of the building, his presence cloaked from mortal eyes.

A moment later, he joined his vampire brother who stood at the edge of the gabled roof. "Looks like you're hard at work, my friend."

"I could say the same about you. I can't help but wonder how much flesh you lost tearing yourself away from Hope."

Miles didn't need to see Hawk's face to know amusement danced in his eyes—he heard it in his voice.

"I told her I'd only be a few minutes."

Hawk finally turned and faced Miles. "I suppose you want to know about Guy?"

"Is there anything to know?"

"He's a strange one. He hates me being here."

"Guess that means he's an early riser or burning the midnight oil."

"Yeah. I just wish I could catch him at something. The man avoids me like there's no tomorrow. Of course the first time he ran into me, he turned white as a sheet. Wanted to know who I was, what I was doing, etcetera. I had parked the security truck Zacke set me up with on a side street. I guess he didn't pay any attention to the vehicle. Since then I've parked in the back but he always pulls around there and then drives back to the front of the store. Tonight, I left the truck at Zacke's."

Hawk gestured toward the street. "I've been watching for him to show up. I'm hoping if Guy doesn't see any signs of me, he'll get in and do something."

"Sounds like a good plan to me. "I think I'll stick around for a few."

"What about Hope?"

"She decided to go to bed early. Bad day at work."

"I bet. I have to hand it to her and Miranda doing what they do."

"You won't get any argument from me."

A car motor purred a short distance away. Miles caught the sound at the same time Hawk did. They shared a conspiratorial grin and waited. Barely a moment later, Guy's late model sedan pulled into the side street that led to the back parking lot.

Hawk had the weasel pegged right. He had been checking to see if security reported for duty. And once again, they were rewarded as the big car purred to a stop right in front of the double front doors.

Two stories above the pavement, both men stayed silent as their prey exited the car and then looked around the surrounding area. Guy wasn't stupid—no question about that. If he was responsible for stealing and embezzling large sums of money, he'd be on the lookout for anything out of the way.

Apparently satisfied, the man unlocked the door and entered the building.

"Let's give him a couple of minutes before we see what he's up to."

Hawk nodded his agreement. "Do you plan on accosting him tonight, if we catch him?"

"I don't know." Miles allowed his newly extended fangs freedom for a moment before retracting them. "I suppose the right thing to do would be to call

Zacke if we witness anything."

"Are we doing the right thing?"

Miles thought long and hard about his answer. His grimace met with laughter.

"Okay, we call Zacke. Now, let's see what's going on."

Miles watched Hawk's form dissolve and then followed suit. They both appeared in the corridor that led to the offices. Light crept from beneath a door at the end of the hallway.

Is that Guy's office? Miles transferred his question into Hawk's mind as they made their way toward the door.

No. Hope's parents used that office. I found some framed photos stuffed into one of the desk drawers.

Miles bit back a curse. Guy needed a beating badly. He so wanted to be the one to deliver it. He wanted to but wouldn't. He'd promised Zacke he'd behave and behave he would for the moment.

Simultaneously, they entered the office in the form of air particles. To the human eye it would look similar to a haze expelled from the heating vents. Once again, in cloaked, immortal form, they watched.

Guy sat hunkered down at the desk, his fingers dancing madly on the computer's keyboard. Moving closer, Miles watched row after row of four and five-digit figures scroll onto the monitor's screen.

Nothing pointed to where the amounts came from or where they were going. For all Miles knew, it could be legit numbers from the business, but he didn't think so. His teeth ached and his sheathed claws tingled. A sure sign something wasn't right.

They watched a good ten minutes more, but nothing else showed up on the screen. Guy's concentration remained unbroken even when Hawk blew a sheaf of papers off the desk. Whatever the figures represented, it had to be important.

Once back on the roof, Miles said goodnight to Hawk. His footsteps when he jumped to street level made no sound as he walked. Traffic was non-existent at this hour, and he welcomed the hushed night. As if it had a mind of its own, his body turned not toward home and Hope, but toward Johnson Square. His personal reminder that life could change in an instant. His life had done just that. The events of the last few weeks had been phenomenal. Whereas once faced with an infinite lifetime of loneliness, he now had a chance for happiness.

If he breathed too hard would it disappear?

He clenched claw-tipped hands. Why the postmortem tonight?

Miles shrugged his shoulders. Did it matter? For too long he'd bridled his emotions—afraid to care, to love, or to live—if one could call his previous existence living.

The square came into view. A breeze, which was reputed to be the product of a long dead general's displeasure, blew across his face. He moved to one of the wrought iron benches and sat down.

Miles sensed the various spirits still chained to earthly boundaries. Some appeared before him—intent on frightening him away. A swift flash of incisors ensured his solitude.

Three weeks until Hope became his wife. Was he doing the right thing? Did he have the right to tie the woman he loved to the creature he was?

Bloody crescents appeared in both palms. As he watched, the blood dried and the marks vanished. Would a year, or a decade from now, see Hope's love vanish as well?

Miles' shoulders slumped with his uncertainty. His mood turned darker.

A second later his form took to the night sky like a bullet. He'd never been a quitter. He would never give Hope a reason to ever stop loving him. He'd make sure she was loved in return every day—every hour—no—every minute of her life.

He soared over rooftops and smiled as his ears picked up on parents listening to children's prayers. His vision blurred with moisture when he spied goodnight kisses between a little girl and her daddy, and he smiled as a young couple hurried to separate when a porch light came on.

Yes, life would be good. He'd see to that. And he knew the perfect place to take Hope for their honeymoon. A place that would show her who he was, where he came from, and build the beginning of a lifetime of memories.

****

Guy shut down the computer and turned off the desk lamp. He'd gotten a lot accomplished tonight—courtesy of Hope's security guard not showing up for work. The figures he'd downloaded and gone over judiciously would pump his bank account up even more. He'd never planned on going this far, but Sam Morgan, as well as his precious little wife had been so trusting. He remembered how blown away he'd been when no one had caught him stealing his first piece of jewelry. He also couldn't believe his luck in finding a buyer right away on the black market.

Since then he'd cached away several priceless objects. It had been so easy coming up with bogus bills of sale for lower amounts, then just sitting back, and watching his profits rise.

But now, Hope was a threat to his extra income. Guy didn't need her digging into the family business. He'd hidden his trail. His quest to make Hope dependant on him by telling her about the missing items had backfired. He'd never dreamed she wouldn't just allow him to handle it, cry on his shoulder, and then be so grateful that she'd fall right into his arms. Instead, she'd tossed him out of his *new* office. Guy laughed, he'd conveniently forgotten to give her the extra key he'd had made and stashed to her parents' old office.

The little—His mind reeled against calling her that name. A name he reserved for the sluts who jumped willingly into bed with him for money. He still wanted Hope, and he would have her before she conveniently died.

But first, he needed to get rid of the man who stood between him and his object of desire. The plan had eased into his mind and then taken concrete form after receiving the wedding invitation. After all, a man inconsolable over his missing love would do anything—even commit suicide.

Chapter Fourteen

Hope forced herself to breathe. Christmas Eve and her wedding day were less than a week away. The last fourteen days had been more than hectic. Miranda's help with the wedding plans had been invaluable. It seemed as soon as the invitations went out the days started flying by. When not working, she'd been finalizing dress alterations. She'd barely seen her future groom. When not sleeping, Miles dogged Guy's footsteps. His frustration had led to a few tense moments when her manager had shown up on Hope's doorstep one evening last week. She didn't think she'd ever forget the visit, or to be more factual, the confrontation.

Of course it hadn't help that she'd been in the shower when the doorbell rang leaving Miles to answer the door. Hope had walked blindly into their verbal match wearing her nightgown and robe just in time to hear Miles' colder than death words.

"I told you Evans, Hope is not available."

"And I told you I wanted to talk to her." Guy's tone was nothing like what Hope was used to. She'd seen his mild-mannered Clark Kent attitude slip several times over the last few weeks but never the fuming and acidic quality he now conveyed.

Miles' snarl compelled Hope into finding her tongue.

"Hi Guy. I'm sorry you had to wait on me." She ignored Miles' wide-eyed stare. "I hope you came by to say you would be coming to the wedding."

She watched as both men got their emotions under control. The tick in Guy's jaw stopped, and the bit of fangs she'd glimpse from Miles were now hidden. Good, just maybe there wouldn't be any bloodshed.

"Actually that's why I'm here." Guy cleared his throat. "I'd like to talk to you privately."

Miles' growl was low but dangerous—so much for no violence. Hope caught his arm in a firm but what she hoped appeared an affectionate grip. "I'm sure that could be arranged, but now might not be such a good idea. We are due at the Kensingtons' for dinner in about an hour. Why don't I come to Morgan's tomorrow?"

Guy's face went from an unbecoming shade of raspberry to an almost pleasant expression. "Yeah, that would be good. We could have lunch." The look he shot at Miles caused Hope a few seconds of trouble as she tried to keep her vampire on a short leash.

"Fine, how about around one?"

"I'll look forward to it. The new girl I hired will be back from her lunch by then."

"I wasn't aware you'd hired anyone else."

"Well, sure, Hope. Someone has to be up front when I'm in the back. You said you didn't want the business to be unattended."

Hope wanted to strangle Guy, but Miles looked like it wouldn't take more than one word from her and he'd beat her to it. She counted to three under her breath. "That's fine, Guy. I just hope she's not going to be hovering over you like the last secretary did."

Guy's face turned red again. "You don't have to worry about that. She's at least sixty with grandchildren."

Hope didn't dare look at Miles. If she did, she'd lose her battle with laughter.

"Great. I guess I'll see you tomorrow."

Guy had said his goodbyes and left just a few moments later. Miles wasn't as easy to dismiss. It had taken her almost an hour to calm him down. At least he hadn't gone out looking for Guy with fangs and claws drawn.

Hope forced herself to forget about what happened last week, turned off her office light, and grabbed her briefcase. She was already late leaving the hospital and had a dozen things to do at home and just maybe, she'd get to see her fiancé for a few minutes before he flew off for the night.

Dusk had fallen while she sat in her office and now night draped the Savannah sky in a cloudy, foggy darkness. Headlights from passing cars glowed eerily as she walked home. The night was mild for this time of the year, but the dampness seeping into her light jacket reminded her this unexpected warm spell would quickly pass.

Nightfall came early, but at least this year she wasn't alone. Miles' presence at home had thawed Hope from a frigid state of drifting though life to a woman who now looked forward to the future. Her nights would be full of the man she loved and that was all she cared about.

She turned the corner onto her street. Not much farther. Miles should be up and if she hurried, she might convince him to stay in after he gave her, as of late, a hurried but extremely thorough kiss.

Hope's pace quickened. She was almost to the house when a cat's loud meow caused her to jump. She stopped for a moment to allow her heart to settle down. Life had been good for the last few weeks. No more phone calls, and although the men who had attacked her were still on the loose, Hope hadn't really worried about it. In fact, that was one of the reasons she decided to walk home alone tonight.

Miles might not meet her at the hospital every night, but someone, Zacke, his partner Gideon, and even Hawk had all taken turns babysitting her when she left work. This evening was different, she'd forgotten to call and let someone know when she was leaving. Anyway, those men were probably miles from Savannah by now.

A whoosh of air caressed her back an instant before a hand descended on her shoulder.

"Hope! What do you think you're doing?"

Her heart did another dive and then sped up in relief. "Hawk! You almost gave me a heart attack."

"What are you doing out on your own?"

"I *was* walking home."

Hawk shook his head, sending several lengths of blond hair flying. "You'll be fortunate if Miles doesn't lock you up until the wedding when he finds out."

Hope gazed up into eyes that glittered bright amber. If she weren't head over stethoscope in love with Miles, Hawk would be someone she could really like. He was always kind and considerate, but sometimes, she noticed the laughter that flowed from his lips didn't quite meet his eyes. He had to be lonely. His very existence screamed solitude. Maybe she should speak to Miranda about finding him a date for the wedding.

"Don't even go there."

"Go where?"

"You know. The matchmaking thing and don't change the subject."

Hawk's discomfiture and determination showed in his posture. He folded his arms across his chest, and looked liked an unmovable mountain. His gaze resembled a deer caught in headlights. Hope would love to know why he was gun-shy when it came to relationships. But now, she needed to get out of the jam she lodged herself in.

"Okay. I'm sorry. I just thought it wouldn't hurt

this once to walk home by myself."

"You know those men haven't been caught."

Hope inhaled and then slowly let it out. "I know. I just wasn't thinking, but do you have to tell Miles?"

"I should tell him."

"Tell who what?"

Hope felt the uncontrollable urge to hide behind Hawk. Miles had surprised them both if Hawk's open mouth was any sign. The man needed a bell hung around his neck.

"That I know Hope wants to fix me up for the wedding."

Miles grin looked like an evil smirk. "You might enjoy it."

"I don't think so. I like my solitude. No offense to Hope and Miranda, but I don't plan on getting shackled."

Hope patted Hawk on the arm, smiled, and stepped into Miles arms. "Hi. I don't suppose, since you're still here, you plan on staying in tonight?"

Miles glanced down into green eyes shining with a hopeful gleam. Lord knew he hated to leave Hope, but he needed to catch Guy in the act. It wasn't just jealousy making him taste the victory of getting the slimy offal out of Hope's life. Something about the man grated on him like a nagging toothache. His senses went into overload every time he thought about or got around him. Guy Evans was up to something—something more than embezzlement. He'd tried reading his mind but it was a like a blank slate. The man hid his thoughts when others were around. Not a good sign. Usually, he could read a person even without touching them. That alone was enough for him, but Zacke said they had to have cold hard evidence.

Hawk had started hanging out in the back room at Morgan's—a beer in his hand and his eyes glued to a small television. Guy had peeked in a few times, but now just came and went. Hawk's plan to lull Guy into making a mistake was a good one, only it wasn't working fast enough to suit Miles.

"Miles?"

His breath blew out in a sigh. "I'm sorry, Hope. I have to go out tonight too."

Hope jerked out of his arms and backed up. Her green eyes sparked fire. "I don't get it. You spend all your time looking for Guy to mess up and still you have no proof that he's really done anything."

"That's not true, Hope." Hawk's tone was soft but defensive. "I saw the numbers on the screen. I feel the same way as Miles—Guy has to be the one."

"But you don't know that for sure."

"No? Be reasonable. No one else is there to steal the items. We've had this conversation before, Hope."

"And we'll have it again, Miles. I'm tired of you going out every night. We're getting married in a few days. Do you plan on continuing your hide-and-seek games then?"

Miles looked over at Hawk who shrugged his shoulders. No help there. "I plan on us going away for our honeymoon. Zacke and Hawk will be here taking care of Guy."

His beloved's eyes glistened. "I hope so, Miles. I guess I'll just have to wait and see. Right now, I'm going inside. And I don't want any company. I'm just a little fed up with men and vampires in general. I need some time to myself. Good night!"

"You going to just let her go like that?"

"Yes. It won't do any good to talk to her while she's this upset. Did she say anything to you on the way home?"

Miles didn't care for the squeamish look on Hawk's face.

"Well, she was fine before you came out."

"That's not what I asked."

"I know, but I sorta promised—I mean I let Hope believe I wouldn't tell you."

Miles was totally confused. "About the matchmaking? You already did."

Hawk's gaze looked everywhere but at Miles. "Uh, that wasn't what I wasn't suppose to tell you."

If the man standing before him wasn't one of his closest friends, Miles would have no compunction in forcing the words from Hawk's throat.

"Spit it out. What did Hope do?"

Hawk looked like someone was pulling out his claws. "Hope walked home by herself."

"What?"

"You heard me. She didn't call, and I got worried. When I went by the hospital, her office was locked up tight. One of the guards said she'd left about ten minutes before. I got here just as she was coming up the street."

Miles' stomach hurt. All the things that could happen to Hope revolved in his mind. Why hadn't she called someone? Why hadn't she called him?

"Miles?"

This time he was the one to look away. If anyone was to blame it was him. No wonder Hope was disgusted. He'd barely spent any time with her and now at a time when they should be closer than ever, he was flying off on a possible wild-goose chase.

"I'm not angry with you. I'm mad at myself. I'm the one who should have been at the hospital the moment she finished work."

Hawk slapped a hand on his shoulder. "Don't beat yourself up. You're doing what you think is best. You have done everything possible to ensure that very thing since Hope's attack. No one could have done any better."

"You sure about that? If I hadn't been wallowing in self-pity in my castle, she wouldn't have been attacked in the first place."

"Miles, she was attacked in broad daylight. Sure, you can stand some sun, but you couldn't have known ahead of time what was going to happen, no more than any of us could know. You want some friendly advice?"

"Do I have a choice?"

Hawk's laughter took away some of the sting of Miles' personal flogging.

"No, so listen up. Stay home and make nice with Hope. You don't want her angry on your wedding day, do you?"

His heart recoiled at that thought. "You're right. Let me know if you find anything."

"You got it."

Miles watched Hawk take to the sky and then turned back to the house. His eyes scanned and found his enchanting, but still disturbed, bride-to-be. Hope sat on her bed with a cup of tea in her hand. Her eyes were wet with tears; the soft moss color he loved had deepened into a hard emerald—definitely a sign of distress.

He entered the house the mortal way and then locked up the same way. He didn't bother with a safety spell, he'd be Hope's protection tonight. And Miles would have no problem killing anyone who threatened her.

Again, he used the mortal way to traverse the stairs to Hope's room. Somehow, he didn't think his vampire ways would endear him to his love tonight.

He raised his hand and knocked gently on the door.

"Miles, I'm not in the mood to talk."

"I know, and if you will let me, I'll do all the talking."

"That's the problem, you've been doing all the talking and thinking for both of us."

Hope's words stung. Had he been that selfish? He'd only meant to protect her.

"I apologize."

"I've heard that before too."

"Please, just let me in. I promise I won't stay long. I just want to explain why I act like I do."

Hope's sigh filtered through the door.

"All right, come in."

He opened the door but paused on the threshold. Hope sat huddled in the center of the bed. Her cup of tea on the bedside table. Her expression made his heart ache.

"Hope?"

"Say what you have to say Miles. I'm tired and really want to go to bed."

He moved into the room, neared the bed but remained standing. "Look, I know I've behaved like an ass. I did what I thought was right but gave no thought to how my absences would affect you. For that, I'm truly sorry. It's just I worry that you're going to get hurt."

Finally, a glimmer of life moved in her eyes.

"I know you think Guy is harmless, but every sense I have is telling me something different. I know a small part of it is jealousy, more is just plain dislike for the man. I swear by all I have ever and will hold dear, that if I didn't think he was capable of hurting you, I'd back off."

Miles waited but Hope remained silent. Should he just go? Leave her to think about what he said?

"Look, I'm going to go back downstairs. You need some sleep, and I don't want to upset you anymore than I already have."

His steps were even slower going to the door than they had been coming in.

"Wait."

Miles turned back. The tousle-haired woman holding her hand out made him want to howl at the moon. He didn't deserve her, but by all God's mercy, he loved her.

He did not need a second invitation and he drew Hope to him and held her. A few moments later, his shirtfront was soaked and Hope was asleep—obviously, she had forgiven him. Not that he deserved it but he thanked God anyway.

He caressed her hair and the curve of her cheek. The tracks of her tears had dried, and he kissed each one. Miles stayed put for several minutes longer before he reluctantly eased his frame out from under Hope's. He gently laid her down on the bed and kissed her lips.

As of tonight, unless something drastic came up, he planned on being at Hope's side every second of his waking moments.

****

Guy smiled. His plan was nearly in place. Hope would soon be a dead thorn in his side and then he would make sure Miles Dunbar joined her in Hell. Just a few more days would see the culmination of all his dreams.

The shrill ring of his cell phone jerked him out of his lovely daydream. "Guy Evans."

"Will you have the merchandise?"

"Yes, but it could be the first of the year before I can broker it to you."

"My backers won't be pleased, but if the shipment is as big as you say it is, it will be worth the wait."

"Count on it. I'll be in touch as soon as I have all my documents legalized."

"Good. If I don't hear from you by the New Year, you'll hear from me." The previous mellow tone took on a sinister cast.

Guy swallowed down his rage at the man's audacity. He was taking all the risks and putting all he had on the line. The other was just a flunky who answered to his bosses. Well, the man and his backers would be bowing to him when he delivered the goods.

"Just be ready to move the merchandise when I call you."

Guy didn't wait on the man's yea or nay, he shut his cell. He looked once more at the document on his screen. A doc that would give him full partnership in Morgan's and a will. One he had predated to right after her parents had been killed. He closed the documents, took out the memory card from his computer, opened a paperweight he'd had specially made, and slid it inside. A second later, he lounged back in Sam Morgan's desk chair. Hope, in her naive and irritating way, really thought he'd do exactly what she ordered him to. Those days were over. He'd laughed long and hard at how all the things she wanted had unraveled. The guard she thought would be so good did nothing but sit on his butt and watch television.

Guy rubbed his hands together. It had been a good few days and the day of reckoning was almost here. He would force Hope to sign the paper, use her like the slut she was until he grew tired of her, and then allow his inept but anxious men to terminate her life.

Chapter Fifteen

The alarm jarred Hope awake. "Ugh." Surely it wasn't time to get up, she could swear it'd only been an hour since she'd fallen into bed. The last few days had rushed by. Her work schedule had been delegated to another doctor. All the final details for their wedding tomorrow had been gone over, and she was exhausted.

Her fatigue didn't stem just from the frantic pace she'd set, but from the long night hours she'd spent with Miles. Each night, they talked until the wee hours of dawn—ever since the day after their quarrel. What she remembered most from that night was how Miles held her while she wept until she fell asleep. He'd been asleep himself when she'd awakened but had met her at the hospital the next two nights when she got off.

They had gone out to dinner both evenings, while the firm decorating for the wedding did their job at the house, and Miles had romanced her with slow dances and whispered endearments. The only fly in the ointment was he still would not take her to bed or at least not in the way she yearned for. The man was a saint, or at the very least a gentleman. Finally, she'd given up her attempts to entice him into forgetting his promise of abstinence until they were pronounced man and wife.

Hope glanced at the alarm clock and then threw her legs over the side of the bed. She needed caffeine—lots of caffeine.

One diet cola and a shower later, she felt more like coping with the upcoming day. She fixed a piece of toast and a cup of tea before heading for the den.

There really wasn't all that much left to do before she and Miles tied the knot. The rehearsal menu had been checked over with the caterers for tonight's late dinner. Hawk and Zacke planned to take Miles out for a celebration drink afterwards, and she and Miranda would be doing something—she wasn't sure what. Miranda had been a bit mysterious about their plans for the evening.

So actually, she had nothing to do but get her hair done and *shoot*...she had to get a wedding gift for Miles. She'd found a gift for Zacke and Hawk, as well as Miranda, who would be standing up as matron of honor. Miles had decided for diplomacy—not to mention he couldn't decide between the two—and have both his oldest friends be best men. She'd been waffling over a gold pocket watch or an antique sword for her groom. Both were great gifts, so she might just get both.

Since her salon appointment wasn't until three, she could go by Morgan's first but she'd rather wait. Hope didn't want to run into Guy if she could help it. Their luncheon had not gone well. From the time they sat down in the restaurant, his attitude toward Miles had been downright ugly, and his pleas that she reconsider her choice of groom had turned into demands. She replayed the scene in her mind.

"Hope, what would you like to drink?"

"A glass of wine, please." Hope smiled at their waiter and wished fervently, she was at home.

After the waiter brought her wine and a glass of brandy for Guy, Morgan's manager smiled before reaching across the table and grabbing her hand.

"I'm so glad we could get this time together. There are several things I want to discuss with you."

She withdrew her hand from his clammy grip,

placed it under the table, and wiped it on the cloth napkin she'd placed in her lap.

"I really don't think we have that much to discuss, Guy."

"I disagree, my dear. What about the missing items? We should really come up with a plan of action."

"We have, or make that I have. A plan I already implemented, remember? We have a security guard, and the police are investigating the thefts."

"Are you sure that's wise? I mean, wouldn't it be better to let our security handle it?"

Hope paced her words to keep from snapping at Guy. "The police are involved because I wanted them to be. Detective Kensington is my boss's husband and a good friend of Miles."

"Miles!" Guy snarled the name. "I'm sick of hearing about him, Hope. I can't believe you are going through with the wedding. You know nothing about him. If you are scared of being alone until those men are caught, I'll stay with you. If you just want to get married, then I'll be happy to step in as groom. We would deal well together. I know we would. Just give me a chance."

She gulped a bit more wine and then wished she hadn't. Her stomach roiled with disgust and nerves. "Miles is not a gift you can exchange for another. He is the man I love and will marry. There is nothing to discuss."

"I think you need to rethink that stand, Hope. The man could be a criminal for all you know."

"Are you ready to order?" The waiter appeared at Hope's side.

Hope shook her head at the returning waiter. "No thank you. I find I'm not that hungry."

Guy waved the waiter off without ordering also. "Hope, there is no need to get mad. I have your best interests at heart."

After downing the rest of her wine, she pushed back her chair and stood, tossing her napkin on the table.

"This conversation is over. If you ever bring it up to me again, I will not just walk out of a lunch meeting. I will replace you as manager."

She didn't wait to hear Guy's rebuttal but left as quickly as possible.

Yes, an altogether horrible scene. One she would make sure did not happen again. She planned to avoid Guy like a thump on the head. As soon as she got back from her honeymoon, she would replace him. It wasn't a plan she'd talked over with Miles. There'd been no time, and she hadn't wanted to bother him. She knew he'd approve.

Advertising the position would only cause her further problems with Guy so after she left their *lunch date* she went by Morgan's and found a list of applicants her dad had put together. The list was less than two years old and never used. Guy, who had been out of the country when the senior Mr. Evans had died, returned for the funeral and offered to take over for his dad. The rest was history. Guy had at one time, or at least she hoped, been a good manager, but his behavior now was erratic and at times frightening.

Yes, definitely better to pick up the gifts when Guy wasn't around.

****

Hope stepped out of the beauty salon and felt like a new woman. She'd had the works. A facial, manicure, and her hair done. She'd even experimented with a new makeup line the salon recommended and rather liked her new look.

Hopefully, Miles would too.

The closer it came to the wedding, the more anxious she got. She wanted to be his in every possible way, but couldn't help wondering if she'd measure up to all the women he'd known over the years—scratch that—centuries.

Beside the fact he made her toes curl when he kissed her, Hope had pushed the issue of their lovemaking so she'd know once and for all if she could hold his attention. She'd rather have that information before the wedding—not after.

She checked her watch. Good. It was past time for Morgan's to close. She'd just pop in, wrap the gifts, and then be on her way. The dinner would start around eight after the wedding rehearsal in the old-fashioned parlor.

Hope made good time in walking the few blocks to the store. Just as she suspected, the lights were dimmed and when she inserted her key into the lock, the faint hum of the alarm greeted her. Another sign that Guy wasn't on the premises.

She disengaged the alarm, sat her purse and a bag of salon goodies down on the counter, and opened the display case. She carefully removed the items she wanted and found a couple of gift boxes. A few swift maneuvers with tissue and wrapping paper and she was finished, all but the bows on top. She penned a brief missive on a card and slid it under the ribbon of the larger box.

She checked her watch. If she didn't get a move on she'd be late for the dinner.

Darkness had fallen by the time she locked up and stood once again on the sidewalk. Few pedestrians were out and about. Everyone was probably home for dinner. Hope wished she'd been quicker in completing her errands, but if she hurried, she wouldn't even notice the moonless night.

Hope rushed to the street corner. She should have called a cab, but hated to waste the time waiting for one.

Footsteps sounded behind her, and her heart

thudded with their rhythm. *Please, Lord, just get me home. I promise to never go anywhere again without an escort.*

She started to jog—the gifts and salon bag, as well as her purse, banged painfully against her hip. The footsteps behind echoed above her pounding heart. Where were her protectors when she needed one? No fair in blaming anyone else. She should have been home long before dark.

Well, home lay just a block away. Hope's jog turned into a full-fledged run—so did the person's following her. Her side hurt and her breath hitched.

Rapid breathing—not her own—assaulted her ears. "Dr. Morgan, hold up."

The use of her name almost stopped her flight but even serial killers could do their homework. Hope kept running. A hand caught the back of her coat and pulled her to a stop.

She turned and faced her attacker.

"Dr. Morgan, it's me, Bobby, from Tapestry Designs."

Hope blinked back tears of relief. The teenager hunched over catching his breath was indeed someone she knew. The design shop was right next door to Morgan's.

"Bobby, what are you doing following me?"

The red-faced kid looked offended. "You dropped your keys. I was trying to give them back."

Hope felt terrible. "Bobby, I'm so sorry. I didn't know it was you. Here, take this." Hope fished in her purse and pulled out a five-dollar bill.

Bobby's expression changed from disgruntled to happy. "Thanks Doc. I've got a date tonight and this will come in handy."

The kid grabbed the bill and waved as he took off in the opposite direction.

Hope took a deep breath and then made a mad dash for home.

****

"To Hope and Miles!"

"Hear, hear!"

The toasts continued and Miles sat, content, with Hope anchored by his side. He'd barely had his eyes open when he heard her steps as she made her way up to her room. They had been light, and the giggles coming from her luscious lips had been a welcome sound.

Miles had looked around while his beloved dressed for the dinner. The parlor room, where their rehearsal would take place, hadn't been used since the last Christmas Hope and her parents had been together. It had always been the center of any celebration. Hope's last birthday, the summer before her parent's death, was also held there. The room was now aired out and clean. The dining room across the hall was a candlelight fantasy with roses and crystal stemware as well as the porcelain china set Hope's parents had used for their wedding.

The decorating service had done wonders; everything looked great.

But Miles' first look at a made-over Hope had rocked him inside and out. The short cranberry dress fit her curves like a sword in a scabbard. Her eyes had a mysterious look, and her lips glowed in a shade almost the same color as her dress. Her legs, encased in sheer stockings, made him want to slide his hands up her thighs to see what else she wore beneath the seductive dress.

When Hope gave him a look promising hot and sinful sex, Miles hoped he could hold out until their wedding night. Yes, he was an idiot for not taking what she offered, but if for some reason she changed her mind about marrying him, he didn't want her to have any regrets about allowing him to make love to her.

A gentle caress on his hand and Miles turned to

the subject of his desire.

"A penny for your thoughts."

"I was thinking about how happy you've made me."

"No more than you've made me, Miles. Thank you."

His *your welcome* reply came in the form of a kiss. Hope rejoiced in his gentle show of love. When the kiss deepened, she returned the emotion. Fire singed her nerve-endings as Miles plundered her mouth. Never would she get tired of his kisses. They were more intoxicating than a sip of champagne. She leaned into him and bestowed some of her own heat.

"Break it up you two." Miranda's teasing tone caused Hope to pull back. Her reluctance to break off the kiss mirrored Miles' frustrated expression.

Due to the late hour, only five sat down for dinner. Gideon had been invited but couldn't make it. He'd traded nights with another officer so he could be at the wedding.

"Stop with the cranky look, Miles. You'll have Hope all to yourself tomorrow night." Zacke's baritone held amusement.

"That's right and don't forget we have plans ourselves tonight." Hawk's satisfied tone made Hope wonder if having a drink was all they had planned for Miles.

"Well, us girls have our own plans too, so I suggest we get started if we plan on getting any sleep at all tonight."

Dinner went off without a hitch. Hope and Miranda ate their share of mortal food while the men sampled a bit here and there. After a last toast of well wishes, Miranda looked at Zacke who stood and then pulled her chair back.

"You ready Hope?"

"I just need to change. I'll be right back."

"Hope, can you wait a minute. I need to do

something." Miles' voice sounded gruff, and he lacked his usual grace as he too stood.

"Miles, what is it?"

Instead of answering, he dropped to one knee in front of her. "I know we're getting married tomorrow, but I want you to have this tonight."

Hope watched as he eased his hand inside his jacket and then brought out a small box with a jeweler's label on the top.

"Open it, please."

Her hand trembled as she took the proffered gift. The velvet lid caressed her fingers when she eased back the lid. Her mouth flew open. A platinum band with at least a two-carat diamond twinkled in the candlelight.

"Miles!"

"It can never show you what you mean to me but I didn't want you to think I forgot to buy you an engagement ring."

The hand that reached out to capture Hope's shook slightly.

"You didn't have to do this. I know you love me. I think I've always known."

"Thank you, my love."

The next moment would be one Hope would never forget. Her big handsome vampire took the ring from its satin nest and slid it onto her finger. His lips warmed the cold metal and a crimson tinged tear, seen only by her, baptized his token.

****

Music blared and lights flashed in the club Miranda had chosen for their night out. Hope would rather have stayed home. Clubbing wasn't something she'd ever indulged in, but Miranda had been so excited when Hope agreed to go out for a pre-wedding celebration. She just didn't have the heart to disappoint her friend.

Miranda motioned for a waiter and shouted out

their drink order. A margarita might be what the doctor ordered, but Hope wasn't sure if the champagne she'd consumed at dinner would be pleased to share her digestive system.

"Relax Hope, we won't stay long. I wasn't about to leave you at home or to let the boys have all the fun."

"I'll try. Though, I've got to tell you I'd much rather—"

The music rose in volume cutting off Hope's words. The overhead lights went down and the stage lights came on. A blend of drums and electric guitars signaled the curtain's rise.

Five men in tuxedoes strutted out onto the center of the stage. Each man stopped and posed for the almost all female audience. Hope wasn't a prude, but knowing what was sure to happen next didn't turn her on. She'd rather be with Miles.

"Miranda." Her shout went unnoticed. She grabbed Miranda's arm. "Miranda!"

The grin her boss and friend sent her way was totally evil.

"What's the matter, aren't you enjoying the view?"

"It's the view I'm afraid of. Please tell me they're going to sing something and then get off the stage."

Miranda's laughter could barely be heard above the club's din but her shoulders shook with amusement. "Afraid not, girlfriend. This show is only here for one night, and those guys ain't gonna be singing or whistling Dixie."

Hope's face heated. Lord, she would have thought being a doctor, the prospect of male nudity wouldn't bother her, but the gyrations going on twenty feet in front of their table wasn't anything she'd seen in medical videos.

The music took on the tone of a bump and grind routine, and the men all with fantastic bodies moved with the rhythm. One man in particular stood out to Hope. He had the same color hair as Miles, but didn't wear it as long as her seductive vamp. The other four men were attractive, but none of them did a thing for Hope.

Maybe there was something wrong with her. The other women seated at various tables were clapping a mile a minute. Miranda joined in their catcalls before leaning close to Hope.

"If you say one word to Zacke, I'll make sure you work nights after you get back from your honeymoon."

Hope's mouth fell open.

"Just kidding, Hope, but seriously, lighten up a bit. Zacke knows where we are, and I bet by now so does Miles."

Great, that was all she needed. As much as she'd thrown herself at Miles lately he'd be sure to think the worse. She might as well sit back and try to enjoy the show. Surely the act would be over with soon, and she'd be able to talk Miranda into leaving. A headache was fast making itself known, and the loud music wasn't helping.

The tempo changed to something slow. Oh good, maybe the floorshow was finished. When the men filed off the stage, she breathed a sigh of relief. Their exodus through the crowd—Hope assumed toward the back of the club, garnered several "woo woos" and "Come here, baby."

Miranda turned and looked at her. Glee crowded her gaze. Uh oh. Hope had a good idea of what was suppose to happen next. No way was she having some man thrusting his gear in her face. Well—no one but Miles. Time to make a strategic retreat.

"I'll be back. Gotta run to the ladies' room."

Hope enjoyed the look of shock on Miranda's face. Deviltry rode her lips as she whispered in Miranda's ear. "Relax, enjoy the show."

The hallway leading to the bathroom was empty. Hope smiled. She really did have to use the facilities. A few moments later, she pushed the door open and started back to the stage area.

A hand jerked her to a halt.

"You're going the wrong way, little darling."

Hope looked over her shoulder and her knees gave way. Her fall to the dirty floor didn't happen. One of the men who had attacked her in the park jerked her against him. Alcoholic fumes assaulted her nose, and the fetid odor of unwashed skin turned her stomach.

The nightmare she'd put behind her was happening again. No way would she survive a second attack. And no way in hell was she going to go down without fighting back.

Hope elbowed the man in his stomach and stomped on his foot. His hold slackened, and she turned to gouge his eyes. A knife gleamed bright in the dim hallway.

"Try that again, and I'll gut you now—instead of later."

Oh God. Sweet Lord. She had to get away before he dragged her out of the club. No telling where he'd take her or if his friend would be there too.

"What do you want?"

"I want you to walk out of this place without making a sound."

"And if I don't?"

"I know where your friend lives. It'd be a shame if something happened to her or one of her children."

Horror clenched her stomach into knots. She couldn't let anything happen to Miranda. Her children needed her. She closed her eyes against the additional nightmare of something happening to one of the twins.

She had no choice.

Hope allowed her assailant to lead her out the

door and onto the street. She prayed she'd see someone she knew—anyone who could help her escape. No one looked familiar. Could she get aid from a stranger? Would she be able to live with herself if she survived knowing she caused harm to another? No—she was in this alone. Not even Miles could help her now.

A dark van pulled up to the curb. Sour Breath held the knife at Hope's sucked-in stomach, opened the door, and shoved her forward. The accelerated motion caused her to fall onto the backseat. Her elbow banged against the seatbelt buckle. She ignored her funny bone and scrambled into an upright position. The man jumped in beside her, and Hope hugged the door.

The door!

She grabbed for the handle. Nothing happened.

"No use in trying to get away. The doors are locked and we're going for a ride."

"Why are you doing this?"

The driver pulled into traffic before he turned his head toward Hope. "Someone doesn't like you, and they're willing to pay big bucks to make you go away."

Who hated her this much?

The man who indeed was the other assailant from the park spoke again. "And after we get rid of you, your boyfriend will be deader than a doornail."

Miles! Could they hurt him? He said he could only die by having his heart plucked out and his head cut off. Did they know he was a vampire?

She had to escape. She had to warn Miles. She had to protect him.

But how?

The man with the knife carried on a conversation with the driver. The weapon he'd threatened her with now lay on the seat. Could she get it?

Hope eased her hand sideways. The slow crawl of her fingers toward the knife felt like a ten-year journey. Her chest hurt and she told herself to breathe. Cold etched metal touched her grasping digits. She closed her frozen fingers over the hilt and pulled the knife, inch by agonizing slow inch toward her body.

Once the knife lay next to her hip, Hope dared to look around instead of straight ahead. Lights flashed inside the interior of the vehicle as they moved farther from the populated area of town. Warehouses rose, stark and ugly against the Savannah skyline. The business district was silent as a tomb. If she managed to escape, she would have to run back the way they came in order to find help.

She needed to make a move—now. She brought the weapon up before slicing downward toward the man's arm.

"What the hell—"

The man held his bleeding forearm and turned toward Hope. His expression one of shock and rage.

Again, she raised the blade. Her momentum this time was deflected. The slap she received stung like a bunch of hot pepper, and her head snapped back. A blow to her ribcage rendered her breathless. The scream of pain begging to be released caught in her throat.

Hope braved the excruciating pain and turned her body toward the door. Her forehead rested against the window, and she welcomed its cool surface. Her eyes burned with tears, and she blinked them back. Her gaze cleared enough for her to take in the sparseness of her surroundings. While she fought to escape, the warehouses had disappeared—replaced by an isolated strip leading to the waterfront.

Reality reared its ugly face. Hope was going to die.

Chapter Sixteen

"Just one more dance."

Miles resisted the urge to pound Hawk into dust. The pre-wedding celebratory drink had turned into an hour or more of cruising. All to satisfy Hawk's quest to reaffirm his bachelorhood. At first, he'd enjoyed the male camaraderie but that had paled as the night wore on. He wanted to see Hope—bad luck or not. He didn't have to speak to or touch her—he just wanted to see her.

Icy tendrils of unease settled on his shoulders. For the last several minutes, Miles couldn't shake the fear that something would stop their marriage. Not a possibility. Hope loved him, and she was safe with Miranda. No one would accost them in a public place, only one of the reasons he'd agreed to the outing when Zacke told him about Miranda's surprise.

Miles didn't want Hope to live in fear, but he didn't want fear to eat him alive when he was away from her either.

Hawk sauntered back to the bar from what hopefully would be his last *dance* of the night.

"You guys ready to go?"

Miles and Zacke shared a who-wants-to-kill-him-first look but said nothing. They both grabbed one of his arms and propelled him out of the bar.

"Look, I appreciate the gesture, but I think I'm going to swing by and make sure Hope is okay and then head back to the house."

"You know Miranda's going to fuss if you get within a football field of Hope before the wedding."

"She's *your* wife, you soothe her feathers. I'm out of here." Miles tone held some humor but the feeling of unease had intensified.

Zacke opened his mouth to reply but his cell phone rang.

Miles shrugged his shoulders. Even if he hadn't been ready to call the night quits, it looked as if duty called for Zacke.

He threw up a hand in good-bye and started walking. "Miles, wait!"

Miles turned back to an ashen-faced Zacke.

"What's wrong?"

"That was Miranda. Hope's missing!"

Dread slammed Miles like a two-ton truck. It had to be a mistake. He grabbed Zacke's arm. "What do you mean she's missing?"

"Miranda said Hope went to the ladies' room and never came back."

"That doesn't mean she's missing. Maybe she went home."

Zacke dislodged Mile's grip. "She left her jacket and purse behind."

"Okay, so we find her, right?" Hawk sounded as shaken as Miles felt.

"Damn straight we do. Is Miranda still at the club?"

"Yes, I told her to stay put until we get there. I've also called Gideon."

"Good, let's go." Miles took off without waiting to see if the others followed or not.

****

"I told you Miles, she just went to the bathroom."

Miranda's voice was husky. Tears welled in her eyes and as he watched, one escaped and rolled down her cheek.

Miles clenched his fists to keep from lashing out verbally. He knew Miranda was torn apart. He knew it wasn't her fault, and he knew that if anyone was to blame it was him. He should have forbidden Hope from leaving the house.

Zacke moved closer to Miranda as Miles stepped forward. He held his hand out to his friend. "I'm not going to hurt her or berate her, Zacke." He closed the scant distance between them and ignored the crowd letting out from the last show.

Miranda's breath hiccupped as he pulled her into a tight embrace. "It's going to be okay, Miranda. I will find her. Hope will be fine." He tightened his grip for just a moment. "Now, go wash your face and then come back and tell me everything you can remember about when Hope left."

Zacke crossed with Miranda to the ladies' room, standing sentinel outside the door. Miles wondered if the look of desolation, horror, and impotence registered on his own features as it did on Zacke's and Hawk's.

****

Twenty agonizing minutes later, between Miles, Hawk, Zacke, and with the help of Gideon, they had interviewed most of the crowd still milling around the club. The manager promised to round up all the employees after they finished closing up for them to be interviewed also.

His fangs ached from being held in check. No one so far remembered seeing Hope. Nor could they pinpoint anybody that looked suspicious. Of course with this being a popular place for strippers and patrons, most folks would probably look like they belonged.

"You okay, Miles?" Hawk's question barely touched his thoughts of what he would do if something happened to Hope.

"I'm not sure about anything at the moment."

"You told Miranda the truth, we *will* find her!"

"What if it's too late?"

"Don't think that way. You have to be strong for when we do find her."

Miles allowed Hawk's hand to rest on his shoulder for a brief moment longer before he forced his frozen limbs to move. "Thanks, Hawk. I can only pray you are right."

"Miles?"

Zacke's unasked question forced Miles to turn back around. "I'm fine. Did you find out anything?"

"Not yet, but the manager said give him just a second, and his crew would be ready for us to talk to them."

"Thanks, how's Miranda?"

"The manager offered her a drink. She needs something to get her to relax just a bit. I need to see about getting her home in a calm state. Cassie, our regular babysitter, is spending the night so she can keep an eye on the twins while we get ready for the wedd—"

"Detective Kensington, we're ready if you are." The manager's voice cut through the silence that followed Zacke's aborted word. What no one wanted to say was there might not be a wedding. Miles wanted to tear out his shattered heart at the thought that instead of enjoying his honeymoon, in a few days, he could be at a funer—

"Thank you, Mr. Bloom. We will be right in."

Miles followed Zacke and Hawk back to the bar area. Gideon remained outside checking with anyone who might still be waiting on cabs or walking about the club district.

"I guess you already know why you are being detained." Zacke addressed the bar help, strippers, and other personnel. "I appreciate your time. This shouldn't take long but bear in mind, we have to find this woman before it's too late." His words painted a gruesome picture in Miles' mind.

"This is the picture of the woman who was abducted. Please pass it around and look it over carefully. If any of you remember seeing her anywhere near the ladies' room or the front doors after the first act started, we need to know."

Zacke stepped back in line with Miles and Hawk. All three waited for the photo Miranda had taken of Hope during an impromptu meeting at the hospital to make its round.

"Hey, I did see this woman." Before Zacke could motion the young waitress forward, Miles escorted her to the front of the room. He ignored Zacke's admonishing frown.

"Okay, miss, could you tell us where?"

The young brunette's dark brows pulled together. "It was probably about an hour ago. I noticed she seemed in quite a hurry to get inside the ladies' room. I had just come off a break when I spotted her." She pursed her lips, squinted at the picture again. "She looked a bit paler then in this picture. I still had a minute or two before I had to get back to work, so I turned around to go back to check on her, thought she might be going to lose her dinner or something. She was leaving—a man was with her."

"Did it look like she was okay?"

"I think. It sorta looked like he was holding her up. Sorry, I thought it might have been her boyfriend, husband, you know helping her to the car or something." The woman bit her lip. "Sheesh, now I wish I'd done something. Maybe if—"

"Ma'am, is there anything else? Can you give us any details on what the man looked like?"

"I'm sorry, I just saw him for a minute." Again she frowned. "Wait a second, there is something else. A customer came in and said something about a van blocking the side entrance. They were pretty steamed because they had to walk around in the cold. I walked out to see and spotted the van leaving. It was so dark, I couldn't really tell what color it was."

Zacke looked at Miles and Hawk. "Would you excuse us just a minute, I'll be right back. Mr. Bloom, you can let everyone else go home. Thank you all for your help. Miss...?"

"Chambliss, Maria Chambliss."

"I might need to ask you a few more questions."

Maria looked at her watch. "That's okay, I can wait."

"Thank you." Zacke, as well as Miles and Hawk, moved to where Miranda still sat on a barstool.

"Are you two thinking what I am?"

"Yeah, we could try to read her mind and see if she picked up on more than she consciously remembers about the van." Hawk's gaze was hesitant. Miles knew he didn't want to get their hopes up.

"I'll do it."

Zacke placed a hand on Miles arm. "I don't think that's a good idea, Miles. Let Hawk do it. You are way too upset. Hopefully, he'll be able to pick up the details we need."

His teeth gnashed together, but he realized Zacke was right. His thoughts had ranged from despair, murderous, and self-loathing ever since Hope had gone missing. If only he'd taken some of her blood, he'd come so close to doing just that a few times but hadn't given in to the urge, then at least he would be able to see where she was. His celibate diet, although noble at the time, could cost him the one spot of salvation in his life.

"All right, I'll stay here with Miranda. You guys do what you have to do."

Miles accepted Miranda's grip on his hand and returned it. The smile she gave him, although filled with sorrow, could not be returned no matter how hard he tried.

****

"Okay, we've got a tag number, Gideon's already at the station and will call me as soon as he runs the plate."

Miles' breath whooshed out in a sigh of hopefulness at Zacke's words. He watched as Hawk gently pushed several green bills into Maria's hand before Zacke escorted her out of the bar.

"The poor thing. Her life's been hard and after reading her mind, I wanted her to have something to buy her kids a few things for Christmas."

"That's good of you, Hawk. I'll make sure we add her to our list of needy moms for the hospital Christmas fund drive."

Zacke's reentry into the bar sent Miles' heartbeat thudding faster than a jackhammer on concrete.

"Okay, we have an address near the waterfront. The house is owned by a man named Bailey. He has a record, and so does the brother who lives with him. Nothing stuck out for Gideon except they have been seen in some of the areas where the purse snatchings took place."

Miles breath seized at the thought that the men who brutally attacked Hope on campus could be the ones holding her now.

"Okay, let's go."

"Miles, this is a police investigation. You have to let us do our jobs."

His fangs exploded with such force, Miles could taste blood on his tongue. "I am going. There is nothing you can do to stop me."

Zacke exchanged a look with Hawk. "That's what I thought. Okay, we have about twenty minutes before Gideon arrives there with the cavalry. I suggest we fly, if one of you two will give me a lift."

Once they saw Miranda home safely, Miles took the address information from Zacke's mind. He jumped for the night sky, praying he would reach Hope in time, the shouts from Hawk and Zacke a distant din as he flew high above the city.

****

Hope worked at the ropes binding her wrists together. The hemp was wet from her teeth marks. She was no closer to getting free now than when they shoved her into the small cement room. At least they had not secured her ankles. The only thing keeping her sane was the fact she could get up and pace. Not conducive to getting free, but at least she felt she had some control over her movements.

A laugh escaped her lips—mirthless and almost hysterical in sound. Hope fought the urge to scream. Icicles of fear stung her spine. She had no control over anything—not since her abduction. Now she faced the ugly truth the men were going to rape her before they killed her.

That fact had been instilled in her when they tied her up.

The taller man had leered at her breasts while the other man's gaze had targeted the apex of her thighs. Yes, they would brutalize her, and then take pleasure in making her feel every detail of her eventual death.

Another quick tug on the ropes and Hope laid back, exhausted. Her face hurt as well as her head where she'd hit the car window when her captor slapped her. Minutes passed. It could have been hours, since she'd lost her watch when she'd struggled with the men after they arrived here.

The irony was, even with a name like Hope, she was ready to give up. Miles... Her heart ached thinking about him and what should have been, even with his powers he would never find her in time. Her wedding day would pass and in all probability, she would be a cold corpse waiting on someone to find her skeletal remains. Tears stung her eyes and made her face itch as they crawled down her cheeks.

Miles! Lord she would never taste his lips again, never be his in every way. His seldom heard laughter would never touch her soul again.

A sound outside her improvised jail cell stalled her thoughts. The men were coming back. Soon, she would be dead and no amount of hope would sway what was to come.

Chapter Seventeen

Miles landed at the back of the house. The interior was completely dark. Before he could pinpoint any sign of life in the shabby wooden abode, Hawk swooped to the ground with Zacke.

"Miles, you should have waited." Zacke's words, although whispered, held a reprimand.

"Hey, I just got here. Haven't even had time to see if anyone's inside yet."

"Good, then listen up. Hawk, you stay with Miles. I want you two to check out the back of the house. I'll go in the front." Zacke seemed totally oblivious to the look Miles gave him. Mortal or not, the man had a stubborn streak when it came to police work.

"All right, ready?"

"More than ready. And watch yourself, Zacke. Remember, you're no longer immortal." Miles punctuated his words with a brief salute before following Hawk to the back door.

Miles reached out to turn the knob. Locked, just as he figured. Without a word, he and Hawk allowed their bodies to dissolve into molecules of air. One vapor trail streamed through the door a second before the other and then both men stabilized into mortal form once again.

A finger to his lips, Miles motioned for Hawk to search the rooms on one side of the hallway, while he took the other. Deciding to use the mortal way he turned the doorknob of the first room on the left and eased it open. A room devoid of furniture, with cobwebs thrown in, greeted him. He inhaled, but found no trace of human life in this room or more importantly, no hint of violence or death.

His search of the next few rooms warranted the same results. A quick look at Hawk confirmed his luck had been no better. Silently they moved through the house until they met Zacke. A quick shake of his head and Miles' breath and fangs exploded. "They have to be here."

Desperation turned his immediate world into a slow simulation of dread and horror. What if Gideon's information had been wrong? What if the van, the witness spotted, had nothing to do with Hope's abduction?

Miles pulled away from his frantic thoughts and read Zacke's. With the upstairs clear, they would check to see if there was a basement.

The steps that led down to the core of the house also ended in a hallway. One door at the very end drew Miles' attention. He crept closer, Zacke and Hawk so close they almost stumbled over him when he stopped. The walls of the basement were solid—at least six inches thick, the door a galvanized piece of steel. No peephole. A silent try of the knob signified it was locked.

Miles didn't wait for the other two, he dissolved into molecules and entered the room. Nothing! Not a damn thing.

Hope had to be on the premises somewhere. The van was the only lead they had, and surely it couldn't be coincidence that the men who lived here might be suspects in the robberies.

They could have gotten Hope's address from her bag and...and what? Would they wait this long to make a move? Why now?

"Miles?" Zacke's voice echoed through the door's thickness.

"Give me a minute." He unlocked the door from the inside and both Zacke and Hawk plowed into the room.

"Hope?"

"She's not here, Hawk, I can't find any evidence she stayed in this room at all."

"Well, she has to be somewhere."

"But where, Zacke?" Miles' nails grew and his fangs punctured his gums.

"Maybe there's another way out of this room. We know all the upstairs rooms and the ones we searched so far here in the basement were all empty, but there has to be another way out."

Zacke began to walk around the room, tapping on walls, moving old furniture.

Miles joined him as did Hawk. It might be fruitless, but it made no sense there wouldn't be a way to exit the basement.

"Give me a hand." Zacke worked to move more old furnishings, and Miles hurried to help him.

Nothing!

Miles felt totally useless. Hope could be dead or dying or worse, and he couldn't help her.

"What if we try the other rooms again? Maybe there's something we missed?" Hawk's face held the same worry nagging at both Miles and Zacke.

"Good idea, why don't we each take a room. It'll speed things up"

"Right, Zacke." Hawk took off, and Zacke came up beside Miles.

"Don't worry, we'll find her, Miles."

"I know. I just hope it's not too late."

Several moments later, Miles stood in the center of the room he searched. So far, he'd come up with nothing. His gaze canvassed the interior again. Several empty bottles of wine littered the floor. A few still rested in the wine rack. He figured it had served as a wine cellar in the past.

The wine rack! It sat cattycorner against one edge of the wall.

Miles put his shoulder into the huge dust-encrusted wood frame and shoved. The rack careened across the floor with a screeching that hurt his ears.

Where the rack once rested was a plain wooden door.

Unsure whether or not the men who kidnapped Hope could hear him, Miles spoke in mind thoughts to Hawk.

I've found another door.

We're on our way.

Good as his word, both Hawk and Zacke made short work of getting to the wine cellar.

"I moved the rack and found the door."

"All right, now we just see where it leads." Zacke stepped around Miles.

"No, I'll go first. You stay behind me."

"Miles."

"Zacke, we're wasting time. Let's do it my way."

Zacke's grunt signaled his frustration but Miles ignored him.

He opened the door and stepped over the threshold onto a dirt floor surrounded by cement walls. He moved out slowly and treaded his way down the long passage. Rats ran across his path, and he kicked them out of his way.

After turning one corner and then another, he stopped. A door much like the one they'd found in the upper basement stood in front of him.

Miles placed his ear flat against the door, closed his eyes, and waited. Three sets of heartbeats greeted his sensitive hearing. A moment more gave him the answer he needed. Two men and one woman were inside. It had to be Hope—it just had to be.

"I'm fairly sure Hope's in there."

"Okay, you two get inside and then unlock the

door. We need to do this by the book."

"To hell with the law, Zacke. We have to rescue Hope."

"Keep your fangs under wrap, Miles. That goes for you too, Hawk. We want them to have no room to weasel out on a technicality if it is the men and Hope."

"Fine, let's go."

Miles dematerialized and reformed inside the room. Hawk stood beside him.

A whimper greeted his ears. Two men were bent over the form of a woman lying on a cot. Miles' heart seized as he spied one flailing arm shoot out between their bodies. A ring adorned the fourth finger on her left hand.

HOPE!

The sound of the lock being turned barely registered as he ran forward. A bone snapped when he grabbed the smaller man's arm and jerked him away from the bed. A cry of agony caressed his ears with joy. Good! He'd hurt the son-of-a-bit—

"Miles stop!"

He ignored Zacke's command. The larger assailant now had Hope by the throat. His hands were clenching her slender neck so tightly her face took on a pink cast. Trusting Hawk to make sure the first man didn't interfere, Miles grabbed the man by the neck and squeezed. He watched as the man's eyes bulged out and his breathing grew rapid as he tried to suck in enough air.

"Let him go, Miles. I mean it! You need to see to Hope."

The words sounded as if they came from a distance. The jade haze obscuring his vision slowly began to fade. Miles shook his head and then looked down. Hope lay still, her eyes closed, the hand wrapped around her throat now gone. As his vision continued to clear, he noticed her sweater was pushed up showing the bottom edge of the peach bra she wore, and her jeans were halfway down her hips.

Thank God, they'd arrived in time. Zacke stood over the man Miles had choked, his frame a dirty mass on the floor. Miles didn't even realize he'd turned the man loose. His hands trembled as he reached down to adjust Hope's clothing, then slid his arms under her shoulders and hips—lifting her up to fit next to his heart. "I'm taking Hope home. Can you call Miranda and ask her to meet me there?"

"Yeah, get going, Hawk and I will wait for Gideon."

****

The night air against her face stirred Hope back to consciousness. Strong arms held her tightly. She fought to break their hold.

"Sssh. Hope, I've got you. You're safe." A small chuckle preceded Miles' next words. "Although, if you continue to struggle, we might find ourselves on the ground quicker than either one of us would like.

Breath, previously caught in her throat, escaped in a rapid sigh of relief and elation. Safe! Not only safe, but with Miles.

"What happened?" Her words came out in a croak.

Miles looked down at her and if possible clutched her tighter. "Don't talk, woman, you need to save your voice."

He kissed her forehead—a gentle caress of butterfly wings. Hope's eyes begin to close once more. "I want to hear you loud and clear when you promise to be mine." Miles' words came from a distance before darkness claimed her.

****

"Miles, I told you I'm fine. And if you don't believe me, remember, Miranda checked me out and said the same thing."

And she was fine. Hope's aches from the

abduction had magically disappeared when she'd awakened this morning. Her prior hoarse voice and the tenderness from the man's grip had also faded.

"I'm just thinking you need to rest for a bit before getting ready for the wedding."

"I just got up a couple of hours ago. I'm already running behind. Miranda will be here in a few minutes and it's time for you to go." Hope reinforced her sentence with a hand to Miles' chest. When he didn't back up, she pushed him again—hard.

"Okay, but at the first sign of anything, I want you to sit down."

"And do what? Miss our wedding? I don't think so, Vamp Boy, I've waited a lifetime for this. Now move—please." Hope's last word came out in a sigh of frustration. Miles had dogged her footsteps for most of the day, and he'd also been in her bed that morning.

It had been quite a rude awakening. She'd seen him sleep but to find his cold body next to hers was a bit different, and totally out of whack with what she thought Miles felt—that she would be repulsed by his corpse like body. Which would be insane if she was right. What did he think he was going to do after they were married? She planned to sleep with him nights and days when she was off. The man needed to realize she was in it for the long haul and it didn't matter that he was a vampire. He certainly wasn't a monster.

"All right, I'm moving. I'll see you at our wedding, my love."

The kiss he locked on her lips threatened to send Hope's knees into a dive toward the floor, and the hand she had placed on his chest wandered northward to grasp a strand of his chestnut hair. His tongue fought for control in the cavern of her mouth, and Hope gave him back as good as he gave. She wasn't sure who pulled away first, but one thing she did know, she couldn't wait to be his.

****

Twilight shadows danced outside with the last rays of the sun as Miles stood under a floral arch. His chest rose and fell with the anticipation of seeing Hope walk down the ivy-colored carpet the wedding planner had installed.

Hawk stood at his side with Zacke on the far left. A man's life couldn't get any better in Miles' opinion. His two best friends, the woman he loved only moments away from being his, and the promise of a lifetime of tomorrows.

"How you holding up?" Hawk's whisper broke his thoughts.

"I'm okay, just can't seem to stop shaking."

Zacke's chuckle was hidden behind his hand, but his words of commiseration took the edge off of Miles' case of nerves.

"It seems I remember you laughing at me when I did the same thing before Miranda and I wed."

"Yes, I know, but for some reason it was funnier when it happened to you."

The men's laughter caused a frown to set between the minister's brows, but it had done its job. The tension embedded in his neck and shoulders slowly dissipated.

The strains of the "Wedding March" began, and his heart picked up speed. Soon, but not soon enough, Hope would be his wife. The woman of his heart and soul. His mate for the rest of his life.

Before he could think on a lifetime with Hope, Zacke and Miranda's two urchins danced down the aisle. Their antics as flower girl and ring bearer were endearing and humorous. Miranda who almost trotted down the aisle in her guise as matron of honor grabbed each twin by the collar and pushed them toward the altar and Zacke. A frown aimed at her husband caused him to pull the children back against his knees. He then leaned down and whispered in first one twin's ear and then the other. Both immediately stopped their rowdiness.

The music seemed to swell in volume as a vision of loveliness dressed in antique lace and cream slowly—too slowly—moved down the aisle toward Miles. Hope's features were covered by her mother's veil she'd unearthed from the cavernous attic, but he knew what she looked like. Her green eyes would be luminous with just a hint of tears, her raven hair with its streak of silver would be pulled back from her slightly flushed cheeks in loose but elegantly disheveled allure. Her oh-so-kissable lips would be parted just a bit, showing a brief glimpse of perfectly straight white teeth.

Just the thought of Hope's face under that lace made him want to go to his knees and thank God for the precious gift he'd been given. As it were, his knees actually weakened as she drew closer. Hope had chosen to walk down the aisle without an escort. She had thanked Zacke and Hawk for their offers to do just that—citing although honored, she would have her father's memory with her.

The music fell silent as his soul mate glided to a halt next to him. Miles waited as she handed the wedding bouquet to Miranda and then he caught both of her hands in a gentle grip.

The preacher's welcoming words barely registered for Hope. She'd feared this day would not happen, but Miles' gentle caress as he held her hands proved that the nightmare was over, the men were behind bars, and she no longer had to worry about being assaulted. Miles had found her, and now, she was to be his—truly his in all ways.

"Who giveth the bride away?"

Shoot, she meant to have that part taken out of the ceremony. Before Hope could tell the minister no one, two male baritones piped out.

"I do."

"I do." Hawk's words were an echo of Zacke's. Hope forced back the sting of tears. Instead, she smiled at both men before finally looking up into Miles' face. Yes, the same look of love remained. She had thought she'd imagined his emotion-filled gaze when she walked down the aisle. She resisted the urge to extract one of her hands from his strong grip just so she could touch his face.

"Very well then, shall we proceed? I believe the bride and groom have some words to say before the traditional wedding vows are spoken."

Hope's throat threatened to close as she sought to get the words she'd rehearsed earlier past her lips. But one glance into Miles eyes and her courage returned.

"Miles, you have made my life complete. You are the owner of my heart, the one that I want to grow old with and you carry the essence of love in your soul. I am so blessed to have found you. I will love you for eternity and thank God everyday for the blessing of having you in my life—as my friend, my lover, and my soul mate."

"Hope, you have given life back to my soul. You are the twin of my heart. You are the one I will grow old with. I too am blessed to have you by side as my woman, my soul mate, my lover. I will love you for eternity and beyond. There will never be another for me besides you."

The traditional vows were then spoken and answered by both she and Miles, but as far as Hope was concerned, they were married when Miles spoke his vow to her. Her heart leapt with the knowledge that they would spend their lives as one. No matter what happened between now and their end days together, she knew Miles would never leave her.

"I now pronounce you husband and wife. You may kiss the bride."

Miles wasted no time in lifting Hope's veil, pulling her into his embrace, and sealing their vows with a kiss. As he tasted the sweet essence of her lips and then further explored the nectar beyond, he felt an emotion swelling inside, almost bursting his heart wide open.

His kiss continued until he felt Hope relax in his arms and the slight burden of her weight as her knees buckled.

"Miles." Hawk's whisper pulled him back to the reality that he and his beloved were not alone.

He ignored the raised eyebrows of the minister, and helped Hope regain her feet, before turning them both to face the crowd of well-wishers.

Hawk and Zacke's back-pounding almost sent him sprawling. Miranda's gentle kiss on his cheek was welcome, but her words caused him to blink back tears. "You and Hope deserve one another. I cannot think of another man who deserves this as much as you do."

He returned her hug and then finally looked down at his bride.

Hope's eyes glistened also with unshed tears. Her hand trembled slightly as she reached up and caressed his cheek. If propriety wasn't at stake, and if Miranda wouldn't kill him with a well-aimed sword thrust, he would transport Hope and himself to where they would honeymoon. He couldn't wait to hold her in his arms, to undress her exquisite body, and to sink into her welcoming flesh, joining them as man and woman. He would also take just enough blood to ensure he always knew where his woman was. Never again would he take the chance of losing her.

****

Several hours later and not soon enough for Hope, she stood at the top of the staircase, ready to toss the bridal bouquet.

The reception had gone off without a hitch. Guests full to the brim with champagne and treats stood gathered, waiting on this one last detail of the wedding. Once this task was finished, she and Miles could leave.

Although not often done, Miles stood with her as she prepared to launch the flowers into the air. His arms encircled her waist as if he was afraid she would disappear. She smiled at the thought that her big strong vamp exhibited the same apprehensions of any groom.

"Thank you all for being here. Now, get ready. Let's see who will be the next in line for a wedding."

Hope pulled her arm back and then brought it forward in a downward arc. The mixture of roses and magnolias, though Heaven knew how the florists had been able to get the latter in the dead of winter, sailed forth to land in the hands of Gideon. His expression of horror caused guffaws from Hawk, Zacke, and giggles from Hope and Miranda. But it was the bark of laughter from Miles that warmed her heart. She looked up into his downward gaze and blew him a kiss with her lips.

"Well, Mrs. Dunbar, are you ready?"

"Yes, but you never told me where we were going?"

"That, my love, is a surprise I think you will enjoy."

Miles, still holding her tightly, withdrew from the head of the stairs to a passage of the hallway obscured from the crowd below.

"Miles, what are you doing? Should we not be going downstairs?"

"On the contrary, we are leaving right now."

Before Hope could say another word, Miles' arm slid under her hips, lifted her into the air, and the hallway blurred into nothingness.

Chapter Eighteen

Hope opened her eyes to see stone walls on all four sides of wherever they were. Miles held her steady until she recovered from their fast escape from the wedding party. Once her head quit spinning and her legs became tangible muscles instead of cooked spaghetti, she eased away from his embrace.

"Where are we?"

Miles sketched a slight bow before responding. "Dunbar's... Lair."

The hesitation in his words made her wonder if he thought she would disapprove of their honeymoon setting.

Hope glanced around what she assumed was a tower room. The tapestries looked new, the shutters were tightly closed but wall sconces held rushlights. A low table held an assortment of food and a bottle of wine with two goblets. A four-poster bed set under one of the closed windows.

As she made a slow circle, she noticed a coat-of-arms on one of the walls. A warrior with a sword extended stood guard against the backdrop of a castle and a cross. She moved closer.

Although the iron plaque was a few feet above her head, she was able to read the words *Dunbar's Keep.*

"Miles, is this your home?"

Her usually arrogant vampire hung his head for a brief second before once again meeting her gaze.

"Yes. I wasn't sure what to do for our honeymoon. I know that you like old things, as did your parents, and I wanted you to have a look at a bit of my heritage."

Hope moved to one of the few windows in the tower room. The shutters on this one hung just a bit askew. She peeked outside. Moonlight coated an inner bailey that stood deserted and beyond that, cottages—then nothing.

"What year is this?"

"How did you know?"

"Well, Vamp Boy, I don't see any cars, any utility poles or hear anything. The silence is like, what, uh, another world, I guess."

"It's the year of our Lord, 1630."

Hope's heart almost stopped. Not only had he transported them to the past, but it was his past. What a wonderful gift, if she could only find out why Miles seemed so apprehensive.

Tracing a path back to her new husband, Hope slid her arms around his waist. "Thank you, my love. This is a wonderful and most welcome present."

"Is it?"

"Of course, don't be silly, Miles. What woman wouldn't count herself blessed to honeymoon in a castle? Not just any castle but a part of you. I'm thrilled you're sharing this with me."

Miles dipped his head and when his lips touched hers, Hope's knees did their usual disappearing act. Once he allowed her to come up for air, she forced out the one question that had been teasing her mind.

"Your family coat of arms says this is Dunbar Keep. Why did you call it Dunbar's Lair?"

In a millisecond, the happiness that had returned to his beautiful eyes dimmed. "What is it? What aren't you telling me?"

"It's a long story, Hope. Perhaps we should eat first and then I will answer all your questions. I promise."

****

The remains of their simple but filling dinner rested next to goblets once again filled to the brim. Miles had only the one refill; citing wine did not mix with his vampiric makeup, whereas Hope took a sip of her third goblet of wine.

"I suppose there's no way I can get out of telling you why I call this place Dunbar's Lair?"

"No, and don't even try. I want to know all there is about you, Miles. There is nothing in your past that I will revile you for. I love you!"

Miles prayed that if she ever found out the truth of that long ago Halloween night that his precious wife would indeed grant him grace. Now, he had the task of telling her the type of despicable character her dead, *thank the saints*, father-in-law had been.

"All right, but it's not a bedtime story, Hope. Times back then or rather now were hard. Here at the castle, we saw more abundance than the crofters that helped till this land. My father..." He stopped as a shudder attacked his shoulders. "My father was not a kind overlord. He beat the men that worked for him and raped the women who worked in the castle."

Hope's gasp cut off in mid-action when he looked at her.

"It's okay, I know this is not something you want to hear after what almost happened to you twice, but for me, my father was worse than the men who attacked you. He had no need to rape a woman, his handsome looks were sung as a tribute to the lord of Dunbar's Keep, but for some reason, he didn't want the women who would come willingly to his bed. He wanted to use the weaker, the frightened, and the ones he knew would be too scared to tell him no."

"What about your mother, didn't she have anything to say?" Hope's hesitant question made Miles want to rip his tongue out for what he had to tell her next.

"My mother was one of those women. The only difference being, my father was caught raping a lady of royalty and then forced to marry her. My mother, Isabella of Ravenswood, was friends with the daughter of the King of England."

Hope's eyes grew round as he continued to speak of his past. "I was the result of that rape. And I paid the consequences almost every day of my childhood."

Hope got up and moved around the table to Miles. She slid between his open thighs and found a perch on one of them. "Hey, just so you know. I will thank God everyday that you are you. That you were given birth, even under horrific circumstances. I love you."

Miles fought the tears that stung his eyes. What had he ever done to be blessed with such a treasure?

"Thank you, my love. I thank God also for the gift that is you." He followed his words with a kiss to her lips. Hope returned it before pulling away.

"I know that way back when or now or wherever, women did not have much say-so, but did your mom not have any say to how your father treated you? And what did he do, Miles?"

"My mother died when I was born, Hope. I was left without any sort of buffer against my father's viciousness. As to what he did, he beat me when it pleased him, and he made me watch him rape the poor souls that were not able to keep away from him. When I was old enough, I tried to stop him—he beat me almost to death. That night I left this place and that is when I met Zacke and Hawk."

"Oh, honey, I am so sorry!" Hope tried to crawl even closer to his body as her heart broke with his testimony of life. How on earth could any one person be so cruel and how on earth had her beloved Miles become the sensitive, loving man he was with such a horrific parent? Thank God for Zacke and Hawk!

"It's all right. I've long come to terms with my past. It is well behind me. I guess I just didn't know how you would take it."

"I married you, not your past. We have the future, Miles and that is what's important. You were the best thing that came from your father. You are the spirit of all the things he wasn't. You do not have to be ashamed of where you came from, just know that you are the man I love more than life itself."

Miles' voice was muffled and if it sounded suspiciously as if tears crowded his words, Hope didn't let on. She just wanted to love him until she made every ache in his heart go away—like he'd done for her.

"All right, Mr. Dunbar. What say you that we get this honeymoon started? I know that I've waited long enough to have you right where I want you."

Miles laughter rang out, caressing Hope's ears and heart with its merriment. Now, if she could get the man on his backside, she'd do her best to make him forget anything else but her.

Before she could blink an eye, Miles scooped, ran, and had Hope in the center of the bed, flat on her back.

Miles gazed upon Hope's beautiful face. The innocence he loved still held sway in her sparkling green eyes but a sensual allure now taunted him with its intensity. Yes, `twas past time they consummated their vows.

His slightly trembling hands brushed disheveled hair away from Hope's face as he leaned down to take her lips with his. She tasted of wine, star filled nights, and warmth. Her soul called to him as a beckoning gift. He eased his tongue between her now parted lips and supped from the sweetness he craved. Desire carved a path from his heart to his loins. His shaft filled with blood and swelled with a lust that could only be satisfied by Hope.

As he pulled away from her lips, he looked once again into her eyes. Desire stared back at him. He left a trail of kisses and light nips down her throat as he followed the path to the tantalizing flesh peeking above her neckline.

Miles began the tedious and agonizing task of unfastening all the hooks that held the bodice of Hope's gown together. The first glimpse of the fullness that had been hidden from his view had his fangs begging to be released. He ignored the ache his creature side brought and continued with his task. Finally, he unearthed the jewels he sought—twin rose-colored nipples ripe with desire. He caught one of the nubs, suckled it, and then lightly nipped the succulent morsel before moving to the other.

Hope's body moved beneath his. He welcomed her passion. He wanted to see the fire that burned him with its flames capture Hope also.

A whimper of sound fell from her lips, and Miles caught it in his mouth. The kiss he gave her was no longer gentle. He had waited so long for this night; he wanted to possess Hope with all the desire, need, and love he'd kept locked inside for so long.

Miles deepened the kiss before he pulled back. "I need to get you out of this gown. I want to see all your body, worship it, and then make you a part of me."

"Well, I say get on with it. I've been waiting what seems a lifetime myself."

Miles bit back a laugh, dropped a hard kiss on his wife's lips, and then stripped the gown from her body. The sight that met his eyes stunned him. A cream satin corset hugged the undersides of her breasts, nipped her waist into an indention he wanted to uncover, and molded the mound of her womanhood.

"God above, Hope, you take the breath from my lungs."

Still held in awe, Miles took a moment to realize her laces were impossibly knotted.

To hell with it.

He concentrated on the barrier holding Hope hostage. A second later, she lay bare beneath his heated gaze, the offensive corset now decorated the stone floor.

"How did you do that?"

"Magic, my love, now hush, I have waited long enough for this moment."

Hope's lips, which had parted with what Miles was sure was a comment, blew a kiss his way before she sent him a smile that could only be described as wicked.

"Darling, I'll explore that smile in a bit but for now…"

Miles' palms traced his desired path from Hope's waist to her thighs and then down her legs. He cupped one of her feet in his hands, pressing his thumb into her high arch. He was rewarded with a low moan.

After giving the other foot the same treatment, he placed a kiss on her arch and then placed her foot gently on the bed. Miles slid his hands up Hope's calves, placed kisses on each of her knees, and then his hands caressed the silky texture of her inner thighs. His breath caught as he cupped her mound and then slid one finger inside her sex to feel her warm welcoming heat.

"Miles!"

"Soon, Hope, soon."

Hope's breaths became frantic as Miles' caressed her. Her body began to weep with the desire he delivered so seductively. Her hips rose off the mattress, her thighs gripped his hand, and a whimper passed between her clenched teeth. The man was going to kill her, but she didn't know if it would be a death of ecstasy or frustration—if he didn't take her soon.

"Miles, please..."

"You're right, my love, it's time."

As she watched, his eyes glowed with green flames—right before he closed them. A second later, his clothing disappeared—leaving a dangerously seductive and definitely aroused vampire. Miles opened his eyes, and the look he gave her would have chilled her to the bone except for one thing—he would never hurt her. She would stake her life on that and nothing on earth could change it.

The almost iridescent jade glow deepened, his lips lifted just a bit and there was just a hint of his fangs. His hands found her breasts again, this time his touch a bit rougher. The nips and kisses pulled her flesh taut and sent a burn of heat straight to her center. Miles' kisses became a form of torture that caused Hope to wiggle and thrust her hips forward to feel the pulsating hardness pressing against her aching flesh.

Before she could tell him what she wanted, his hands grasped her hips, spread her legs, and pulled her closer. A brief but thorough caress of her nether region was followed by a smile from Miles. The more than substantial display of his incisors almost caused her heart to stop, but again she told herself her new husband would never hurt her on purpose.

Miles forced his lust to retreat for just a moment. He had to get a grip or he could seriously injure Hope. Sex with a woman always held a danger of allowing his beast free, but with his soul mate the risk was even greater. His arousal throbbed, engorged with enough blood to fill a blood bank. He needed to be inside Hope *now*.

A second later, he nudged the opening to his desire. Hope's face went still, her movements of seconds before stilled.

He renewed his efforts to not thrust into her

brutally to claim what belonged to him. Slowly and agonizingly he pushed forward, an inch at a time, until he pushed against her virginal barrier.

The pain he glimpsed in her eyes tore his heart asunder but he had to have her. Miles eased his hand down and stroked the nub within her feminine valley.

Hope's eyes went wide for a moment before she thrust her hips forward—to take more of him. He continued his strokes until her whimpers turned to moans. His own arousal strained to achieved the same orgasmic goal but still he held back. Only when Hope's body lay still once again did he slide forward through the barrier of her innocence. Her inner core gripped him with a welcome that not only signified his release was near but bore with it the knowledge she had given her heart and soul to him.

Miles' thrusts became harder as he now braced his hands on either side of Hope's head. A groan found its way from his loins to escape through lips that had gone dry. His fangs punctured his bottom lip, and he tasted the sweet tang of blood. Blood was what he needed, but only a taste. Would his wife be disgusted, horrified?

Again, Hope's hips begin to move. She met his thrusts with a grinding expectation of experiencing more. Miles had shot her world to bits when she met him, and now he threatened to send her to Heaven with his touch. A whirlwind of sensation started once more in her core—spiraling faster and faster until she feared she would be torn apart with the ecstasy. The tempest rose higher, carrying Hope with it. "Miles!"

His teeth scraped her overly sensitive skin and then his fangs punctured her flesh. Before she could even yelp at the sharp pain, she was bathed again in passion so strong, spirals of ecstasy built deep within her core. She not only knew Miles was close to his climax, she sensed him reaching the pinnacle of lust before falling over the edge, taking her with him. Her last thought as she spiraled back to earth was how would she live through this night after night.

Chapter Nineteen

Miles licked the puncture wounds on Hope's throat. His tongue swiped the last drop of blood from his lips. He savored the blend of honey, woman, and spice that made up his love's life nectar. The jade glow faded from his vision, and he looked down at Hope. She lay still, but the slight rise and fall of her chest reassured him she just rested. Her blood had been just as potent as he knew it would be. The urge to take more than what he required to ensure he could always find and protect her had been crushed. How he'd found the strength to stop his thirst, Miles didn't know. He only knew he thank God he had.

"Miles?"

"Yes, my love?"

"I don't know what to say or if I have any breath left to say it with, but what just happened?"

"What do you mean?"

Hope pushed at his chest. Miles gave her some room and watched as she sat up in bed. Her luscious breasts taunted him, but the look on her face and the question in her diamond bright eyes, deserved an answer.

"Are you talking about what happened when we made love?"

"Yes, Vamp Boy, the mind-blowing sex, where somehow, I got to experience what you felt."

Miles felt a shout of exultation creep into his lungs. She actually thought it was mind-blowing. He also felt his face heat just a bit, because she probably knew how close he came to losing it.

"Well, it's like this, Hope. When vampires make love, they can heighten the sexual experience by taking blood from their..."

"That had better be 'wife' you were planning on ending that sentence with. If not, then I don't want to know how many women you have seduced."

Miles chuckled. He couldn't help it.

"You are really asking for trouble, my new husband."

"I know and I'm sorry." He took her slight nod as a forgiving sign and then scooted around and behind Hope. He pulled her up and back against his chest and flush against the unmistakable resurrection of his manhood.

"Okay, explain, Miles."

"Wife. I meant to say wife, Hope. Now, if you could keep your sweet sexy mouth closed for just a few moments, I will tell you the rest."

Miles didn't have to see Hope's face to know she probably had a pout on her lips. No matter, he would kiss it away after his explanation.

"Most vampires always take blood from their *wives,* it is a way to bond. Of course, in most cases, both are vampires. That means they would take blood and give it. Does that make sense?" Miles wasn't sure if it was the fact he was telling Hope information that might not sit well with her or if the blood flow to his shaft was cutting off the blood he needed for his brain but his explanation seemed disoriented.

"Okay, so are you are telling me you took my blood? Is that why I was able to see and experience what you did?"

See? God above, he hoped not. There were things in his mind and life that Hope did not need to witness.

"What did you see, my love?" His breath stalled

in his chest and the beating of his heart slowed to a snail's pace.

Hope turned her head and looked up at Miles. "I saw colors—dark shades of green. They whirled faster and faster as you..."

Miles' relief knew no bounds. She had not seen anything she shouldn't have. But, just to be on the safe side, he closed his eyes for a brief moment and entered her mind. His wife's thoughts were of confusion, sated passion, and love.

His sigh escaped and stirred strands of Hope's hair that had escaped their jeweled constraints during their lovemaking.

"Miles, you okay?"

"More than okay, wife. So do you understand what happened now?"

"I think so. Were you able to experience what I felt also?"

"Yes, I could even intensify your desire if I wanted to."

He silenced her gasp with a kiss. Once he tasted the depths of her sweetness and he felt her relax against him once more, he reluctantly removed his lips from Hope's.

"I didn't, I swear. What you felt was your own body welcoming mine and then the sealing of our love."

Hope's mouth snapped closed and then opened again. "Well... that might be a bit much, since you almost killed me with passion anyway. Is it possible for me to be able to do that to you, since you took my blood?"

"Well, you could if..."

"If what, Miles?"

"Never mind." Miles shuddered to think what Hope would say if he told her he could turn her into a vampire.

"It's not important, Hope. However if you are

ready for something besides twenty-questions, I think I have something in mind that you will like even more."

Hope wasn't sure she believed Miles' statement about it being nothing, but the shadows in his eyes made her want to hold him and take his mind off of whatever bothered him.

"Well, if it's what I have in mind, then I say go for it."

Miles' laughter relieved the tension that had crept into their chamber.

"So are you going to laugh or play, Vamp Boy?"

"Boy? I'll show you things a boy could only dream about."

"Yeah, in your dreams, Miles."

"No, it won't be a dream, so be silent, wife, and let me get started."

****

Hope gazed in awe at the outside of the castle. It was twilight of the second day of their marriage. After Miles had made sweet and incredible love to her off and on during the night, they both had fallen asleep. Expecting to wake with a cold stiff almost corpse by her side, she'd awakened to find Miles gone from their bed. He'd returned just moments later with a tray of fruit, cheese, and fresh bread.

Although, her new husband had only nibbled at the breakfast fare, Hope had been ravenous. Once she devoured all but the wooden trencher, she'd bathed in an oak tub Miles had carried in on his shoulders and water he'd also carted from a nearby lake. When confronted with all she had to wear was her twenty-first century clothing when her husband was now dressed in early sixteenth century garb, Miles had found her a dress to wear from an old trunk in his mother's chamber.

"So what do you think, wife?"

Hope heard the uncertainly in Miles words. She

wanted to smooth away the slight frown on his forehead. "I love it. This castle is extraordinary. You couldn't have chosen a better place for us to honeymoon."

The grin he shot her way made him even more handsome and seductive—if that were possible. Miles' height and girth only emphasized the fact he was once a warrior. Black tights cupped his sex, outlining the bulge of an almost constant arousal. The plain doublet he wore pulled tight across his shoulders and chest.

"Glad you approve, wife."

Hope wondered if she looked as good to him in her black gown without the farthingale that usually accompanied Renaissance women's clothing. She'd pulled on a silk chemise but left off the linen underdrawers. Her clothing was bit more dated than Miles' since the garments had belonged to his mother.

Their exploration of his home had begun outside earlier since Hope's eyesight couldn't pierce the darkness of full night and she wanted to see the castle's exterior in all its glory. Now, with her curiosity satisfied, she wanted to delve into every room in the castle.

"Miles, do you think we could go in now? I want to see everything there is to see about Dunbar Castle."

For a moment, her husband's smile slipped but then he nodded, grabbed her hand, and pulled her back through the oak doors. Once they were fastened tight, he turned to look at her.

"Where do you wish to start?"

"Why not at the bottom and work our way up?"

Miles frowned but caught her around the waist to lead her to the kitchens. From there, he opened a door that led deep into the bowels of the castle.

"Where are we going?" Hope wasn't sure she

wanted to see what lay beneath the castle's first floor but it had been her idea. Maybe next time she would keep her mouth shut.

"The dungeons."

The steps they traversed leading ever downward were damp and slippery in spots. Without the firm grasp Miles had on her arm, Hope feared she would turn coward and run back to the safety of the upper regions.

"Just a bit farther, Hope."

"Okay, I'm right behind you."

The slight chuckle he gave helped her to calm down just a bit. She really needed to forego watching any type of serial killer movies. This was just too close for comfort. Any moment, she expected something or someone to jump out with a knife.

Finally, they reached the bottom. The area before them stretched wide. An almost circular array of stone greeted her gaze. Miles let go of her hand and stood still as a statue as Hope moved forward into the open space. Chains and manacles were positioned at ten-foot intervals about eight feet off the floor. She didn't want to know how the poor souls who hung there had been placed into the iron implements of captivity.

As she slowly turned to survey the rest of the dungeon, her gaze lit on a wooden table with a pulley and chain contraction. It could only be a rack—a torture devised to stretch a person until they screamed their confessions of guilt or whatever else their captor wanted. The chill that touched Hope's spine made her wish for the warm fire in their chamber far above this monstrosity of dark judgment.

"I've seen enough, Miles. Let's go back."

"Hope, I'm sorry, I truly didn't want you to see the things that my mortal life was made of. Although I never used torture to elicit information, I did hear the screams of my father's victims. Not a good time in any part of history." His words were tense, his gaze a fathomless pool of green.

"It's not your fault. I should have realized with us being in this time, there would be things that were horrific."

She caught Miles' hand and brought it to her lips.

Miles clutched Hope to him and then transported them to the first floor of the castle. Once his bride recovered her breath and leg usage, he captured her lips with his own. The kiss was brutal as he relived the images the dungeon stirred. He could still smell the copper scent of blood as it dripped to the floor while his father tortured each victim. His incisors begged to be released, and his claws ached to be free also. Miles pulled back from Hope's sweet taste and ignored the startled look on her face.

"Hope, run!"

"Miles?"

"Run now!"

Hope obeyed his guttural order—allowing Miles a moment to leash the beast within him. His shaft, which had lengthened with the desire for blood, throbbed in time to his over-accelerated heartbeat. He just needed to calm himself. Yes, he would take Hope, but he didn't want to hurt her with his physical and blood lust.

Instead of transporting to their chamber, for that was where his wife had escaped to, he forced his legs up the stairs. All the while he paced his movements to slow his heart rate—he had to be calmer when he reached Hope.

The door of their chamber slammed against the wall and his gaze found Hope. She stood dead center in the room. A brief look of horror crossed her face before she squared her shoulders and moved forward toward him.

"Hope, don't. I'm not sure I can control myself."

"I'm sure. You would never hurt me."

She walked closer, and his back hit the wall next to the door. He couldn't have moved if his life depended on it—the horrific fact being Hope's life would be dependent on his next few moves.

Combinations of green and red once again assaulted his vision and mingled with a crimson haze. He was fast losing his hold on the beast.

Her hand slowly lifted and caressed his cheek.

The gentle touch should have calmed him, but his inner beast began to growl for escape. He snatched her hand away, noticing he'd sprouted claws. Not good—not good at all.

"Hope, please, stop. Leave me be."

Maybe he could transport back to the future and get Hawk to come after Hope. NO! He would not allow his beast to hurt her.

"Miles, I'm not going anywhere. We are in this together, so do your worst, Vamp Boy."

Crimson began to fade from his vision, the other colors soon followed. When he could see Hope in just the firelight of the room, he wanted to drop to his knees. His woman had stuck by his side. He had not lost her.

"Woman, I don't know what I did to deserve you, but I'll never stop thanking God for putting you in my life."

"I feel the same way, so are you okay?"

"Yes. I'm more than okay."

Miles slid his arms around her waist and then spun her around and around. His kiss, this time, was gentle but still full of the fire Hope loved. She reveled in the touch of his tongue as he caressed her mouth and the heat from his hands as he dipped into the neckline of her gown. Her breasts swelled with his caresses and her nipples peaked with want for

Miles to touch, to taste them.

Once again, his eyes changed color but Hope no longer feared the vampire within him. Miles was her husband, lover, friend, and soul mate. A tug on her knee and her thigh rode his, opening her to his searching fingers. Without a word, Miles slid his hardness into her center, connecting them together with more than a physical bond. The love she saw in his gaze permeated her soul.

In and out, he thrust until Hope felt the corkscrews of passion filtering through her feminine hub and her entire being felt as if it rode a wave of ecstasy. Miles moved even closer, his mouth nuzzling the side of her neck. She knew what he wanted and arched her throat to give him better access. The first prick of his teeth stoked the fire within her. Flames burned higher as he tasted her blood. Hope jerked as once again she felt his desire roar out of control. Her climax hit hard and fast—on its heels, she felt Miles reach his fulfillment. Her body tensed, her nerve endings went haywire, and once she fell back to earth, her lids closed in fatigue and rapture.

Chapter Twenty

Miles landed unobserved behind the police station. He'd called Zacke and Hawk when he and Hope arrived back from their honeymoon. Both men were working but promised to meet with him after he dropped Hope off at Miranda's. He dissolved into air molecules and made his way through the back door of the building and down the hallway to Zacke's office. His hearing picked up the sound of one mortal heartbeat and then Hawk's. Good, they were already there.

"Evening, you two."

Zacke barely jumped when Miles rematerialized in front of him. Hawk just laughed.

"So, how was the honeymoon?" Zacke's grin resembled the one Miles could feel on his own lips.

"How do you think?"

"All I know is, you don't seem as bad-tempered as you were before the wedding." Hawk's chuckle followed Zacke's.

Miles gave a mock snarl before responding, "I was not bad-tempered, just a bit anxious."

"Afraid you couldn't keep it up to snuff?"

Before Miles could reach out and grab Hawk, Zacke stepped between them.

"Enough. Let's leave Miles some peace, shall we? You know one day you could be in this same situation."

"No woman would have him!"

"Not going to happen, I am a very contented

bachelor. Not to mention I get all the perks without the chains."

Miles exchanged looks with Zacke. Both of them knew it wasn't just the extraordinary lovemaking but the emotional feeling of being loved that made them want to put a fetter around their neck for eternity.

His snort preceded his question, "So anything new on Guy?"

"No, he's kept pretty much quiet since he got Hope's invite to the wedding—that is, after he threw a royal tantrum."

Miles propped himself on the edge of Zacke's desk and resisted the urge to growl. Guy was an odious piece of crap, but hopefully he realized by now Hope wasn't defenseless. She had him to protect her and if the man kept on destroying his bride's peace of mind over Morgan Rarities, he would have more than a heart-to-heart with the man, more like a fang-to-neck conversation.

"So he's not made anymore midnight visits to the business?"

"No, he's pretty much become a model businessman. However, he did have a visitor while you were gone. The guy looked like a dressed down version of a television lawyer. The man only stayed about ten minutes, but Guy was smiling when he left."

"I still don't trust him as far as I could drop him when I'm airborne."

Zacke who had remained silent spoke up. "Has Hope mentioned anymore of those phone calls?"

Miles blinked. "No, there haven't been any. It's strange—they seemed to stop not long after I met Guy."

"You think he was behind them?" Zacke leaned back against his desk.

"I wouldn't put anything past that scum, but I

can't figure out how he could do it. Or why he would."

"Well, one thing's for certain. Guy's got something up his sleeve. I would keep a close eye on Hope."

"No problem there, the woman is not leaving my side at night, Zacke."

"Just make sure you let the woman get some sleep, Miles. She does work a day job." Hawk jumped out of the way of Miles' mock slap.

"Let me worry about her sleep. You find something on Guy."

"Believe me, I'm trying. I don't like the little dandy either."

"That makes three of us. Just get me something I can arrest him for and I'll be happy. And Miles—"

"I know. You want to handle it the legal way. That's fine as long as he doesn't hurt Hope."

****

Hope handed Miranda a Christmas ornament to go into one of the many boxes lined up in front of the tree. Her boss had corralled her into helping take down at least one of the four trees the Kensingtons had put up for Christmas.

"Don't just stand there, tell me."

"Tell you what, Miranda?"

Miranda pointed a porcelain candy cane at Hope. "You know very well *what*."

Hope burst out laughing. "My honeymoon? Well, what can I say. It was fantastic!"

"Dish, girl, I want to hear where you went and almost all of the down and dirty details."

Hope's cheeks burned as she thought of some of those details. "Okay… you talked me into it." She crossed to the couch and settled back. "We went to Miles' home in the sixteenth century for our honeymoon. It was like you wouldn't believe, Miranda. A real honest-to-goodness castle."

"I would believe. I saw the twenty-first century version, when Zacke and I flew to Europe for a second honeymoon after the twins were born. Now tell me the rest. Did Miles make your bones melt? Your toes curl? Come on, Hope, don't leave me in suspense."

Hope laughed again, Miranda's words had flown from her mouth like a gaggle of geese. "Let's just say, you could fantasize all day long and still wouldn't get the mind-blowing sex I had."

"Hope Morgan, make that Dunbar, I can't believe that came out of your mouth. Still, sex does have a way of making you lose your inhibitions. Guess we are two lucky girls."

"I couldn't agree more. So do you and Zacke have plans for New Year's Eve?"

Miranda sighed. "I wish. I will be on call at the hospital, since someone who shall remain nameless is still on her honeymoon until after the first of the year. Zacke will probably have to work also, but he will try to pop in around midnight."

"I would say I'm sorry, but it would probably not sound too sincere." Hope giggled. "I'm hoping to get Miles to take me to Atlanta or we might just celebrate at home. I love the teleporting thing. It's so neat to just *arrive*."

"I bet. I never got to experience being teleported. Zacke was beginning to suffer all types of symptoms by the time we married. And of course you know the story of how he almost died, became mortal again, and settled down to be a dad."

"Yes, Miles told me. I'm so glad it all worked out, Miranda. I hope one day we have children too. Of course, if they are anything like Miles when he's being stubborn, I'll want to pinch their necks in two."

"I heard that!" Miles' voice came from behind the couch, and Hope restrained herself from jumping out of her skin. But, she could not keep her heart from beating double time, nor could she stop the dampness coating her panties.

"Well, you shouldn't have such great hearing, Vamp Boy!"

Miles leaned over the couch, planted a kiss on her neck, and then sniffed.

"I think it's time we went home, Mrs. Dunbar."

"Miles, I'm helping Miranda. Can't we stay a bit longer?"

"We could, but I don't think Miranda would appreciate me stripping you naked and taking you on her couch." His whispered words sent another wave of dampness to her sex. Her nipples tightened until they ached.

"I guess we should go. I'm sure there are things we need to take care of back at the house."

"Yeah, I bet. Go on you newlyweds. Just make sure you get in some food for Hope, Miles. I cleaned out the fridge when I watered the houseplants. You might be able to live on love and blood alone, but your wife needs more sustenance."

Miles jumped over the couch and kissed Miranda on the forehead before responding verbally. "Yes, Mom, I'll do just that."

Her husband turned to her, pulled her up off the couch, and locked his arms around her waist. He lowered his head and took her lips in a scalding promise of what was to come. Hope's arms crept to his shoulders as she gave herself up to his kiss. She thought she heard the faint sound of Miranda's laughter, but when she opened her eyes, both she and Miles stood in her bedroom.

Once, he removed his lips from hers, Hope spoke, "Miles, it was rude to just pop out like—"

"I told you what I wanted to do and now I plan on doing it."

Miles had been crazy with lust ever since he

smelled Hope's arousal. The nectar of her womanhood was more potent than the finest blood in the world. Just a whiff and his shaft hardened like set mortar. It was a miracle Miranda hadn't seen the evidence of his desire.

He backed Hope up until her knees hit the bed. A gentle push and she lay back against the bedspread. Miles pushed her legs apart and moved between her thighs. A brief touch and the skirt she wore rode her hips. He slid his hands under the waistband of her lavender underwear. A slow glide and her panties slid down her legs and onto the floor. He eased off her high heels and allowed his hands to travel up the path her panties had descended.

Hope's body jerked just a bit as he caressed her flesh. The closer he got to the apex of her thighs, the more she wriggled. "I think you like that, my wife."

"What makes you say that, my husband?"

Miles grinned. "Because you can't be still, and I can smell your arousal stronger now than I could at Miranda's.

Hope's cheeks took on a deep rose color as her mouth flew open. "Oh, well, it's your fault. You know I can't be responsible when you're in the room."

"Yes, well, if it helps, I feel the same way. Now where were we?"

Hope raised her hips and pressed them against his engorged sex. Miles almost saw stars as she rotated her body and then pushed herself closer to him.

"You are killing me, woman."

"Then put us both out of our misery."

Miles ripped the zipper of his jeans down so hard, the metal came loose from the material. He pressed his shaft into the dew of Hope's love and then pushed forward until he was buried to the hilt.

"Miles!" Hope's breathless saying of his name

ended in a moan as Miles pulled out and then pushed back into her heat. She locked her legs around his hips, and he moved his palms under her sweater, cupping her breasts. Her moans grew louder as he tweaked her nipples with his thumbs, and he leaned forward and took one of them in his mouth.

Blood rose beneath Hope's skin as her passion grew. Miles watched the pulse beat in her throat as she became more frenzied to reach her climax. Now, he felt the craving for more than his sexual fulfillment. He could almost taste the rich, sensual flow of Hope's life-giving fluid. His fangs extended with his need, but he forced them back. Twice he had taken Hope's blood and the third time would see a changing taking place. He would not do that to her. He would keep his beast chained.

"Miles?"

"It's all right my love. I'm just thanking God for you."

He prayed his lie would be forgiven, but he did not want to see any fear in his beloved's eyes. Hope had soothed his creature self at Dunbar's Lair, but he'd seen her fright before she'd hauled it deep inside her soul. He would never allow the creature free rein. To do so would risk Hope realizing the part he'd played in her childhood.

His thrusts became faster, harder as he rode out the blood lust on a wave of physical ache for Hope. The closer he came to reaching climax, the more his wife gave of herself. Just before he reached the pinnacle of fulfillment, he touched the hard nub between her nether lips. Hope's hips rose higher, meeting his downward movements. His sight went blind but for the green haze covering everything in sight. He heard her moans grow louder, her nails bit into his arms as she reached for the same thing he did. The culmination of their passion and love.

****

A long while later, Hope moved closer into Miles' embrace. He held her tightly and wrapped one hand into her raven hair. His wife lay still, her inhalations and exhalations now quiet after their night of lovemaking. He'd taken her several times more as the sun began to wake up after he'd opened his belated wedding gifts. Her consideration in choosing something he loved made him want her more. And Hope had not only stayed with him in his desperate need to prove she was not going anywhere, but had met him more than halfway, proving the woman he loved indeed was his, and her promises of eternal love helped to mend long ago hurts.

Miles prepared to sleep now. The sun had long since crawled from its bed, and his death slumber tugged at his body with arms he wished he could reject. He would love to awaken Hope again—not so much to make love to her, but to just tell her how much he loved her. Promises given in the dark of the night were meaningful, but he wanted to see her face in the bright light of day. Zacke had found a way to brave the heat of the sun without too many side effects. Maybe he would ask him how he did it.

His lids began to lower. His heartbeat slowed and his mind began to turn off. With the last vestige of his strength, Miles pulled Hope even closer as he finally allowed sleep to claim him.

Chapter Twenty-One

Hope heard the peal of the doorbell and covered her head with her pillow. Who on earth would be calling at—she glanced at the wristwatch Miles had left on her arm—good grief! It was four in the afternoon. She had slept through what was left of the night and most of the day.

She slid her feet onto the floor, eased into slippers, and grabbed a robe to cover her nudity, before half-walking, half-limping out of the bedroom, down the hall, and then the stairs. By the time she made it to the front door, her legs trembled from their wild night.

A quick peek through the curtained side panel by the front door revealed Guy. Lord, the man had no sense of timing. Not to mention, it was plain out rude for him to just drop in. She had sent a brief note with the wedding invitation, stating she would be on her honeymoon until the first of January.

Rejecting the idea to leave him standing there—he would probably keep ringing the bell and there was the slight possibility he could awaken Miles, Hope unbolted and opened the door.

"Hope, so glad to see you." Guy's smile turned into a sneer as he observed her apparel. "A bit lazy are we?"

"Guy, I'm on my honeymoon, in case you've forgotten, so I can be as lazy as I want. Besides, it's really not any of your business."

Her manager's face turned the color of a beet

before he spoke again. “You’re right. I do apologize. And that’s why I’m here in the first place. I wanted to apologize for missing your wedding.”

Hope wasn’t sure what was going on with Guy, but he looked sincere. “That’s really nice of you, Guy. Was there anything else you wanted to talk about?”

His grin resembled a shark’s—full and toothy. “Yes, actually, there is. Do you mind if I come in?”

“Well, I’m not really dressed for company, and Miles will be up in just a bit.”

Guy zoomed past her and headed for the den. Hope had no choice but to follow him.

“It won’t take but a few minutes. And, Hope, if you don’t mind me saying it, your husband seems to be a bit on the lazy side. You’ve never mentioned him having a day job. Is he letting you foot all the bills?”

Hope resisted the urge to slap the smirk off Guy’s face. She couldn’t wait to fire his sorry ass, but for the moment…

“Guy, what my husband does or does not do isn’t any of your business.” She eased around him and headed for her desk. She slid onto the wooden chair, leaned forward, and spoke, “Now, what was so urgent it couldn’t wait?”

Guy looked miffed but took a seat on the sofa. “Well, I was thinking, you being a newly wed and all, that you might want to consider turning over Morgan Rarities to me.”

The idea to kill him lodged in Hope’s mind, but she hated to ruin the carpet with his blood. How dare he? They had already gone over this subject, and he knew her stand on the management of her parent’s business.

“Guy, we’ve been over this before. I plan to take part in running Morgan’s.”

Guy shifted forward on the couch. His features took on an anticipating and hopeful expression.

Almost like a kid who has a great idea and is sure it will work.

"No, no, Hope. You misunderstand me. I don't want you to give me sole managerial rights; I want to buy into Morgan's as a partner."

"What part of no don't you understand? If I'm not going to let you run the business without consulting me, why do you think I would allow you to become a partner?" Hope stood up, moved from behind the desk, and stopped in front of Guy.

"A partner in the business my parents broke their backs to build up and, in essence, died for. No way, Guy. I do not want a partner in the company. Besides, this is not just my decision any longer, I have a husband now. I'm sure Miles would be happy to hear your idea."

Guy's face paled a bit. "No, it's not necessary to run it by him, I'll just table this talk for now. Maybe in a few months you would be willing to hear me out."

"I don't think so, but if it makes you feel better to believe that, go ahead. Now, I think it's time for you to leave." Hope walked to the den door and stared pointedly at Guy. A moment later, he stood up, passed her, and headed to the front door. A sharp crack as the door slammed shut signaled his exit.

"Who was that?"

Hope jumped but settled back against the broad chest and body that cradled hers. "Guy."

"What did he want?"

Hope's sigh disturbed Miles. Except for that one brief instance at the castle, he'd seen her eyes filled with happiness and laughter since their wedding. The sweet essence of escaped air signified one thing—his wife was troubled. Not something he would allow.

"I don't want to talk about it, Miles. It just

upsets me to think how crazy that man can be."

Miles waited to see if Hope's upset would cause her to spill more of what Guy said or did. When she said nothing, he turned her around to face him. "I'll let you keep your secrets for now, wife, but if I hear one more sigh from your lips, I will read your mind or go after Guy and force him to tell me what he said."

"Miles, you wouldn't, would you?"

"Oh yes, I would, my love. Now, let's forget about that despicable excuse of a man and find you something to eat."

"Aren't you forgetting, we have no food in the house."

"To the contrary, after you wore me out with your lustful endeavors, I took a brief nap and then went to the store."

Hope's giggle was manna to his heart.

"*You* went to the store, the mortal way? You didn't just think it and have the food appear?"

"Damn it woman, what do you take me for?"

Hope laughed harder. "I get it—you forgot to act like a vampire, didn't you?"

Miles tugged Hope closer, untied her robe's sash, and cupped her breasts. "I'll show you a vampire, wife—just get your butt up those stairs.

****

Guy slammed through the front doors of Morgan Rarities. His hands trembled with rage, and his brain screamed with his frustration. Hope would not even listen to his idea. Not only had she tossed him out, but she'd also defended that wastrel of a husband she claimed.

He'd never trusted Miles Dunbar. All his careful research to find anything devious on the man had turned up nothing, but he knew a con man when he saw one. Something wasn't right. No one Guy had talked to remembered seeing him during the daytime. If he had more time, he'd put a private investigator on his trail, had even talked to one, but money was getting tight. With the new security guard watching his every move, although most nights he barely saw the man, he'd had to use the time during Hope's wedding to get the shipment ready for his buyer. Still, it wasn't enough. His creditors were getting more than a bit edgy.

If only Hope had listened to his idea about Morgan's. If only the imbeciles who'd kidnapped her hadn't been caught before he forced her to sign Morgan's away. Well, at least, they didn't know who was behind Hope's abduction. Guy really didn't want to soil his own hands with Hope's blood, but he had no choice. She had to die if he wanted to keep his own skin.

Chapter Twenty-Two

Hope leaned over and kissed Miles on the lips. Her vamp looked sexy as hell. The sheet draped just low enough below his waist that she wanted to ditch work and jump his bones, but Miranda would kill her. This would be her boss's first non on-call day in a while.

Miles' tongue teased her bottom lip, and her knees threatened to put her on the floor. Dang the man—he knew what buttons to push. "No Miles, I have to go to work. Besides, it's almost dawn, you need to rest."

"I can rest later. Come back to bed."

"No way. I have barely enough time to get to the hospital as it is. If I even lie down next to you, I'll be in deep water—not to mention naked."

"Don't you trust me?"

Hope evaded Miles hand. "Of course I do—with my life—but I have to go." For just a moment, the sensual light in his eyes dimmed, replaced by a look of sadness. Her heart ached for him. She wished she knew what caused these brief lapses. When they had first met, he'd been such a man of mystery. Remote in a lot of ways but always able to pull out a smile—unless he was angry. Something she hoped never to see.

"I promise, I'll be home right after work—as soon as I go by Morgan's." She closed her eyes and waited for the storm to erupt.

Miles pushed the sheet off, leapt from the bed,

and began to stalk her. "I forbid it, Hope. You are not to go near Guy."

"Forbid? Are we back to that? Every time you pull that I am vamp-piglet act, it gets one of us in trouble."

"Then please listen to reason. Guy is dangerous. He is doing his best to steal you blind. He constantly upsets you, and he looks at you with malice in his eyes every time you disagree with him."

"Oh pooh, he's harmless, Miles. There are times he gets a bit on the temperamental side but then he stops."

Miles continued to move forward as Hope continued to back pedal towards the door.

"Until you get out of range. I'm telling you, he is not to be trusted."

"You all keep telling me that, but where's the proof?" Hope took a step toward Miles. "I don't like him that much either. And just so you know, I plan on looking for another manager. But it will be because I think he's just not the manager for Morgan's, not because he's stealing or dangerous. That hasn't been proven yet. Look, my parents gave him the manager job after his Dad died, and he did graduate with a master's in business. Up until the last couple of months, I left everything to him. It has to be a shock that I want to handle more of Mom and Dad's legacy. It's probably the reason he's acting so unlike his usual self."

She pried open Miles' clenched fist and slid her hand into his. "I know you all have been looking so hard to find something on Guy, but what if you're wrong? I don't want to live my life in fear. I just want to be happy, Miles."

"I know, my love. I just wish I didn't get this gnawing feeling inside my gut every time he's near you."

"Well, perhaps it's just that green monster."

Miles laughed. “Me? Jealous of him? Please Hope, that’s ludicrous.”

“Really? Then how come your fangs come out whenever he’s around?”

“Maybe because he’s dangerous, remember?”

“Yeah, pull my other—” Hope glanced at her watch. “Yikes, I have to go—right now. Can we talk about this when I get home? I promise I’ll just be at Morgan’s for a minute. I just need to talk to Guy.”

“Can’t you call or email him?”

“I could but I don’t think that would have the same emphasis as in person. Relax, hon, I’m sure if he doesn’t like what I have to say, he’ll get mad and quit.”

“Good, that will save me the trouble of killing him.”

****

Hope decided to take Miles’ suggestion and call Guy instead of going by. Her day had been hard——maybe because it was her first day back, but the trauma cases coming in had stolen a bit of her happiness in her marriage and Miles. She needed to go home and ground herself in their love. To know that life went on no matter what.

She hit the speed dial button for Morgan’s and put the phone to her ear.

“Morgan Rarities, how can I help you?”

The voice on the other end sounded like an older woman. Probably the new secretary Guy hired.

“Hi, this is Hope Dunbar, I need to speak with Guy please.”

“Oh yes, Ms. Morgan, I mean Mrs. Dunbar, Mr. Evans said to put you right through if you called. Just a moment, please.”

Hope heard the beep signaling she was on hold and then just a second later, Guy’s effusive voice greeted her.

“Hope, so good to hear from you. Will you be

dropping by, I hope?"

"Hi Guy, that's why I'm calling, I had thought about it but my plans have changed. I've had a really tiring day and just want to go home." She held her breath for his reaction.

"I thought we could talk some more about the partnership, Hope. I know you said no, but surely after sleeping on it, you see the merits in this arrangement."

The urge to just hang up before things got ugly was rejected. She needed to show him her stand had not changed. "Look, Guy, I already gave you my answer. There will never be a partnership. I plan to hand Morgan's down to any children I may have."

"I see. You would rather give it to children you spawn with your husband than allow me a chance to make good."

"I am not going to talk about this anymore, Guy. I suggest you forget about your suggestion and continue to manage."

"Or what, Hope?" Guy's irate question was low but still reeked with venom.

"Or, as much as I hate to say it, I'll have to let you go."

"You would fire me after all I've done for Morgan's?"

"You have been a good employee, Guy, that's true, but in the long run, I will fire you if you keep badgering me."

"Well, I'm sorry to hear you say that, Hope. I'll be talking to you later."

Guy hung up before Hope could respond. Maybe it was for the best. She was more than a bit angered by his attitude. There would definitely be some changes made at Morgan's in the immediate future. But for now, she just wanted some quiet time with Miles, hopefully, he would not have to go out.

Again, she hit speed-dial.

"Hi love, I'm on my way home. Where are you?"

"By yourself? Hope, you know I would prefer you wait until one of us can be with you."

"Miles, the men that attacked me are behind bars. I just don't want to have to call someone every time I leave work. Besides, you didn't tell me I had to have a guard. You just said you didn't want me to see Guy."

"Surely, you are not going to use that as a defense? And why aren't you seeing the little—"

"Miles! Just because at the moment I agree with your attitude doesn't mean I want to hear you call him names. His dad was a good guy, but I'm really beginning to think Guy fell a long way from any paternal branches."

"Forget about him. I'll be there in a minute to walk you home."

"No need, I can—MILES! Stop doing that. You scare me to death every time you pop up."

"Sorry my love. I did check to make sure no one else was around."

Hope suppressed a smile. Her husband was entirely too cute when he looked chagrined.

"Never mind, let's just go home."

"Ah ha, I knew it."

"Knew what?"

Miles leaned in closer and gave her a wicked wink. "That you regretted not coming back to bed this morning."

"So what if I did, are you going to keep talking or—"

"Get you home so I can make passionate love to you?"

Hope's answer was breathless. "Yes, that would be the right answer."

****

Guy watched from his car, a block down from Hope's house, as her husband exited out the front door. The man walked as if he was in a hurry to get someplace. Good, that would work well for Guy's plan. He needed Hope alone. One way or the other she was going to sign that paper. After that, he would laugh when she died. The only thing that would have made his plan better was if Miles could watch her slow and painful demise.

Chapter Twenty-Three

Hope pulled a hamburger casserole out of the oven and placed it on the countertop. She stripped off her mitts and tossed them down beside the dish. Miles was gone. One call from Zacke and off he went. She knew it had something to do with Guy. Her husband's face had lit up as if someone had given him a gold fang. Just maybe, the question of whether or not Guy was guilty would soon be settled.

Pulling a chair out from the table, she sat down and propped her head in her hands. Lord, she wished it would be over and done with. Then they all could get on with more important things. Hope shook her head, no use stewing about it. Miles said he wouldn't be long, and she needed to finish dinner. He might not eat a lot but the man had confessed to having a fondness for chocolate. The ingredients for brownies sat on the counter, and she needed to get to fixing them.

Just as she stood up to do just that, a light knock at the kitchen door sounded. Hope pulled back the curtains. Guy!

What on earth could he want? Too late to pretend she didn't hear him. She might as well let him in, although, Miles would probably have a fit.

Once she opened the door, Guy moved over the threshold—forcing Hope to back up to keep from being run over.

"Look Guy, I don't want to get into anything with you. Miles—"

"Your husband is gone, Hope. I saw him leave. So we have all the time in the world to take care of business."

Hope's thoughts spun. How could he know Miles was gone? He'd been gone for at least fifteen minutes. The only way Guy could possibly know that, is if he watched him leave.

"There is no business and Miles will be home in a few minutes." Maybe that would get the man out of her house before Miles did come back. She just hoped it would be only the few minutes she quoted.

"Good, I really want him to be here for the finale." Guy's expression turned icy as he continued. "I had hoped to get this settled peacefully, but you've left me little choice, Hope."

Hope scanned the kitchen area for anything she could use to defend herself if she needed to, but she prayed that Guy was just being obnoxious. That he truly wasn't the danger Miles believed him to be.

"What are you talking about?" Hope eased back until the table stood between her and Guy.

"The partnership, Hope. All you had to do was just give me half of Morgan's, and I wouldn't be forced…"

Hope's blood began to slow down as she realized the brightness in Guy's gaze signified madness. Okay, she could handle this, she'd had one on one experience with psych patients during her residency. Always stay calm—she could do that—if only her heart would quit hammering in her ears. Praying her hand didn't shake, she reached out tentatively. "Guy, why don't we go into the den, sit down, and talk about this."

Guy moved around the table so fast, Hope had no time to react. He grabbed her arm, and his short nails dug into her skin as she tried to jerk free.

"You're hurting me. Let go."

"Oh no, Hope, I'm not letting go, but we will go

into the den. I think your crime scene would look better there."

Terror shot up her spine, crawling toward her brain. If she couldn't get away, Guy could kill her. She never would have believed it, but the man was totally unhinged. If she could buy some time, hopefully Miles would be home soon.

Dragging her heels on the hardwood floor earned her a slap. She refused to cry, she'd be better served to kick him but no telling what he would do. So far, she'd not seen a weapon on him. Would he strangle her with his hands? Bludgeoned her with a hard object?

Stop! She had to stop thinking that way. She refused to leave Miles a widower. He would never live without her. He'd sworn that and she believed him. Dang the man for being an honorable vampire.

Hope grabbed the threshold and flinched. The blow when it came almost knocked her down. If she lived after tonight, she would be sporting a black eye.

"Come on, I don't have all night."

"Well, you don't want to leave before Miles gets back, isn't that what you said?"

Guy pulled back the desk chair and shoved Hope onto the seat. "That's correct; I do want your husband here. After I finish with you, then he and I will have a final goodbye."

"Guy, you can't really believe you're going to get away with this? Zacke Kensington is already suspicious of you and there is no way Miles is going to let you kill me without exacting revenge." Her voice was shaky but she hoped she got her point across.

"I suppose you think your husband is something special. Just like you thought your parents were." Guy moved away until about three feet separated them. "Well, let me tell you something about your dearly departed mom and dad. They were scum. Lying, deceiving scum."

Icicles of fright begin to melt with the fire of temper now coating her veins. "Don't you dare say anything about my parents. They gave you a job, Guy!"

"Sure, out of guilt."

"Hope's fingers tapped on the desk. "Guilt? They had nothing to feel guilty about."

"How would you know, you were at that medical school up north. You have no idea what they did to my dad." Guy's upset was more than apparent. His lips pulled back in a parody of a smile.

"Yes, you, the sweet little princess always had everything you wanted. I had to work for my education. All it would have taken would have been a tenth of the money they spent on you or one of their trips to make my life easier." Guy began to pace. "Instead, my dad who worked for Morgan's for decades ended up dying."

"Your dad was sick. My parents wrote me about him. It was an inoperable tumor, Guy. There was nothing—"

Guy moved so quickly, Hope jumped. She watched as in slow motion his hand lifted and reached for her hair. His grip caused her eyes to burn—Hell would freeze before she allowed him to see her pain.

"Don't. You. *Dare* say there was nothing to be done. Maybe if my dad hadn't worked his fingers to the bones, and if he had retired at an earlier age, things would have been different. Instead, your parents kept him bound to Morgan's like a dog on a chain. The pittance they paid him was hardly adequate for necessities."

Hope forced her words out through clenched teeth. "You are the reason he had nothing. Luke sent all his money to your school. You might think you were paying your own way, but the money you paid was refunded to your dad and put into a saving's account. Something for you to have when you graduated. I don't know why he never told you."

"Another lie." His grip tightened, pulling her neck into a burning aching arc. "Why couldn't the high-and-mighty Morgans give him a break? But you will, Hope. You'll sign a paper giving me a full partnership in Morgan's and then a will giving me everything when you die."

"They did…they tried to help. Your dad refused the money they offered. And I am not signing anything. You're crazy."

Guy released her hair. For whatever reason, Hope was grateful. With her neck pulled back that way, she was defenseless. She needed a weapon. Her parents had never believed in guns, so there were no firearms in the house. The only knives were in the kitchen. Could she stab Guy if she had to? Damn straight!

"Liar! Your parents didn't help anyone. But I helped them." Guy's face took on a gleeful look. His eyes shown with an evil gleam. "I helped them right out of the sky. I stood at the airport and watched as they fell thousands of feet and then crashed and burned."

"What are you saying?" Hope's skin crawled with the implications of what he could mean.

"I'm saying that I sabotaged their plane. My only mistake was you not being on it."

Rage as she'd never known ignited inside her body. A trail of red fire made Hope throw herself out of the desk chair as she lunged at Guy.

****

"Where did you find it, Hawk?"

"Inside a paperweight on Guy's desk. He must have been in too much of a hurry to make sure it was closed. I'm sorry, Miles, there was no way I could have seen it. When the pieces came together they locked but for some reason, he didn't lock it this time."

Miles didn't want to think about why Guy had been in such a hurry, but he had a good idea. As he contemplated all the ways he would kill the bast—"

"Okay, it's loaded." Zacke's words pulled Miles back from a green-tinged view.

A second later, a document box showed up on the screen. Zacke clicked one of the docs and Miles' exhale was echoed by the others.

"Is that what I think it is?"

"Yes it is, and now I can arrest Guy." Zacke's jubilation rang in his words as he stood up and moved toward the door.

"I want to be there when you do."

"Hey, you two need to see this." Hawk's tone was somber.

"There's more?"

"Yes, and we need to get to Guy before he gets to Hope."

Miles' gaze caught and read the words on the screen. "Does he really think Hope won't dispute a partnership agreement?"

"I don't think he cares." All their gazes lit on the third document Hawk had opened. The document title read Last Will and Testament of Hope Samantha Morgan Dunbar and Miles Dunbar. The date inserted was today's date.

Chapter Twenty-Four

Miles eased the kitchen door open. He could have transported but didn't want to take a chance on startling Guy. He tried to call Hope before they left the station, but she didn't answer the house phone or her cell. The blood he'd taken on their honeymoon assured him she was at home but it wasn't until they spotted Guy's car that he knew for certain she wasn't alone.

Hawk and Zacke followed behind him. Their stealth reminded him of the night Hope was kidnapped. Too much had happened to the woman he loved. He'd march right into Hell itself before allowing someone to take her from him again.

As one unit, they moved toward the den. The sight that met his eyes turned Miles' blood into sludge. His breath stopped, his pulse died a slow death as Guy jerked a struggling Hope to him. A bruise marred the flesh on her cheekbone. The delicate tissue under her eye was already turning colors, blood dripped slowly from her bottom lip, and her knuckles were bruised. Neither she nor Guy noticed their arrival.

All Miles needed was one moment to get across the room and yank her away. Yet he hesitated. Guy's eyes glared with wildness. The man was totally, certifiably insane.

Hawk and Zacke flanked him as they all waited for an opportunity to step in without causing Hope any further abuse.

A mistake—Guy looked up and spotted them.

"We have company, Hope. A few more than I anticipated but no matter. I welcome the additional witnesses to your death." Guy twisted Hope's arm up and behind her back, turning her so Miles had a complete view of her face.

Her eyes were clear of tears, and her gaze held fright that quickly turned into relief. The woman trusted him to get her out of this mess and that was what he planned to do.

"It's over, Guy, we found your computer files. You will be going to jail for a long time. But, I promise if you don't let Hope go, you will not make it to jail."

Hawk and Zacke remained silent.

"I don't think so. I've been patient waiting on Hope to turn to me after her parents were killed. When she didn't, I decided to give her more time. You and Hope ruined that, so I don't think I'll listen to anything you say."

"He killed my parents, the worthless piece of—"

Guy pulled Hope further back against his chest. Her whimper of pain caused the world around Miles to turn a dark, portending jade.

"She speaks the truth, gentlemen. A proud accomplishment on my part. I also generated the late night calls to Hope. I just couldn't resist when I found some home movies at my dad's house. It seemed like the thing to do, since Hope missed her mother so much."

Mile's incisors exploded from his gums so quickly he tasted blood. His vision cemented on the man who had taunted and now threatened Hope. His nails turned into claws. Hawk's hand on his shoulder pulled a deep guttural snarl from deep within.

A part of Miles that still contained some semblance of mortal morals recognized the look of shock and terror on Hope's face as he released the monster he kept chained. His immortal heart actually shattered into miniscule pieces. Now, she would know the beast she had married. The animal that had been a part of her childhood nightmares. A part of her life he had planned never to reveal to her. Guy deserved to die for that alone.

The man's face lost some of its smugness and slowly took on the guise of terror. The hand that wasn't holding Hope's arm slid slowly upward until a knife touched the flesh of her throat.

"Stop! I'll kill her. I mean it." Guy's words were shaky in utterance but the threat was real. As Miles watched, Hope struggled and the knife pressed inward just a bit. A crimson drop of blood dripped slowly down the pale column of her throat to land right above her heart.

Time slowed as he lunged toward Guy. Time became suspended as the blade cut an arc across Hope's throat, severing the life that sustained her and Miles. Her body slumped and Guy released his grip. The body Miles loved to caress hit the hardwood floor with a sickening thud just as he reached Guy. His hands became manacles of death as he asserted pressure against the man's windpipe.

He heard the shocked yells of both Zacke and Hawk but ignored them. Hope was dead. He would kill the man who stole his soul!

A spiky shard of pain right below his heart caused Miles to loosen his grip on Guy. He watched in disbelief as the mortal sliced the air a second time with the blade that had killed Hope.

Bam! Guy's body jerked as a bloom of blood blossomed on his shirtfront. Miles released him and spun to see Zacke holding a gun.

"You should have let him kill me. Hope is dead. And so am I."

"No!" Hawk knelt by Hope's body. "You have to

turn her Miles. You can't lose her. There is still time if you hurry."

"I can't. You saw the horror on her face—she would not want to be like me. I can't change her."

"Then I will. She is carrying your baby, Miles. A baby that deserves a chance at life."

Miles legs collapsed under him. A baby! When? How could he not have known? He crawled to Hope's side. "You're sure?"

Hawk's smile was slight as he confirmed his previous words. "Yes, she is tiny, almost perfect, and newly made. God's miracle, Miles."

A girl! A tiny piece of Hope. They had to save her.

He placed a hand on Hope's chest. Her heart rate was almost non-existent. She had to be turned now and even then, it might not work.

"I'll do it." Miles moved into a seated position and pulled Hope onto his lap. He'd never turned a mortal before. Wasn't even sure he could. He'd tasted Hope's blood twice before so now he would need to drain her body and give back his own blood to restore her to life or death—for that would be what it would be—a living death.

She would hate him for eternity.

As he suckled Hope's blood, he was aware of Gideon arriving. Zacke must have called him. He probably handled any neighbors that heard the gunshot. The more he tasted her essence the more he hated himself. Hope would not be dying if not for him. He would turn her, make sure she was all right, and then leave. The agony of watching her despise him day after day, night after night for infinity was not something he could handle. He'd rather have his head and heart taken.

Moments dragged as he drained Hope's life-blood. Finally, he straightened up, wiped his lips, and looked at his friends. "What if it doesn't work?"

"It will, just believe it, Miles." Hawk's words came from his right side. Apparently, he'd not moved since Hope went down.

"I guess now I give her my blood." Miles opened a gash in his wrist and laid it against Hope's lips. Nothing. She didn't even try to drink.

"Not positive, but I think you have to dribble some of the blood in her mouth, then she might suckle." Zacke shrugged his shoulders, so Miles knew he was shooting in the dark also. He tilted Hope's head back farther over his arm and allowed the blood to drain down her throat.

Collected breaths held as they all waited.

A second passed—a minute. Each tick of the clock signaled another slash to Miles' heart. It had to work, it had to.

The slight movement of her throat caused his breath to catch in his chest. Was the movement real or was he seeing what he wanted to? No! Hope was swallowing. No, not just swallowing, her lips locked onto his wrist and tugged. The blood began to flow once again from his not quite healed gash.

Miles wanted to laugh with joy, but it was too soon to celebrate. Too many things could go wrong. He could still lose her!

As he contemplated again, a life without Hope, he fortified his intent to end his own life if she died. His head began to feel light, his breathing slower. So intent with his thoughts, he almost missed Hawk's proffered arm. A twin cut to Miles' own pinpointed a bubble of blood.

"Miles, if you would allow me, it would be my honor to give Hope some of my blood. You need to rest and replenish what you lost from the knife wound and what you've given already.

Tears burned his eyes as he looked at one of his oldest and dearest friends. His gaze also took in Zacke and Gideon who both held out their wrists.

Although, they had not yet made the cut, he knew both men would not hesitate to offer what he and Hope needed.

"Thank you all." Miles eased Hope onto Hawk's lap and then tried to stand. His vision blurred, his legs trembled, and he would have fallen if Zacke and Gideon had not grabbed him. Both men walked him to the couch and sat him down.

"Okay, Miles, here's the deal. I don't do blood, you know that, so when you bite my wrist, go easy."

Miles chuckle surprised them all. Gideon, God bless the mortal's heart, really meant what he said. And it would have to be Gideon, he didn't want to take Zacke's blood unless necessary. He would need his strength to take care of the mess Guy had left behind. He conveyed his thoughts to Zacke, who nodded his head in understanding.

"Okay, I'll try to make it painless." He reached out and touched Gideon's face and then bit down on his wrist. Zacke's partner's blood consisted of a blend of flavors, a faint taste of beer, salty peanuts, and candy. He wondered how much exercise the man had to do to get rid of the calories. Another gulp and Miles pulled back, he swiped his tongue over Gideon's wrist and then looked up. "Thank you, man. I owe you."

"You owe me nothing. We're friends and that's what friends do. But don't tell anyone or I'll have to hurt you."

Although, laughter seemed out of place, Miles welcomed it. Maybe things would be all right. "How's Hope?"

"Still drinking. Soon, we should move her to your bedroom. She will be more comfortable there as her body converts."

"How's the baby?"

"Her heartbeat is growing stronger. We just have to get both of them through the change."

Chapter Twenty-Five

Hope struggled against the nightmares taunting her. Her mind would not respond. She was locked inside a vast array of memories that forced her to look at the monsters chasing her.

"Treat or treat?" Hope held up her Halloween bag and waited for their neighbor to drop in an assortment of candies.

She was only allowed to participate in the annual candy bash if she went to neighbor's houses and only off her street if her mom went with her.

She hopped back and forth on first one foot and then the other as her mom's friend told her mother about something her kids were doing. Hope wanted to get on with her trick-or-treating. She was never allowed to go for more than an hour and she worried the hour was almost up.

Still her Mom stayed. Both women were talking now. Hope looked around. If she couldn't go for more candy, then she would just go home. She eased off the porch. Her Mom didn't notice. She continued down the driveway and then turned left. At the end of the street, she looked both ways. Neither one looked familiar. But she didn't remember it taking them long to get to Mrs. Staples' house. Surely, her home was down the next street. Her candy rattled in the bag, making delicious sounds as she almost drooled at the prospect of eating her bounty.

Hope stayed on the sidewalk but soon the smooth pavement turned into concrete with cracks and litter. She didn't remember this on the way over. She stopped and looked around again. A light in the distance. Oh goodie, that must be where her street was. Her footsteps in her ballerina slippers made scarcely a sound as she moved forward. The farther she walked, the more her feet began to hurt. Surely, her house was not far.

Maybe her mom was looking for her because Hope had a sinking feeling in her tummy that she might be lost. She turned a corner and the light looked brighter. Hopefully, she was on the right street or close to it. As she walked along, an older man with a cap on his head came out from one of the buildings. She wanted to ask him where Twelve-Sixteen Victorian Lane was. But her mom and dad always told her never to talk to people she didn't know. Would that count now? She hoped not, because she knew she was totally and completely lost.

"Hi girlie, are you lost?" The man had moved closer while Hope wondered what to do. His breath smelled funny, but he looked a bit like the janitor at her school.

"I need to find my house. Can you help me?" She prayed the man was a nice one. If only she had stayed with her mom.

"Why don't you tell me your address and I'll get you home."

The man's stance was relaxed, his smile a bit crooked, but his eyes held a gleam of laughter. Maybe she had made the right decision.

Hope told the man her address, and he promptly took her by the hand and started to lead her back the way she came. Okay, she had taken a wrong turn but soon she would be with her mom and dad.

Another man fell into step beside them as they approached an alley. He grabbed her arm and along with the first man tugged her into the dark dank space. Hope started to scream but one of them put a hand over her mouth.

A grownup Hope fought the memories of what happened next but could not stop the vision of the man who saved her. He looked like an angel with long hair. His eyes shone like green glass as he pulled the men away from her. But then, his face contorted into a hideous mask. His teeth became long jagged spikes, and she screamed.

Another memory pushed that one aside. Miles, her lover, her husband, her heart, telling her he would always protect her. Making passionate and sweet love to her and never hurting a hair on her head. That was the memory Hope's mind locked on and held until the dreams disappeared completely, and she floated in a void of darkness.

****

Miles wanted to pull his hair out as he watched Hope thrash around on their bed. The change had started not long after they brought her to their bedroom. Dawn was fast approaching, but he couldn't leave her like this. Zacke promised to bring Miranda over but they needed to wait until a babysitter could get there to watch the twins. Both he and Gideon had gone in and finished up their reports on Guy. A simple statement from both men that Guy had tried to kill Hope and had been behind her parents' deaths, not to mention stealing from Morgan Rarities, and their captain marked the case closed. Guy had no living kin, and the coroner confirmed one gunshot to his chest had killed him. Zacke had surrendered his weapon but been assured that IAD would probably not reprimand him for the shooting.

"How is she?" Miranda's soft whisper came, a welcome sound to his ears. She was always a calming influence on him and Hope. He counted on her influence to help Hope if—no when—his wife awoke as a vampire.

"Still in the throes of the change. God above Miranda, I had no choice."

Miranda slid an arm around Miles' waist. "Of course you didn't. You had to try to save her and your child. Now, go sit down or stretch out somewhere and rest. You won't be any good to her if you can't keep your eyes open or your senses about you."

He squeezed Miranda's hand, dropped a kiss on her cheek, and then settled down across the bottom of the bed. "I can't sleep right now. Maybe later when she's through the worst of the change."

"Well, at least try. I'll be here if she wakes up."

Miles sat up so abruptly he startled Miranda. "Miranda, you are to call me if she shows any signs of waking up."

"That's foolish, Miles, I can take care of Hope."

"No, she will wake up with an intense hunger for blood. You would never be able to subdue her. I need to do that and then get her the blood she needs. She is going to be confused and then frightened once she realizes what is going on."

"Oh. I guess, I never thought about that aspect. Does that happen to every turned vampire?"

"I guess. All three of us behaved that way when we were first turned. I just hope she doesn't hate me for what I did."

"Hope loves you. I don't see that changing whether she's mortal or immortal. Her heart will still know her other half. Just trust that it will be okay. Look at Zacke, you know what he went through. Just have faith in Hope, Miles."

The sun had long passed the noon hour when Miranda shook him awake. "Miles, I think she's coming around. What do I do?"

"We have to get blood in her some way. I don't think she will be still long enough for us to give her an injection like Zacke use to take, nor take it fresh from a bag. Any ideas?"

Miranda scrunched up her nose. "What about hot tea? Hope loves that raspberry blend and if we mix it with the blood, she might be able to drink it that way."

"If I wasn't already married and if Zacke wouldn't stake me, I'd marry you, Dr. Kensington. I think that might work, but first, I have to make sure she doesn't hurt herself when she awakens."

****

Hope eyes flickered once and then again, before she opened then to see a greenish glow encompassing the ceiling. Strange, it almost looked like Miles' eyes when he was in his vampire mode. Why was she in bed? She didn't remember lying down. In fact, she wasn't sure what she remembered. She closed her eyes to concentrate and heard thuds and then more thuds. If she didn't know better, she'd swear it was heartbeats. Impossible. No one could hear a heartbeat without a stethoscope unless they were a vampire.

A kaleidoscope of images hurled through her mind—starting with Guy and then she witnessed again Miles' change into a monster. The last thing she remembered was the cold steel of a knife cutting into her throat. After that, everything went blank.

Miles! What had happened to him?

Blood seemed to gather in her skull, a slow pulse beat that intensified as she turned her head slightly. Miranda sat still as a sculpture—watching her with eyes full of trepidation. She wasn't sure why Miranda was here, but at least maybe that meant she was alive or did it? Next, she glanced gingerly to the right. Miles' eyes were bright with blood-red tears. His gaze also looked frightened.

"Hope?"

"Miles, what's going on? I don't remember a lot

after what happened in the den."

"Well, you were, uh, Guy is dead."

Her gasp was met with a compassionate stare from Miranda and a satisfied one from her husband.

"Did you kill him?" Hope really didn't care who had done the job, Guy had been out of control and would have killed her. Wait, she still hadn't established the fact of whether or not she was alive or dead.

"No, Zacke did when Guy tried to stab me a second time."

Hope sat up in the bed and reached out to touch Miles. "Are you okay?"

"Yes, remember, vampires heal pretty quickly."

Her slight smile hurt her lips. "My lips and tongue feel funny. Like my teeth are too big for my mouth."

"Uh, that is normal."

"Why is it normal, and why is my vision colored with a tinge of green? Something's not right. I need to know what happened after Guy put that knife to my throat."

"I'll just go fix that cup of tea." Miranda smiled tautly at Hope, gave Miles a look Hope didn't understand, and left the room.

Miles slid closer to her and pulled her into his embrace. "Hope, there's no easy way to say this. "Guy cut your throat, you died, and I turned you into a vampire."

Laughter exploded from Hope's lungs. "Yeah right, that is not even feasible or funny, Miles."

"It may not be, but it's true, darling. I can show you the scar."

"I thought you told me vampires don't scar."

"No, I told you we heal quickly. You have been a vampire less than twelve hours, the scar will disappear once you have some nourishment."

Hope slid out of Miles arms, jumped off the bed,

and ran for the bathroom. The T-shirt someone had put her in was a crew neck. She tugged it away from her skin. The sight that greeted her eyes as she peered into the mirror caused her knees to buckle. "Sweet Heaven!"

"Hope, it will be okay. I'll help you through this. I just don't want you to hate me."

"Hate you? At the moment, I don't know what I feel, Miles. Can you just leave me alone for a few minutes?"

"I wish I could, but in a few moments, you are going to become really hungry. I need to make sure you know how to handle the changes your body has undergone."

"Five minutes, okay? I promise if I get an urge to bite my arm off or yours, I'll give you notice." Hope ignored the hurt manifesting itself in Miles' face. At the moment, she couldn't pamper him. She had to think. Would she be a monster preying on innocents? Would she become the ogre that surfaced in her dreams?

Oh, dear God! Miles was the ogre. All of her dream came tumbling back. The near childhood abduction and him saving her. Her head reeled with memories and dizziness. Why hadn't he told her? Hope shook her head, probably because he knew she wouldn't believe him. Why would she? All memory of that night had disappeared until she dreamt it earlier. Miles! Had he taken that memory from her and were there any others that he'd stolen?

Hope spun on her heel and noticed her body moved with fluidity that she'd never had. What other differences would she discover? Would she be able to fly? Transport? UGH! She'd have to drink blood. That was so not happening.

When she hit the threshold into the bedroom, she was ready for a fight. Could be interesting, since she had some fangs and claws of her own.

"Miles, we need to talk."

Hope watched as her tree-sized husband literally shrunk before her eyes. "What's the matter, darling, aren't you feeling up for a chat?"

****

A bit later, Hope sat at the kitchen table sipping a cup of tea. Miranda sat across from her and the vamp pack, which she refused to include herself in, staggered themselves around the room. Miles stood farther away than Zacke or Hawk. Although, in fairness, she couldn't classify the detective as a fang-toting individual, his history and concern for Miles put him right there with the other two.

"Come on, Hope, you need to drink all of it." Miranda's soft tones prevented Hope from lashing out at her friend. After all, she was only following orders. Orders from Miles who she still refused to speak to after his disclosures. How dare he wipe her memory of what happened and to do the same thing after she met him at Miranda's party? Oh yes, she'd gotten every little bit from him—even the part about him healing children in the cancer ward. Did she feel good about it? NO! She felt like she kicked a puppy, and that made her even angrier.

She took a sip of tea mixed with something she didn't want to think about and glanced at her husband. His eyes still held sorrow of a magnitude she'd only felt when she buried her parents. Hope tried her best to ignore him, instead she drained the cup of tea.

"Okay, we've established what Miles did. Now tell me how long before I start sprouting fangs and claws?"

Her statement and question was met with disbelief from Miranda, a glimmer of a smile from Zacke, and a snicker from Hawk. Nothing from Miles.

"Well, I thought your fangs would descend when

you first had the tea, but since they didn't it might be a few hours. Just be careful when they do come down, you don't want to split your lip."

"Thanks, Zacke. If I taste my own blood will that make me want to bite someone?"

"Not necessarily, Hope. We all controlled our urges after the initial turning. You don't seem to be following the same path. It could be because you were so far gone when Miles turned you, or the fact it wasn't a brutal change."

"Humph. Not sure what you mean by that, but I'll wait to see if I get any long canines or need to start seeing a manicurist for my nails. So, will I be able to fly or transport? Throw men across the room with immortal ease?" This time she shot a look at Miles that left no one in doubt who she wanted to toss.

"I don't know. Your change was the first one I've ever seen. I'm not sure what you'll be able to do or when you will get any immortal powers."

"Thanks, Hawk, guess it's a waiting game now."

Hope turned to Miranda. "Is this going to affect my job at the hospital?"

"Well, the guys here all sleep during the day. Whether you will or not will depend on what I can do about your job. If you can work days, then you will stay on them, if not, I can have you assigned to the night shift."

"That's fine, I just don't want to lose my job over something that is beyond my control." Again, she shot Miles a killing glance.

"Uh, I need to get home, Hope, if you don't need me. The babysitter has an evening class."

"I'm sorry, I wasn't thinking. Thank you for being here, Miranda. Zacke, thank you for taking care of Guy. I don't know if he had any life insurance but if not, I'll make sure he gets buried."

"That's generous of you Hope, considering all he

did."

"Let's just say his dad was a sweetheart of a man. That's why I'll do what I need to do."

Hawk crossed the kitchen and dropped a kiss on Hope's forehead. "I have to head out soon too." The blond-haired vamp leaned down and whispered in her ear. "Cut Miles some slack, Hope. He wasn't going to turn you but he had no choice."

Hope opened her mouth to ask why, but a finger on her lips stopped her. Another whisper in her ear, "Ask Miles and if you love him like I think you do, put him out of his misery. He loves you more than he loves himself."

Hope barely registered when Zacke, Miranda, and Hawk left. All she could think about were Hawk's words. She knew Miles loved her, she just had to figure out a way to rationalize what he did. Before she could voice any sentence at all to him, her husband brushed past the table and left the room.

She allowed him all of two minutes before she followed. Hope found Miles in their bedroom. Lines fanned out from his eyes, not happy ones, but more like ones of stress. He didn't acknowledge her presence, but instead kept packing a small bag.

"What are you doing?"

"Leaving."

Hope sat on the bed before her legs collapsed. Why would he leave? Then a speck of illumination went off inside her brain. It was because of her. She'd hurt him. The very real threat of Miles leaving put everything in prospective. She loved him. No matter that she was no longer mortal, her heart still wanted to be with him. She had to make it right.

"Miles, no. Please don't leave."

"I have to…I can't stand the…"

"Stand what?"

"The thought of you hating me for eternity and beyond."

Hope moved forward, grasped Miles by the arm, and tugged him around to face her. Her brief move caused him to almost fall into her arms. She could get use to vampiric strength.

"Now, Mr. Turns-Me-into-a-Vamp-and-Leaves-Me, let's get something straightened out, shall we?"

Miles did not have to fake his confusion. His beautiful wife wasn't mad any longer or he didn't think she was. What had changed?

"Sit!" Hope pointed to the bed and waited for him to do as she ordered before she continued.

"I'm sorry. I was upset. All the things that happened last night and even in the last few months have been hitting me hard and fast lately. I look at you, Miles, and I still wonder how you could have fallen in love with me. After you told me you saved me when I was a child and then watched out for me over the years, I realize how fortunate I am to have you."

Miles hesitated, but then went with his instincts. He tugged Hope closer and pulled her gently onto his lap. When she didn't slap or bite him, his breath escaped in a breeze of joy.

"Hope, you know that I only did those things because I wanted to protect you."

"I understand about what happened when I was a kid, but why did you take away my memories—the ones of you making love to me in my dreams? They were beautiful. Although, I'm not sure how you managed them in the first place."

"They were beautiful for me too. I did it through thought transference. I was afraid to really touch you. When you spooked at Miranda's, I realized I had to make you forget, because I wasn't ready to tell you the truth about me. I believed you would think I was a monster. My life after death, turning into a vampire, was not a sad one except when it came to you. Then it became a curse. I didn't see how you could ever separate what I was from the creature who terrorized your childhood."

"I can see why you would think that. I did behave horribly." The way Hope accepted his actions almost did Miles in.

"Thank you, I don't deserve your understanding, and I certainly don't expect you to forgive me for then or for my turning you. I just don't want to lose you."

Hope popped him in his forearm with her fist. When she'd done it in the past he laughed, but now it actually hurt. "Okay, enough, my vampire fistanator. You're going to bruise my tender skin."

Hope's laughter bubbled forth and for the first time since the events of the night before, he dared to dream everything would be okay.

"For someone so smart, you can be such a dumb-ass. You are *not* going to lose me. Yes, I was and still am upset about not being mortal, but when I look at the alternative… Well, I could be dead."

His heart stuttered at what had almost happened. He never wanted to relive the moment of Hope's almost death again.

"Hope, my love, I thought I lost you last night. The only reason I was leaving was to give you time. I just didn't think I could wait to see if you would banish me from your life. I couldn't live that way."

"So you thought it would be better to just leave, period?"

"Yes, but now I'm rethinking that."

"You do that, Vamp Boy. Now, tell me, why did you change me?"

"Why do you think, Hope? I couldn't fathom living without you."

"Miles, weeks ago, we both decided that I would grow old as a mortal and then die. You would age by artificial means and then you would die also. You seem to understand why I didn't want to be a vampire." Hope caught his hand in hers. "For you to change me there had to be something else."

"Yes, there was one little detail I couldn't ignore."

"Well, what was it?"

"Why don't I show you instead?" Miles placed his hand on Hope's forehead and allowed her to view what she'd missed the night before."

"Oh my sweet Jesus. Are you sure?"

"Yes, after you finished your changing, Miranda used a fetal stethoscope and heard our baby's heartbeat. It's a girl, Hope. We are going to have a girl. I don't know how Hawk knew but he did."

Hope threw her arms around his neck. "Miles, I love you. If you remember nothing else, know that I have never thought you a monster. Even when I was a child, I felt safe, as if I had my own angel. You are that angel and now you have given me a treasure I never thought I would have."

Tears scalded Miles' chest as he held Hope and patted her back. "I know, baby, I never thought I would ever be a dad. I love kids, but always thought I would be their favorite uncle or something. One of the reasons I went to the cancer ward."

"Again, I love you, my wonderful vampire."

"I love you too, my vampire wife."

Miles caught Hope's lips in a kiss that melded their hearts and souls together. A long time later, he pulled her naked body next to his, her buttocks cradling his spent manhood. He listened as her breaths became slower and finally she slept. He too closed his eyes and allowed sleep to catch him in its grasp.

"Oh God above!"

Miles startled awake at Hope's exclamation. He bared his fangs and prepared to fight off any enemies only to realize they were safely ensconced in bed.

"Hope, what is it? Did you have a nightmare?"

"No, I just realized we're having a baby and we have no idea if the baby will be vampire or mortal."

Miles kissed the back of his wife's neck. "I have no idea, but I have a feeling our little one will take us on an awesome ride."

Hope relaxed back against Miles chest. "Well, as long as you're with me, I'm sure we'll manage just fine, Vamp Boy."

"I'm sure you're right, my darling wife."

Miles and Hope both fell asleep, missing the sound of a tiny child's giggles. A sound that touched the stars in Heaven before their child of eternal love curled up under her mother's heart, embraced by the love of parents who survived the curse of evil to achieve perfection on earth—faith, hope, and charity.

A word about the author...

Faith started her journey to publication when she joined the Romance board at iVillage.com, where she became a community leader. She has written book reviews for *Bridges* magazine, MyShelf.com, and, until her first book was published, for Romantic Times Book Reviews. She also pens a column for a local magazine. Her path veered into editing and marketing for a small press before she joined The Wild Rose Press staff. Her dream of having her own work published is a blessing and an honor. Faith resides in the South with her daughter Amanda, memories of her now-angel husband Rick, and a special zoo crew of furry babies.

Visit her at www.faithvsmith.com
www.faithvsmith.blogspot.com

Other books by Faith V. Smith:

Beware What You Wish
Kensington's Soul

To my readers,

I hope you enjoyed reading Miles' and Hope's tale of love as much as I did writing it. Please look for Gideon's story in Book 3 of the series "Bound By Blood, The Legends" coming soon from The Wild Rose Press.

~*Faith V. Smith*

www.ingramcontent.com/pod-product-compliance
Lightning Source LLC
LaVergne TN
LVHW020539100826
845148LV00010B/1536